A Sherlock Holmes Mystery

THE MAKING OF A MAN

John Worth

Paperback ISBN 9781780924748
ePub ISBN 9781780924755
PDF ISBN 9781780924762

Published in the UK by MX Publishing
335 Princess Park Manor, Royal Drive,
London, N11 3GX
www.mxpublishing.com
Cover design by www.staunch.com

For my sister Irene
la coragiosa

INTRODUCTION

He lay still, curled in a protective ball; the kicking had stopped, but he feared any movement might cause it to commence all over again. He did not know how long he had lain there in the dark, face pressed to the uneven cobble-stones, so cold and muddy. The idea of fighting back was not entertained. All of his focus was upon survival, just to lie there and protect his head and vital parts. The filthy wet pavement was almost a comfort, a refuge - at least it was not attacking him. Hands over his head, he pressed closer into it.

After what seemed an age, it suddenly started again. He could not suppress a whimper of anticipation as a boot poked experimentally at his ribs.

'Come on get up – I know you are alive. Get up man, this 'ere is not the best place to spend the night at all, it aint.' The tone was rough, but there didn't seem any malice in it. It was a deep mellifluous voice, with gutteral overtones.

'Come along young fellow; I don't know about you but I fear I might get my death if this bloomin' rain don't 'old off. Come on, here, let me give you a hand.' So saying the stranger grabbed him under the armpits and attempted to lift the figure lying there before him. The deep groan of distress made him desist.

'Looks like you've been done a damage – hang about and I'll round up a couple of lads. Stepping back from the prone figure, the speaker put two fingers in his mouth and gave two sharp whistles.

Slowly he lifted his head from the muck; the tone of the voice had not indicated malevolent intent. He lowered his arms and looked up, tried to make out the figure dimly perceived before him.

The fellow appeared bulky, dressed in a long coat of some heavy dark material that he took to be some sort of dressing-gown. On the stranger's head perched a small tight cap upon long dank curling hair. The massive head sat seemingly without neck upon his shoulders. From beneath the man's brow jutted a very generously proportioned nose, between bushy eyebrows and straggly beard. The

2

dim moonlight fairly gleamed upon it as the bulky figure stood head turned side on, at an angle, as if listening for something. Shortly he heard it - an answering whistle. Satisfied for the moment, he turned back now to the figure lying there. As he approached, the crouching man spoke;

'Look I haven't got any money – ' he coughed then, it obviously caused him pain to say that much, as he now lay panting, unable to continue. Unexpectedly the other chuckled.

'I didn't expect you might have any, my dear, seeing as you have just had a right good blaggin.' He turned away then, calling out.; 'Over here lads; come on, look sharp. We got us a toff 'ere as had a right bit of a kicking by the look of it.' Two and then a third boy had come upon the scene, their heavy boots clattering on the cobbles.

'Ere – cast about a bit and see if you can find something we can carry him with.' Without a sound the three darted off to carry out the instruction.

Now that he realized he might be out of further danger, the injured man slowly uncurled from his defensive crouch. He began to very gingerly make a catalogue of his injuries. - *His ribs of course, a badly bruised shoulder, hands that had suffered as he had endeavoured to shield his head* – his whole body was in pain. The effect of the adrenalin was now beginning to leave him, the full consciousness of his pain rising rapidly - as he was lifted he gave an involuntary cry and sunk into merciful darkness.

This was probably for the best, as it enabled his rescuers to handle him with rough efficiency. In a short while he was lying helpless, flat upon an old door. He felt neither the cold drizzling rain upon his upturned face, nor being badly jostled and once nearly dropped entirely, as his unknown rescuers carried him through a maze of darkened back alleys and courtyards.

The busy din and clatter, voices calling out, snatches of

raucous laughter; - all this bombarded his still somewhat deranged senses, as the recumbent figure in the corner upon a straw palliasse was recalled reluctantly to consciousness. Reluctant, for he dimly knew that consciousness promised to be painful.

For a time longer, he kept his eyes closed; despite the noise, the mingle of unidentified unpleasant smells, he felt safe like this, wishing only to prolong this inert state for as long as possible. He was warm, he was almost comfortable. He knew too well that this would all cease when he fully awoke. Awoke to a new day, and to the ongoing misery of his life.

Still in this semi-soporific state, he gradually became aware of a tantalizing smell, an odour so delicious it overwhelmed the pervading noisome fug. He opened his eyes.

There before him squatted a boy, just in the act of placing a steaming earthenware bowl of soup before him on the floor. The boy turned his head, and spoke out of the corner of his mouth to another urchin standing behind.

'Ere –nip 'round and tell the old gaffer that this'ns alive'. His grin was derisory as he turned back to the man lying before him. '- Fought a sniff of that soup in 'is hooter might bring 'im back from the dead.' Laughing, the boy jumped to his feet and went off whistling, hand in his pants pockets.

Slowly he sat up; mindful of his many tender areas, it nonetheless gave him pain just to move. So much so that he found it very difficult to suppress a groan. His ribs in particular hurt like the very devil.

Halting half raised, he rested on his elbow and took in a few careful shallow breaths. Whist he rested, the injured man took the opportunity to take in his surroundings. As he began to do so, he marvelled that he had been sleeping through what seemed mayhem.

He lay in the corner of a cavernous, ill-lit place. It's furtherest reachings were not discernable in the prevailing gloom. The only light source he could make out came from several small barred windows high up on one wall.

To further hinder visibility, and greatly add to his confusion, the whole place was billowing with steamy vapor. It was difficult to make out a ceiling in what he took to be some kind of vast dungeon. Gradually he became aware that he appeared to be inside some kind of giant laundry.

People scuttled about on various duties, mostly women and boys, as far as was apparent. The din in this steaming great space contributed to the confusion. Some of the women were very busy around a row of great boiling cauldrons, sleeves rolled up, faces red, as they stirred the contents with large wooden paddles. Due no doubt to the amount of water being sloshed about, he noticed that the washerwomen worked bare-footed. They worked with their outer garments tucked up near to their waists, showing plump white legs contrasting with reddened feet and toes. To keep their feet clear of the wet stone flagged floor, they stood upon pinewood duck-boards.

As they toiled, an old man carrying a short handled shovel and a bucket pushed amongst them, shouting for the women to get out of his way as he attempted to throw coal into the boilers. This was obviously a familiar occurrence, as the washer-women showered him with good-natured insults in return. The watcher deduced by their accents that the women seemed mostly to be Irish.

Now and again there was a shouting to and fro, several of these women would together begin fishing out the contents of a boiler into an even larger vat of obviously cold water, which then sent up even more clouds of water vapour as it's contents were stirred and poked by a very stout woman, who also shouted a lot.

Amidst this flurry of activity, boys, scruffy urchins, were constantly trotting about, delivering more basket-loads up to the women at the cauldrons. On the other side of the cold water tub stood a great iron mangle, with wooden rollers. This was operated by a woman at either end each turning a crank handle. This pace of work went on continuously.

On benches along the walls of this great steaming place sat others, mostly older women but among them some younger boys, busy with the piles of clothing before them. The observer had no idea as to how he had come to this place.

Totally bemused by it all, unable to take it in, he turned his attention back to the immediate task at hand. To get himself at least sitting upright.

Finally he was able to sit with his back supported by the rough wall. As comfortable as he could make himself, the young man prepared to drink some of the soup before him. He noticed then the heel of a loaf lying upon a piece of newspaper alongside the soup. He was greedy for both, but began first gingerly to drink the soup from the bowl. He'd felt the piece of bread; it was stale and hard.

His mouth hurt, his teeth ached, but the need for nourishment overrode any accompanying pain. He began breaking up his bread, crumbling it to soak it in the soup until soft. With his whole mouth very tender, he wasn't about to try and chew anything.

'Well well my dear; you are looking remarkably well this morning, considerin' like.' He looked up, and suddenly it all came back with a rush –standing before him was his rescuer of the night before.

Looking down at the man whom he had brought in the night before, the speaker observed the fellow closely, despite the bad light. But he was used to that; - the gloom, the half light – the shadows were always his *milieu,* he thought. The notion amused him.

As the man returned his greeting with a painful half smile, he urged him with a gesture to continue with his breakfast.

He studied the man's face closely as he returned to his bowl of soup.

-*Dark straight hair, an unusually high and broad forehead, deep-set strangely hooded eyes; imperious aquiline nose upon a lean, wolf-like face – all indicated a character of great intelligence, perhaps marred by arrogance.*

-*Could be cruel perhaps, but in a sort of counter-point, although the chin indicated a resolute character, the mouth was curiously sensitive, indicating perhaps a poetic soul – very interesting head indeed -*

There was something about this man's appearance that had from the first moment of seeing him, had engaged his interest and attention. As his unexpected guest went on with his breakfast, he noted the fine-grained skin on the back of the man's hands, olive rather than the London pallor of his face, the long fingers, the fine straight black hairs on the backs of his fingers and hands.

- very interesting indeed – a true type -

All this impression gained in mere seconds – he prided himself in instant character reading, and believed himself rarely wrong. It was something his people had by necessity to become good at – it was a gift, he thought, earned by blood.

Having finished his soup, the man sighed with satisfaction, carefully lowered the bowl. Tenderly he wiped his bruised lips with the back of his hand. Raising his head, he essayed a half smile.

'For the soup I thank you heartily, sir. For rescuing me, I am truly indebted.' He paused for breath, it obviously caused him some discomfort to speak. The man standing before him noted the well-modulated vowels, the civility of his address.

So like I thought; -, a bit of a toff...but there is this something else there…

Then somewhat to his surprise, the man held out his hand:

After a slight hesitation – *this was unusual -*, he bent to take the proffered hand. Although the fingers were long and thin, - *like that of a musician, perhaps* -surprisingly, the grip was quite firm, despite the obvious bruising to the hand;

'Shiloh Coombes sir – at your service.'

As their hands were still clasped, his rescuer now gave his name in return. He wished to note any reaction, an involuntary twitch of the hand, perhaps.

'My name is Isidor Feigenbaum.' He looked closely into the eyes of the other as he spoke. He detected no start, no sudden withdrawal in either hand or eye. On the contrary, upon hearing the name of his rescuer, the injured man shook his hand even more firmly.

'Mr. Feigenbaum sir, I am very grateful for your kindness -.' The effort to speak caused him to suddenly begin to cough, obviously causing some considerable pain.

'Now now Mr. Coombes sir, just you lie quiet for a bit. I've got a bit of business to attend to, but I'll have one of my lads take a bit of a look at you in a while - see if you need anything. I'll come back soon enough and we can have a bit of a chat.' He turned to go but the man on the floor, having caught his breath again, motioned him closer. He looked somewhat embarrassed,

'I wonder if your lad might bring me a large bottle of some kind. I am absolutely dying to piss.' Feigenbaum chuckled:

'I should have thought of that myself,' he was serious as he continued, 'I would advise you to have a good look at your piss, if you will pardon my frankness. If you have a show of blood, we might have to get you to a doctor -' Coombes face was closed as he cut in.

'No - no thank you, no doctors, please,' he tried to soften his abruptness, ' But thank you, I will indeed do as you suggest.'

It was some days later, and although he still felt like he'd fallen beneath a steam roller, Shiloh Coombes was beginning to believe he might recover. The man Feigenbaum had arranged for his removal to smaller room, not so much more salubrious in it's general aspect than that strange dungeon full of noise and steam, but at least quieter, and private.

The bare room in which he now lay, he soon discovered to be some kind of storeroom. It contained no furniture at all, but racks of shelves ranged along three sides. High up on one wall a narrow window let in some light, but the grime of ages kept this to a minimum. The shelves containing what appeared to be bundles of rags, old clothes. He owed his present comfort in fact to the great heap of such old rags upon which he lay.

He was as comfortable as his various injuries permitted. Although somewhat improved, the same injuries still prevented him from doing much more than sleep and swallow the bowls of soup which various boys fetched for him at times.

These boys, right street urchins by the look of them, would come in and without ceremony place his food, the inevitable bowl of soup and piece of bread, and with nothing more than a grin or perhaps a wink, take themselves off. Of his benefactor Feigenbaum, he had seen little. The man would dart in, exchange a few words then he would hurry off.

Since that first morning when he had woken in what he called the dungeon, he had noticed that everybody whom he had observed seemed to be always in a great hurry and rush. If he made an attempt to speak to the boys delivering the soup they would only grin and dart off.

Shut away in this dim room not much bigger than a broom cupboard, with no distractions, he eventually found himself missing his earlier accommodation. All of that noise and vitality might at least afford him some diversion in his recuperation. Left alone now for long hours, he had spent much of it in recrimination and self-loathing.

It was late afternoon, judging by the light filtering through the one grimy window; he lay there, still sunk in such unhappy reflections, when the door slowly opened. Peering around the door came the face of his rescuer, Mr. Feigenbaum himself, preceded by his distinctive nose.

'Ah, my dear; I was hoping you might be awake. Feeling a little better are we?'

He smiled ingratiatingly, 'I do apologize for not attending to you for these past days – pressure of business, you understand; pressure of business,' all the while rubbing his hands together, apparently well pleased with himself over this same piece of business.

'Sorry to have deserted you, leaving you to the tender mercies of my young villains…'

The man Coombes waved away his apologies. 'No not at all

good sir – goodness me, I have been looked after very well indeed by your – er –assistants.' He saw a quick gleam of ironic humour in the eyes of Feigenbaum, who chuckled at this.

'My assistants; yes, well indeed so they be, but sometimes I think the scamps will be the death of me. Assistants indeed.' The notion continued to amuse him. He went to the door and called something out into the adjoining room. There followed a slight scuffle with the door as a chair was first thrust into the small space, followed by a bucket containing hot water, judging by the vapour rising from it. Then to further crowd the space, the bucket was followed in by a young woman, who was in fact carrying the bucket. 'This 'ere is our Molly; she's goin' to give you a bit of a sponge over like.'

Startled by the idea that this young drab was about to wash his body, at the same time Coombes had noticed a singular thing: Mr. Feigenbaum, although admittedly having a discernable accent, in conversation with himself alone, the man had spoken in a grammatical, even educated voice. Now in front of this girl his voice was the pure argot of the East London streets.

So matter of fact was the girl Molly as she proceeded with her task, she could have been washing a table down. Coombes soon lost all considerations of modesty as he concentrated on avoiding her most vigorous and hence painful ministrations.

Leaving his guest to the care of Molly, Feigenbaum took himself off once more upon his busy schedule. He wanted to supervise the weighing of rag bales, preparatory to bargaining with the rag collector on the following morning. He rubbed his hands in that familiar gesture of his as he hurried along the passageway. He always enjoyed this weekly battle of wits. As he went, his thoughts returned though to the situation regarding the young man lying in his storeroom.

In rescuing the fellow, Feigenbaum had acted out of some spontaneous spirit of humanity. Since then he had also intuited things about this same young man that had interested him

10

exceedingly. He would be keen to know if his intuition was right, but now right he had to make some decisions as to his future. In this regard Feigenbaum had already done some serious thinking.

Earlier on it had occurred to him that as the man was obviously of a good background, there was a possibility of obtaining some reward from Coombe's family connections. This plan was soon shelved, when in conversation with the man himself, Feigenbaum had come to understand that young Coombes was in some sort of deep disgrace; his family had in fact disowned him and thrown him out. As a consequence, it was not likely that they would be eager to buy him back.

Coombe's refusal to have a doctor attend him, his reluctance to notify anybody of his whereabouts led Feigenbaum to the conclusion that the man wished to remain in hiding – if not hiding, at least unfindable.

All of this smacked to Feigenbaum of some mystery, but his agile mind had come up with an alternative plan for young Mr. Coombes. A plan he could turn to good profit if it came to fruition. He would be patient; Shiloh Coombes had first to be brought back to health.

At the rear of his laundry premises, Feigenbaum had a big old shed, or warehouse, and it was to this that he now hastened his steps. He entered, looking around as he did so. Everything seemed to be going well, as he stood in the shadows watching.

The shed consisted only of a roof with walls lined only with slats. Black stalactites hung down from the broken tiles, where they had been patched with repeated applications of tar. Nevertheless it as sufficiently water-proof for his purpose. The side facing the lane at the rear was closed by two large wooden doors, somewhat sturdier in appearance than the walls.

Two lanterns hung high upon the walls at either end, dimly illuminating the scene. Several lads were busy packing rags from a great wooden pen off to one side into large jute sacks. As the sacks were filled, the contents were being jumped upon to pack them

11

tighter by a couple of smaller boys. The boys seemed to be making a game of it. As the bags were filled to the top, another boy deftly stitched them closed with a bag needle and twine, leaving one corner unstitched. They were then lifted up onto a hook and weighed upon scale hanging from the roof timbers. If a bale was too light or too heavy, it would be adjusted through the still open corner, and the stitching completed.

Pleased to see it all going along well without his supervision, Feigenbaum was nevertheless not about to tell these scamps that.

'Ere, stop all that foolin' abaht you lot. I want all this schmatter packed tonight, not next flamin' week. This should 'ave all been finished already', was his only greeting. Judging by the general laughter, this was about what they had expected from the 'old gaffer', as he was generally called.

'You can laugh all you want but there'll be no supper until its done, mark my words. This aint a flamin' charity 'ouse.'

It was still dark, early next morning, but despite the cold drizzle still coming down, the shed was once more a lively scene. The doors had been thrown back, and a horse drawn lorry stood there, the horse stood steaming, his head into a nosebag full of oats. A brazier had been lit in one corner of the shed, around which stood several figures warming their hands. One man, apparently the carter, was toasting bread. A couple of young lads were wrestling each other upon the heaped bales.

'Oh this is just marvellous innit,' cried Feigenbaum who had just arrived once more upon the scene. 'That's right, burn up all me winter coal.' Belying his words, he pushed in to warm his own hands by the fire. 'Ere - where's that bloody thievin' goniff buyer then eh?' he asked of nobody in particular. Nobody answered him; this was a weekly performance. This was weigh up and pay up day, as Feigenbaum would say.

The bales which they had packed and weighed the previous

evening would have to be weighed up all over again, once the rag trader arrived. He was a man who trusted nobody.

CHAPTER ONE

Shiloh Coombes woke to a short knock on his door. Upon his call, It opened and the girl Molly presented herself. In her hands she held a small pile of neatly ironed and folded clothing; he recognised it as his own. Since shortly after his arrival, he had worn only a voluminous nightshirt provided by his host.

The girl was brusque, merely placing the clothing upon the chair in the corner before leaving without a word. It was on the tip of his tongue to say something to ease the tension between them, but she had hastened from the room. He knew that he had offended Molly, the last time when they had met.

She had returned some days after his first bathing to ask if he would like her to give him a second sponge bath. As he was rapidly on the mend, he was about to decline her offer. Before he had been able to answer, the girl had closed the door behind her. In two steps she reached where he lay and knelt. Smiling, she'd put a finger across his lips.

'Ssh – If you don't want me to wash you, I could do something else.' And her hand had slid beneath his covering. Caught unawares, Coombes had grabbed the girl by the arm, perhaps with a tighter grip than he had intended. His voice perhaps harsher than the situation warranted.

'Stop that – Please go now.' Snatching free her hand, she had fled the room, leaving him with a mix of conflicting thoughts.

Today was the first he had seen of Molly since this mutually embarrassing episode. Once more he was thrown into a perplexed state of mind. He felt he had handled the situation badly.

Coombes was still mulling over this unfortunate situation that had risen between himself and the girl Molly, when Feigenbaum himself entered. He was carrying a pair of shoes, the same shoes Coombes had been wearing on the night he was attacked. They gleamed with polish.

'Ah, I see Molly has returned your clothing my dear fellow –

seems they got most of the mud off – socks here as well – well hullo, the old girl stitched up that nasty tear on the knee right enough.' This as he checked the clothing still neatly piled upon the chair by the door. Satisfied that things were all in order, he placed the shoes upon the floor. He turned then to speak directly to the young man.

'Young Sparrow gave me your message this morning. He said you felt well enough to get up and go about your business,' he looked keenly at Coombes.

'Just what is your business, if you don't mind me asking squire?' The question was accompanied by a smile, but Coombes could see the gleam of interest in those deep-set eyes. He sat a moment more in silence, measuring the man before him. He had absolutely nothing to lose, and he did owe this man Feigenbaum some explanation.

Despite all of his natural inclinations, the reticence instilled by his upbringing, reinforced by his schooling, he decided to tell his benefactor all – well almost all.

'Actually Mr. Feigenbaum I must confess that not only do I have no business, but that I do not know what I shall do,' he paused to marshal his thoughts.

'I did tell you that I am in a state of disgrace with my family,' he began again, launching into his sorry tale without further ado, and without any outward show of embarrassment or self-pity.

'I will try to cut a long story short. To begin, I might as well tell you that I stole a sum of money from my uncle. To forestall the necessity of my uncle resorting to the people at Scotland Yard, my elder brother himself repaid the money.' His face was pale, but he looked Feigenbaum directly in the eye as he continued.

'My brother was naturally furious with me, but when I went to face my uncle it was worse. He was as cold as ice, contemptuous. He has forbidden me to contact either him nor any member of our family. So you see, I am effectively cast out,' his smile was thin, but he spoke with a touch of irony,   'A fate which I admit I richly deserve.'

Feigenbaum had listened to this frank confession without uttering a word, but now he spoke. As Coombes completd his bleak account, he had placed the folded clothing upon an adjacent shelf and now pulled the chair close. The two men sat facing each other now in the room.

'I already figured out you was in a spot of bother. I admire that you told me all this. It sounds like the unvarnished truth, and you didn't try to blame others, nor give me any guff, or spout self pity,' he chuckled, low in the throat and not entirely humorously. 'I don't take kindly to those who give me guff'. I get to hear an awful lot of bullshit around here, and I reckon I have a good nose for it,' as he tapped the side of that appendage with his index finger, 'a right good nose for it.' He turned his face this way and that, to better show off his superior proboscis. He tapped it once more for emphasis:

'This is a bullshit detector my dear,' Feigenbaum continued on, 'not knowing of your particular circumstances like, I was nevertheless thinking you might be in some sort of trouble. It wouldn't take a genius to twig that -gent like you, lying in the muck, late at night in a dodgy part of town, ribs kicked in – you probably got a couple of cracked ribs, you know – yes my dear, you could say you looked like you were in trouble.' Shiloh Coombes gave a rueful half smile at Feigenbaum's deft summation.

'Added to which you wouldn't hear of getting a doctor, no friends or family either – I thought to myself: - 'ullo 'ullo, what have we here?'

As he spoke, Feigenbaum watched keenly for the other's reaction to his words. Coombes seemed as if he was weighing up those same words. Eventually he nodded his head several times, as if listening to some inner voice. He raised his eyes to meet the other.

'You seem to have smoked me out pretty well; my story no doubt only served to reinforce your opinion,' at that he began to rise, somewhat painfully still, from his make-shift couch.

'Once more I thank you for your kindness, for which I cannot offer any recompense. But now if I may, I shall dress and take myself off.' Feigenbaum put a hand upon his shoulder, gently pushing him back down.

'I haven't judged you – I don't have the right, believe me. Anyhow, you appear to have given yourself a harsh enough judgement.' Coombes sat silent, neither indicating Feigenbaum should continue, nor that he shouldn't. He appears indifferent to praise or condemnation, thought Feigenbaum, and that state of mind could lead to despair, and even suicide. He decided to continue.

'I have been thinking about your situation. As you say yourself, you don't have any business to attend to, nor even any place to go right at the moment, right? Well I might have a proposition for you.' Shiloh Coombes received this offer with an enigmatic face. For some seconds he looked keenly into the eyes of Feigenbaum. Finally he broke the silence.

'You are indeed correct; I have no recourse open to me at this time,' he paused for a second or two, then continued.

'Whatever you have in mind to offer me, Mr. Feigenbaum, I thank you unreservedly. However I cannot believe that I could be of any use to yourself, or for that matter anyone else. I feel I cannot impose further upon you sir, and will take myself off. I do not wish for you to believe that I distain your offer, but in the present circumstances I cannot conceive how I might be of use to you.'

At this Feigenbaum laughed out loud, smacking his knees as he did so. 'That is probably correct, as far as it goes at the moment, but if you are willing to learn a new sort of life, well you might indeed be of great use to me – and for that matter yourself.' He fell silent, allowing the younger man some time to take in the implications of his words. Eventually Coombes looked up from his melancholy gazing at the bare floorboards before him.

'It seems sir that I am in your hands; I have no inner resources left to me,' as he put his face down into his hands.

Feigenbaum leant forward, his hand upon the shoulder of the despairing young man, his head close to the other. His voice was low and steady, but with an iron inflexion.

'Listen to me now; like a lot of my people, I have endured my share of troubles, and one thing we Jews have learnt is this – flexibility. We have a saying; when a strong wind hits a stiff reed, it can break, see, but the reed that bends... you have to learn to bend, to adjust to your circumstances. I'll tell it to you straight how I see it. The truth is you have led a soft existence, good school, university - you've never had to fight for your life. Am I right? For someone like you, it takes a bit of adjustment to pick yourself up when fate knocks you into the shit. Nevertheless I see you as a sort of investment.' Shiloh remained silent, listening without interruption to what Feigenbaum had to say, as he continued.

'I said I haven't judged you regarding your actions, but I have judged you in yourself, and I see a man of considerable intelligence and strong will. If you were some weak milksop, some foppish young sod, I wouldn't waste the steam off my piss on you, understand? But If you are willing, I will help you build another life.' Coombes had listened without any sign, but then he slowly looked up again at this man Feigenbaum. He looked intently into the others eyes.

'I don't know why you should offer this, nor what it entails, but I accept your offer. It is either that or a leap into the Thames, I suppose.' Feigenbaum accepted the dark humour in the remark as a sign of inner resilience.

Shiloh Coombes had at first thought he could never accustom himself to this; the mind-numbing work, the conditions. But after some days at it, he seemed to have found a rhythm, a pace to carry him through the day. He was seated as he had been for the past days, at the long bench against the wall in the same dank steamy cellar laundry workshop in which he had first awoke.

All along the bench, others were doing the same work as he. Most were older women, a couple of old soldiers, both with missing limbs, some young boys but only a few girls amongst them. Girls were not often here, he'd learnt. Their mothers, working themselves at the boiling vats, needed them to stay home to look after their younger siblings. Occasionally a girl might fetch in a squalling infant, at which the mother would without ceremony stop her work and put the infant to her breast.

Coombes had at first been embarrassed, he had never seen such behaviour, but like everything else going on around him, he was quickly growing to acceptance.

Only the reed which bends, survives... Feigenbaum's words still resonated.

He was dressed not in his own refurbished clothing, but in a miss-matched set of workman's clothes. Upon his feet, wooden soled heavy leather clogs. The task he and his fellow workers performed, was the tedious unpicking of old clothing that had been washed. The articles which would bear re-selling were sorted aside for pressing, those beyond repair now needed to be disassembled into rags. These were further classified into stuff for re-weaving, the worst of it into piles for paper-making. No sooner was one heap finished, than another load was dumped before them. It was unending, tedious drudgery.

Feigenbaum had spoken to him before he had begun this work. 'Now you don't have to do this, but you said you are willing, so here is what I think you should do.' And here he broke again into the dialect of the east London streets.

'Nah listen up a bit,' his face was very earnest as he began, 'it's like this, see; if you want to live 'round 'ere wivvout notice, you 'ave to study 'ow to talk like 'em, an' all. You'll 'ave to learn to get yourself invisible, do you follow? You can't stand aht; you'll 'ave to be exackly like 'em. Wiv luck you might be able to fool some stranger comes apokin' abaht, but you can't fool the people of this manor. The first lesson to learn - poor is not stupid, eh. You only sees the poverty and the squalor, but vey is as cunnin' as shit'ouse rats 'round abaht 'ere, I'm tellin' you. Like vem rats, vey can smell aht any stranger.' There was an amused light in Feigenbaum's eyes as he watched Coombes difficulty in understanding his quick staccato delivery.

'That's your first task, see; learn their way of talking. A lot of the women are Irish of course, and some of their way of language could come in useful and all. But mainly I want you to study the boys way of talking, the street sparrows. Keep any conversation to a minimum. Don't talk to them until you feel you can carry it off. The aim is to make them think you are one of them, see. This is all part of my plan, and it will stand you in good stead bye and bye. Tell 'em nothing about yourself; I'll put about that you are a relative of sorts, and your name will be Samuel, or Sam for short.'

Shiloh Coombes found that he had adjusted to the day's routine well enough, but the nights, which he still spent in the small storeroom, were difficult. Working during the day, he was preoccupied, but as evening fell, over and over he would find found himself agonizing over his fate; in bitter self-recrimination he would re-hash his recent history, his fall from grace.

Eventually Feigenbaum had provided him with a mixed collection of second-hand books, they at least gave him some respite from his melancholy thoughts. With only the dying light of day through his one high small window, he could at most manage an hour of reading before the light waned. He had a candle for the night but feared for his eyesight to read by it. He was still recuperating his strength after the savage beating he had received, the long days work left him tired in any case, and he usually managed to sleep through the night. Before falling asleep, he would try to memorize expressions he had heard during the day, and re-ran snatches of conversations overheard in his head. Sometimes he would practice sentences out loud, to test his pronunciation. He'd always fancied himself as a mimic. With wry irony he told himself;- *a fellow who had excelled at Latin and Greek should surely be able to manage the East London street cant -*

Shiloh had not seen the old rag dealer for some days, but he was becoming used to the old man's erratic appearances. He was pleasantly surprised though when Feigenbaum did appear at his door; he had hardly spoken to anybody in days.

'Well and how are you getting on my dear fellow,' asked Feigenbaum, rubbing his hands together as was his habit.

'Right enough, guvnor, right 'nough, fank you for askin'; carnt complain, like', he'd answered, straight off. Feigenbaum was delighted, clapping his hands..

'I knew you were a clever chap, I did, but that was capital, capital indeed. You are coming on in great bounds, if I might say so,' his eyes held the hint of a twinkle.' He regarded his protégée with avuncular pride. 'No doubt your ribs and all are still very sore, but I 'spose your mouth is healing up all right? Good - when you have fully recovered, and I think you are up to it, I want to put to you a proposition which could be of great advantage to us both.' Feigenbaum solemnly tapped his nose, then made to go. At the door he turned back.

'I don't doubt you could probably tackle something a bit solider than soup, eh,' he said with a broad wink.

That evening the boy known only to Shilo Coombes as 'young Sparrow' came to his storeroom with a plate covered with a chequered cloth. With his usual grin and a nod, he then took himself off. On lifting the cloth, Coombes was confronted with the first solid meal he had seen in some time.

A large slab of corned beef, accompanied by potato, carrots and Brussels sprouts sat steaming before him. Slowly, carefully at first, he began to eat. There was some pain still in his jaw, but he found his teeth were up to the task.

As he ate, Shiloh Coombes went back over the conversation he had earlier shared with Feigenbaum. He decided to follow the advice of his benefactor:- have patience, and allow himself time to heal completely. Whatever lay in the future for him, probably was in the hands of this old Jewish rag trader.

After a couple of days of solid food, one evening Feigenbaum came to visit his recuperating lodger one more.

'Ah my boy, you are looking better and better.' He rubbed his hands in that typical way of his, to indicate his satisfaction, as he looked his guest up and down.

'Bit of solid nosh sets a man up, eh?' He had found Coombes dressed in his own clothes and sitting up; he'd been reading a pile of newspapers the boy had fetched for him. He certainly presented a far different picture that that at the time of his rescue. The cut lip was all but healed, though there was still evidence of bruising around the face. He had availed himself of the shaving equipment sent by Feigenbaum earlier, and was almost presentable.

'I've taken the liberty to bring you some pipe tobacco, my dear.' This he handed to Coombes. The eyebrows raised in surprise, followed by the grateful smile this generosity evinced was enough to cause Feigenbaum to chuckle.

Carefully he produced from his voluminous great cloak an object wrapped in tissue paper. He unfolded it to reveal it's contents.

'We found a pipe in the pocket of your jacket but it had unfortunately been broken; I brought you one of those Dutch clay pipes for the nonce. You will have to pardon me for not doing so earlier, as I daren't risk fire, you understand.' He grinned widely.

'To give a man the wherewithal to smoke and then deny him the possibility would have been right cruel, I thought'. They both laughed together at that.

'Once more I am in your debt, Feigenbaum. Shall I then be offered some place to enjoy a smoke?'

'Yes indeed my friend; if you are up to it, I thought tonight might be a good opportunity for us to attempt a walk outside, if you are so minded.'

There was not much of a fog, but Feigenbaum had chosen a

dark overcast night for Coombes to essay his first steps outside in the street since the time of his beating. Coombes wore a shapeless half cloak, half coat, similar to that worn by his companion, which Feigenbaum called a *kaftan*. Feigenbaum had been highly amused when Shiloh Coombes told him how he at first meeting had the vague impression that he had been wearing his dressing gown.

As they made their way along the dark narrow way, Coombes was assailed by various malodorous smells; of stale cabbage cooking, effluent flowed down the uncovered gutter, the all pervading smell of excrement mixed with the overriding pungent odour of badly burning cheap coal. He still had difficulty walking. his legs were stiff, still bruised and sore from the kicking.

Holding on to Feigenbaum's elbow, Coombes found himself often stumbling upon the uneven slippery cobbles beneath their feet. The older man seemed to handle the going better.

'Ah yes; I think I know every toe-stubber in this bleedin' alleyway. It can be a good thing to study if you ever find yourself pursued, know what I mean,' said his companion when he remarked upon their unevenness. 'We'll take a turn along the river, if your legs are up to it like. You could take the opportunity for a pipe.'

Standing now with Feigenbaum alongside him, Shiloh Coombes smoked his pipe as they gazed out across the Thames. The dimly seen moon cast a sulphurous yellow light upon the surface. It didn't resemble water so much, thought Coombes, as some sliding great serpent, roiling and eddying as the tide ebbed. In the crapulous light it gleamed with an oily metallic sheen.

'Beautiful, isn't it ,' commented Feigenbaum, after they had stood there for some time in silence.

Coombes turned to him, eyebrow quizzically raised, but he detected no irony in the voice of the old Jew, who remained gazing out across the river. 'An awful thing, but I suppose beautiful in it's own way,' he said.

'Yes', went on Feigenbaum, still gazing before him, 'the old river forgets and forgives; we do terrible things to her, a lot of

London's sewerage still empties into her, all the rubbish, dead rats – and dead people too, eh, don't forget that. And yet when the tide has gone right out, and the upstream water begins to come through, people 'round about here can still take water out of her, more or less fresh.' He cocked his head up at his taller companion. 'If you boil it with a handful of charcoal, it's drinkable. Hard to believe, eh?' He chuckled, but without mirth. 'Poor ignorant buggers though, they don't often do that, and the typhoid gets 'em.'

Coombes regarded his companion for a moment or two, meanwhile taking a couple of reflective draws upon his meerschaum.

'But you seem to love the river; you are aware of it's dreadfully polluted state, yet you see poetry in it.'

The massive head of head of Feigenbaum swivelled around upon his squat neck, as he peered up into the face of his young companion. His eyes were fierce, compelling.

'If a man can't see the poetry in the essence of things, regardless of them being pretty or not, then he is a man spiritually blind,' he paused for this to sink in, 'given this shitty world we live in, my dear, without this, life would be intolerable.' He fell silent, as he turned again to his contemplation of the dark swirling waters below.

Coombes for his part also was silent. A strange mood had overcome him, he felt as though in an altered state of consciousness. He seemed to see himself from above, standing beside this companion, an old Jewish rag trade man, looking out over this river of the night. He experienced the most compelling emotion about the scene. It was strange, and yet somehow familiar – no not familiar, but perhaps expected – no, not expected, stronger than that; fated was the concept he reached for.

- it's as if my whole life has been a journey, a preparation for this moment -

To add to this air of unreality, Feigenbaum spoke again. It was almost as if he had read the thoughts of the younger man beside him, meanwhile still looking out with moody gaze at the Thames. At that same moment, Coombes understood that the man looked with unseeing eyes, his real attention was inward, to his own deepest thoughts.

'Yes it is strange, this meeting of you and I. I find I speak for myself as much as to communicate with you. I think we understand one another. It feels as if we were somehow fated to meet. Anyhow, to get back, here's what I think. I believe that one cannot have joy without knowing to the full it's converse - the bitterest dregs, the pain of unhappiness. You cannot conceive of beauty without it's concomitant ugliness, nor goodness without evil.' He turned then full face to his companion.

'A lily growing alongside of a cesspit, taking it's nourishment from it, its still a beautiful bloom, isn't it?. It's why we love great composers, isn't it, we honour our great artists and writers, for they have the grace given them to remind us all of such higher truths.' He shrugged his shoulders, with a sudden self-deprecating rueful half smile.

'And yet we usually treat them like shit, starve them to death. Only then we can we properly venerate them,' he grinned now, fully, 'I think it's because we sort of fear these soothsayers, wouldn't you think? You got to be careful what you say in this world of woe, or they nail you up like the good Rabbi Issa Bar Jussef' – Jesus to you. Come on; let us keep walking, you need the exercise.'

Feigenbaum linked arms then with Coombes, and the two men continued their riverside walk. It was late in the night, but given the usual life of the river, Coombes had been struck by the fact that during their stroll they had seen no other person, either along the river, or upon the river itself. He now remarked upon this.

'Oh yes; see with tide running out like this, the riverboat men will all be at mooring; upon the ebb turn you'll see the buggers, common as fleas on a dog.' He pointed towards the buildings up ahead, which seemed silhouettes backlit by a greenish yellow glow that was reflected from the murky surrounding atmosphere.

'No sleeping down that way; Rotherhithe docks that is, 'round the bend on the other side of the river. Night and day unloading, all lit up by bloody great gas lamps.' Feigenbaum held out both arms, as if to encompass the scenario of which he spoke. There was almost a wistfulness in his voice as he spoke again, 'just think of it, the vast fortunes to be made, all that trade, stuff from all over the world.'

Coombes was struck not for the first time by the complexity of his companion's character, his mercurial switching from high philosophic discussion, of poetry, to this sudden enthusiasm for commerce. Once again Feigenbaum seemed to intuit his thoughts. He now chuckled, digging his companion in the ribs with his elbow.

'We Jews find beauty in good business too, you know,' he regarded the younger man with eyes bright with shrewd interest, 'because you have led a privileged life, never had to go out in the world to grub for money, you think all trade is *schmutzig*, eh?' Again the elbow in the ribs, hard enough this time to cause Coombes to wince; he was still tender there. After a profuse apology, Feigenbaum continued.

'Here is a story to illustrate my point. Once I was in Stamboul – oh yes, I've got about a bit – and I saw this fine little bit of business. A friend of mine was selling bales of wool out at the camel market, see, where caravans load up. This buyer was a very sharp trader, and he just wore my friend down with his haggling. Very hard to best a Jew, you might think, but this fellow was Armenian. They can be right cunning buggers, believe me.

Anyhow to cut a long story short he got my friend to eventually agree to a price, down to almost three quarters of what he had originally wanted to sell at. I must admit I was a bit surprised, but my friend accepted a price of five Dirham a bale, when I knew he had wanted to try for seven or eight. The deal was done, they shook hands, the money changed hands. The agreed ten bales to be delivered to the caravanserai of this Armenian.' Feigenbaum halted, wishing to finish his story with a dramatic flourish.

'Here is the best bit. It was marvellous, and I learnt from it; it was a classic piece of business. As soon as the buyer was gone, my friend called to his assistant Ali. Here Ali, he sez, undo these eight bales here, take out a bit of the wool from each and re-bale it, then sew them up tight again and deliver the ten of them to Mr. Jossarian, with my compliments.'

Feigenbaum smiled broadly at Coombes. 'What a trader eh! The wisdom of a Solomon! Now both seller and buyer could feel satisfied!' Noting the somewhat sceptical look upon the face of his young acquaintance, Feigenbaum sighed.

'For you see, and many don't understand this, it is the cut and thrust one enjoys, the play of wits; the money is really only secondary.'

They had not proceeded along the river more than twenty paces when they were accosted by a man stepping suddenly from the shadows. As they had so far met nobody on their nocturnal stroll, it came as a surprise. The fellow was silent, but in the dim light Coombes nevertheless thought he saw the gleam of a knife held down close to the man's thigh. He was about to warn his companion when Feigenbaum hissed at him from the side of his mouth;

'Stay back, you're still not well.' He then began an amazing pantomime. Flapping his wide sleeves, he began to wail and cry out, 'don't rob me, please don't rob me. Oh weh is mir, oh God help me, I'm just a poor old jew, I have nothing, nothing,' all the while still flapping and hopping about, from foot to foot, for all the world like some great crow.

His would-be assailant was like Coombes somewhat taken aback, but he soon collected himself and proceeded with his plan.

'Shut up that fuckin' screamin' you old barstid and give me your purse, or I'll cut your fuckin' greasy neck,' as he brought up the knife, flourishing it before him. Seemingly daunted by the sight of the blade, Feigenbaum called in a quavering voice, hands held out entreatingly; 'Oh yes, oh yes. Here it is, take it but don't do us no harm, please don't hurt us.' He had pulled from his sleeve a leather pouch, and held it out abjectly towards the robber.

It all proceeded so quickly; Shiloh Coombes, thinking to come in from the side to assist his friend, was just manoeuvring himself around to the left of Feigenbaum when it happened. As the unknown assailant snatched at the proffered money pouch, Feigenbaum hit him a tremendous slap on the side of the head with his other hand. The sound of it was like a report of a pistol as the fellow screamed with pain, his eardrum burst by the blow. Too late he swung up the knife, Feigenbaum has swept up his loose kaftan of heavy felt as an impenetrable shield.

Coombes was left flat-footed by the speed of the scuffle; the squat figure of Feigenbaum swarmed over the would-be robber, enveloping him in the folds of his garment, at the same time kneeing his opponent in the groin a time or two.

Coombes stepped forward but Feigenbaum threw out a restraining arm. By this time the attacker lay on the ground, retching and groaning. 'Come along my friend, let us go on,' breathing hard, but seemed oddly cheered by it all.

They stepped out again along the river wall, and it was only when his companion had gained his breath and composure that Coombes commented upon the incident.

'I must say you handled that well; I thought for a moment you were all for giving that villain anything he wanted.' Feigenbaum grinned up at him, pleased by the comment.

'Hah hah, fooled you as well eh. Learn this well; never give a blagger like that one back there the idea you might want to confront him, my dear. My old grandfather used to say this: Anybody can sit on my face, but don't complain if you get teeth marks on your arse.' Then he laughed a booming full-hearted laugh., 'tell you the truth my boy, and I should be ashamed to admit it, but I enjoyed the whole piece of nonsense.'

Shiloh Coombes awoke next morning to what was for him an unusual sight; sunlight came streaming in through a window alongside his bed. He lay awhile, enjoying his new surroundings, and thinking over the events of the previous evening. He brought back the image of Feigenbaum and his amazing pantomime, begging for mercy. The way that the robber had accepted the old man's abject surrender, dropping his guard and reaching for the proffered money purse... Coombes had the impression of a spider trapping a fly.

This Feigenbaum never ceased to amaze him, no sooner did he think he understood his new acquaintance when some other facit of his complex personality would be revealed.

Up until the previous evening Coombes had not known that Feigenbaum did not live somewhere within the labyrinth of what he called the rag factory, but some streets away in this house where he now found himself. Upon the completion of their interrupted walk, Coombes having had to admit to being tired out, Feigenbaum had with a touch of formality, invited him to spend the night under his roof.

Shiloh looked about him, examining for the first time the room in which he had slept the night. The evening before, his view had been constrained by the small light of a candle, the stub of which stood now in it's candle stick upon a bedside table, alongside a stoppered cut glass water bottle and glass. Also lying upon the table the clay pipe and tobacco that Feigenbaum had provided for his use.

Looking further, he saw that the room was quite plain, sparsely ordered, with few items of furniture. Although sparsely furnished, Shiloh judged the pieces to be of reasonable quality. These included a polished wardrobe, a small sideboard with mirror. Upon this last stood a china pitcher of water and basin awaited his morning ablutions. He noted a small towel for this purpose hung upon the foot rail of the bed. A single chair upon which he had placed his clothes upon retiring, and of course the side table and bed. There were no pictures upon the plain white walls, nor any ornament of any kind. It brought to mind the notion of a monk's cell, or more exactly a hospital room. Comfortable, but not comforting.

Acting upon an intuition, he rose from the bed and began a closer examination. He felt with his hand above the wardrobe, then checked underneath it at floor level. Coombes then lifted one leg of the bed, after first examining the carpet beneath.

His suspicion was justified; there was no dust above the wardrobe, nor any fluff beneath it, nor did he find any under the bed. The leg of the bed left but a faint impression upon they carpet. All of this furniture had only very recently been installed in the room. He went close to the wall, and sniffed. The odour of distemper came to his nostrils - it had also not long ago been painted.

A knock upon the door, and the voice of his host called, 'breakfast awaits us, my dear Coombes.'

After a surprisingly good breakfast cooked by his host, Coombes spoke to Feigenbaum about the room, voicing his discovery of it's newness. Feigenbaum clapped his hands, seemingly pleased at his acuity. 'Yes, you have smoked me out there, I must admit,' rubbing his hands together with satisfaction.

'I have noticed your sharp powers of observation upon a couple of occasions. We will do well together you and I, very well indeed.' The older man seemed very pleased about this, as he bustled about stacking the used dishes and cutlery. Coombes made as if to assist. 'No leave all that,' he cried, 'a woman will come in later to do all that.'

CHAPTER TWO

The evening past, before retiring to bed, Feigenbaum had opened up the topic to which he had several times alluded. He'd mentioned some ideas he had been mulling over, projects in which he hoped to involve Shiloh.

They had been seated at the kitchen table of Feigenbaum's surprisingly neat and tidy kitchen, drinking Feigenbaum's own recipe for what he termed a night-cap posset, consisting of warm milk and brandy.

'Before I get down to what I have in mind though, you should know something of me, and what sort of enterprise I have in mind. You will remember earlier this evening,' he'd begun, 'just as we were about to go off for our constitutional along the Thames, I had occasion to draw aside from you for a few minutes. I had a certain conversation with that fellow we met.' Coombes of course recollected the meeting, and as he had stood apart for Feigenbaum to converse with this man, he had been able to study the fellow. For he was a singular man.

Noticeably short, in a part of London where people were often of stunted physique, he stood no more than about five foot three or four inches. The man nevertheless carried himself with a particular vigour, a quickness of movement, somehow light on his feet like a trained dancer - more likely boxer, perhaps, had been his assessment. Although short, his body was thickset, his coat tight fitting almost to the point of splitting across his back. All in all, with his blunt ugly head and face, he reminded Coombes of one of those bull-baiting dogs. Not all that big, he'd judged, but quite possibly ferocious enough to make up for it.

As Shiloh had waited, politely out of earshot, he had taken the opportunity to fill and light his new pipe. Meanwhile the two had quite an animated conversation, heads close together, eventually breaking off and parting without further ado. Although nothing was said about it, Shiloh had got the distinct impression that the stranger

31

had been waiting about in particular to engage Feigenbaum in that conversation.

Feigenbaum had been delighted at his impression of the diminutive man. 'Oh Mr. Birtles will be delighted with that, he will. A pit bull terrier, hah! Oh yes, I must tell him. He is indeed a fierce little animal, our Mr. Birtles', all the while rubbing his hands with glee, 'he's a right terror, that one. He hates Jews, he always says, but when I reminded him that I was one myself, do you know what he said? 'Oh but Izzie,' he says, you ain't a proper four by two, is you. You gave me a great bleedin' breakfast of bacon and eggs once, didn't you.' He looked at me crafty; bacon and eggs, he said again. He grabbed me by the lapel of my kaftan and whispers in my ear; 'an' I won't be mentioning that around the synagogue neither.' Feigenbaum laughed his heartiest laugh.

'I haven't been much in a synagogue for years, but it seems if all the Jews in London ate bacon, our Mr. Birtles would think much better of 'em.' He laughed again at the recollection, then leant forward, still grinning, 'actually it was a couple of slices of pastrami, smoked beef, which he enjoyed so much with his eggs.'

Feigenbaum had been all seriousness once more, as he'd continued. 'See, Birtles is a Bow Street runner, and he and I have a sort of business arrangement. This arrangement comes into play over certain delicate matters. In such a case, I've had occasion to act as what you might call a middleman. A fixer. Sometimes some item of serious value gets pinched, see, or mislaid you might say. Usually so valuable that the poor *goniff* can't get rid of it, the fences are mostly too scared to touch really hot items. That's where I come in, see. It has to be done quickly, speed is of the essence, as Mr. Birtles says. Otherwise the stuff might go over the water to Amsterdam to be broken up, perhaps re-set or even re-cut if it's diamonds, melted down if it's gold or silver.

So for a negotiable fee, I endeavour to locate the said item. As I say, could be a prized family possession, a piece of jewellery for example. Birtles goes to the owner, and they come to some

32

agreement; after paying off the other party, all is well and happy.'
He paused to assess Shiloh Coombes response. The young man
appeared very thoughtful, and his question showed his lingering
reluctance.

'Isn't this sailing into murky waters, if I may put the question?
Doesn't all this throw suspicion upon yourself, ostensibly an honest
rag trader?' To the surprise of Coombes, his host had laughed,
reaching across the table he patted Coombes upon the shoulder.

'Delicately put my dear, delicately put. I see I shall have to be
as honest with you as you have been with me concerning yourself.
So here's the truth of it; many years ago I was sent down for
handling stolen goods, oh mostly small potatoes. I was living over
Saffron Hill way, in them days.

It all started from doing favours for others; some of the lads
about the place, street urchins and the like, used to bring
handkerchiefs and the like which they had lifted. If it was good
stuff, expensive like, we would unpick the fancy monograms, wash
and iron 'em, and then Bobs your uncle, sell 'em off again.' He
smiled to himself at the recollection. 'Like I said, small potatoes, but
sometimes it was a watch or two, money purses these young villains
would make off with. Anyhow, some crusading newspaper schmuck
made a mountain out of a molehill, and I was made out to be some
awful villain, corrupting these poor lads. The long and the short of
it, I finished up in the dock, accused of running a gang of
pickpockets.' Feigenbaum looked over at his companion Coombes.
'Honest to god, I never set out to be some crime boss, or anything, as
they made out. Whatever, they decided to give me a lagging and I
finished up transported to New South Wales for seven years.'

'That certainly must have been something of an ordeal,' began
Coombes, but Feingenbaum cut in; 'Oh it had it's moments, but to
tell the truth, it turned out not too bad. I finished up in Hobart town,
on Van Diemen's Land island – Tasmania they call it now. All that
hard work on the road gang, it made me awful thin, but I reckon it
also made me fit.' Feigenbaum chuckled at the memory, patting his

present waistline. 'Anyhow, I eventually got my ticket-of-leave and then managed to get financial backing from one of the military officers out there. Before long I was running a drapers and ironmongers shop.

All these officers see, they were making heaps of money on the side, running the rum trade and other dodgy enterprises. Some of 'em were bigger villains than any of the cons, I'm telling you. By acting as a sleeping partner in my business, this army captain, Rogers was his name, he could make it all look kosher, if you see what I mean.' He chuckled; 'We did right well, the captain and I, but for various reasons I wanted to get off the island. I made enough within a couple of years to buy myself out.' He paused now, looking intently at his young interlocutor.

'There now; I was lagged and transported, yes, but my conscience is clear. And this here business we are talking of, is totally legit and kosher. We set out to provide a valuable service –' here he broke into a grin; 'if you'll pardon my pun.'

Feigenbaum felt he had said enough – Coombes could make up his mind as to his course of action in his own good time. Reaching out to finish his milk and brandy posset, Feigenbaum stood and suggested as it was late, they should retire early, as they had a big day on the morrow.

Early next morning, as soon as they had finished their breakfast, Feigenbaum asked his guest Shiloh Coombes to accompany him on what he called 'an informative tour'.

'Where are we off to, if I may inquire?'

'Well you see,' continued Feigenbaum as they had stepped out into what appeared to be a rare fine day, 'we are going on an errand for Mr. Birtles, we spoke of him last night. You will remember I mentioned our special arrangement. Pausing only to peer both ways along his street, Feigenbaum locked his front door and they set off.

Feigenbaum again took up the conversation. 'This little

inquiry for our Mr. Birtles is very much in the line of what I have in mind for our enterprise. I won't go into long explanations, better that you get the drift of things as we go about today. ' He looked keenly at his companion, 'keep shtumm, and your eyes open.'

Leaving the short street, more a close, in which lay the house of Feigenbaum, they turned off into a narrow covered alley, and then out into a quite a busy street. Despite the fact that it was Sunday, they had to thread their way through a surprisingly large morning crowd, tradespeople already going about their business, the carts of bakers and milkmen.

Turning off from this busy throng, they made their way then through a maze of small mean streets, an area of the city unknown to Coombes, and as they walked, talking all the while, he looked back several times, but was unable to maintain his orientation and was soon convinced that he would not be able to navigate his way back, even on a bright day like this. Once more Feigenbaum seemed to intuit his thoughts.

'It does take a bit of learning right enough; these lanes and alleys go every which way. No plan at all, it seems. They say around here that this is because this is the original site, when old London was just a collection of hovels.' He laughed, 'still is, eh.'

Eventually they reached their destination near Houndsditch, a great open space filled with noise, busy with people scurrying about. It was, as Feigenbaum explained, the Rag Fair, the great old clothes market of London.

It was a Sunday morning, hence the market's busiest time, Feigenbaum explained. Shiloh admitted himself astonished by it. He had thought that he knew London. Of course he'd spent years in the country, at Willsden, his father's old school deep in the wilds of Yorkshire, but after coming down from Cambridge he'd stretched his rather modest allowance to explore the distractions of fashionable Mayfair. He had lived in London, admittedly on the west side, and had never so much as heard of this Rag Fair.

After hurrying to get there, Feigenbaum seemed content to

now stroll about, now and again greeting acquaintances, exchanging gossip, often as not in Yiddish. It seemed that ever second person knew him. Coombes had time to take in the many impressions offered by this busy scene. There was noisy bidding going on for baled rags of all kind. Much of it traded for paper making, and some for re-constituting, Feigenbaum explained as they made there way through this noisy throng..

Apart from the rag traders, there seemed to be great trade in new and second-hand clothing, selling anything from quite decent looking second hand clothing to cheap new clothing. Houndsditch, Feigenbaum told him, is also a cheap jack fair on Sundays. It was also the headquarters of the fancy warehousemen, mostly Jewish traders, supplying all the hawkers and small shopkeepers of London with what he called the small necessaries of life; from combs, razors, soap, sponges, toothbrushes etc. to cheap jewelry for the ornamentation of the poorer classes.

In yet another part of the vast market they came across traders who specialized in leather ware. From new boots and shoes, to furs, caps, and all items it was possible to make from animal skins. Further down, for the London building workers and other tradesmen there were laid out all the tools of trade.

As they progressed along Petticoat lane, Feigenbaum paused and sniffed, tapping his impressive nose. 'Smell that my dear? This is where one may buy all the sticky sweet spicy confectionery dear to the heart of the children of Israel —we shall have to take coffee along here a piece, and sample some of that brown butter cake, or this one,' as he hurried towards the next stall like an excited child. 'This is a special favorite of mine; it's a sort of pudding made of eggs and ground almonds. Come along quickly, we shall order our coffee, and the waiter will come back and fetch something for us.'

Shiloh Coombes was still somewhat bemused, he stood looking about him. It was like being in another country. The rows of food stalls carried all kinds of things, mostly unknown to him. The smells arising were exotic, alien to his English nose. It was here that the poorer Jews of London came seeking the foods they especially like to eat, from shining heaps of Spanish olives to wooden barrels of Dutch cucumbers pickled in salt and water. Here they came for such delights as herrings steeped in brine, pickled in vinegar, smoked sausage, the dried flesh of beef and mutton, smoked salmon, and, indeed, fish of all sorts. He saw fish being sold in every guise; fresh or fried in oil. Chickens, ducks geese added to the noisy scene. Further along Petticoat-lane, as Feigenbaum told him, were the kosher meat butchers, who prepared the meat according to strict religious protocol.

'So have you come here to do some rag trading Mr. Feigenbaum? asked Coombes, as they sat now together in a coffee house. The coffee house was situated in the area that appeared to be mainly concerned with the sale of second-hand jewellery and plate. Feigenbaum had told him that it was here in certain public rooms of certain well-known Jewish coffee-houses, where valuable and portable property readily changes hands. The old trader sipped his coffee. His eyes held a mischievous twinkle as he answered, 'oh indeed no - this my dear fellow, this is our aim this morning.'

Upon entering the premises of the coffee shop, Feigenbaum had been greeted effusively by the owner, a skinny little fellow with soft spaniel eyes who had rushed forward to embrace him. This he had suffered with good grace, only rolling his eyes at Coombes over the man's shoulder.

'We Jews are a demonstrative lot, eh?' he'd chuckled, 'he owes me a sum of money, you see.'

As promised, Feigenbaum ordered several of the various cakes and sweetmeats which he had pointed out to Coombes, and he appeared to all intents and purposes to be sitting there to enjoy a leisurely morning of coffee and cakes.

Shiloh was therefore surprised when Feigenbaum suggested after they had finished their refreshments that they return to his quarters. As they retraced their steps, Coombes could not resist asking why they had visited the rag fair – was it just for his amusement?

Feigenbaum's answered him with a loud laugh, clapping Coombes at the same time upon his back: 'Remember what I said as we set off; keep shtumm and keep your eyes peeled, again he laughed, amused by the look upon the face of his young companion.

'No my son, in fact I have completed our business on behalf of Mr. Birtles, and I should imagine that we might expect a visit from an interested party tonight. While you were having a look around, I passed the word about that if a certain necklace was to appear at the jeweler's market, there was a reward on offer. You see, the traders do not want any trouble; now that I have put the word about, no trader will want to touch the goods with a barge-pole. The smartest thing the *goniff* can do is take the reward whats on offer, and scarper, see.' he winked at Coombes, 'or if he is extra dodgy, he might sell it off for a part of the reward, and then the trader will pass it on and cop the rest.' They walked on a pace, as Coombes digested all this.

'You obviously then pass the goods on to Mr. Birtles, and he in turn to the owner. It would seem that perhaps these things are dealt with through too many hands.' He looked inquiringly at Feigenbaum.

'Yes! Capital! I knew you was sharp!' cried Feigenbaum, much pleased. You see, my plan is to cut out all these middlemen, and that is where you might come in. You are presentable, a right kosher young man about town. I believe we could advertise, yes in the Times itself; reliable and discreet, oh yes must be discreet, gentleman to arrange such business as we have just completed. What do you think?'

Coombes was silent as they continued on their way, obviously giving serious thought to these suggestions, and Feigenbaum wisely allowed him to digest the idea.

He had high hopes of this young man, and didn't want to hurry his thinking, nor make him feel pushed into making any hasty decisions. *Softly softly...*

Now and again he stole a sideways glance at his companion's

face, now set in concentration. The deep hooded eyes, the high beaked nose, once more reminded Feigenbaum of some bird of prey. This young man had intrigued him from the start; he had recounted a story of his troubles, yet Feigenbaum felt sure he told only part of it, he was open and at the same time oddly inscrutable. He often had the feeling that there was something deeply troubling Coombes; some problem or circumstance which bothered him constantly.

When he did focus upon something, Coombes was alert, alert with a total giving of his attention; it was this facility that had first commended itself to Feigenbaum's attention. He had seen within this young man, great possibilities. And yet at other times, he seemed to be so preoccupied with his own thoughts and concerns, and to such a degree that he seemed almost oblivious to the presence of others.

Feigenbaum considered himself a keen student of the human psyche, and this dichotomy puzzles him greatly. This private distraction within Coombes he felt was something quite apart from the recent family scandal about which Coombes had discussed so openly with him.

Shiloh continued on with his role in the laundry cellar. Feigenbaum could not fault him there; he had applied himself with single-minded tenacity to his primary task – that of 'becoming invisible', in the words of Feigenbaum. He also prided himself that he had become quite a proficient unpicker, and was at least to this extent useful to his benefactor.

From the shadows, his old mentor sometimes observed him. He still kept much to himself, but when spoken to directly, he would answer with ease, in accents now indistinguishable to those of the lads who would on occasion banter about with him, as boys will. Nevertheless, on the next occasion of their now frequent night walks, Feigenbaum did offer some criticisms.

'I heard you the other day, telling the boys a joke: very good I must say, but there is still something gives you away.' Coombes looked at him sharply, 'I saw you there; I thought I did well enough.'

'Oh yes well enough to fool a couple of lads, but I'm talking about playing the full monte, see. It's not just how you talk, is it, it's how you act, your whole stance. You stand confident in the world. You have to imagine yourself as being a man who has had to get by, who has had a few set-backs – in short someone who considers himself a bit of a loser, like.' Coombes snorted; "I should have thought I fit the bill', but Feigenbaum demurred. 'Oh yes you've had a bit of bad luck, but I'm talking about a man who has been a loser all his life. He is shifty. His stance is a bit cowed, he's always looking over his shoulder, perhaps expecting a blow. You have to adopt the whole persona, see. You have to not only talk the part, but to look it as well. In short, you have to be him.' Coombes was silent as they walked on apace, and Feigenbaum thought that he was disappointed, stung at this criticism of his attempts.

Suddenly his companion stopped, and took him by the collar. 'Ere,' he hissed, head close to Feigenbaum's ear, 'I've got somefing for you – bit of information like '- he glanced about, eyes nervously darting. 'Come over 'ere, over in the shadows. I din't nick it see, but I know 'oo did, like.' His eyes now glinting with a cunning light, 'If I can steer you right, wot's in it for me, eh?' again glancing back.

'Bravo!' cried Feigenbaum, 'that's it to a tee,' impressed with the progress of his protégée. 'Well done! I think you might well go on the stage, my dear fellow,' and he continued to chuckle as they fell again to walking.

When the weather allowed, they went on increasingly long walks, giving Coombes the opportunity to regain his full strength, and also to give him an increasingly good understanding of the surrounding streets. What at first has seemed to him a confusing maze of lanes and narrow crooked streets, was now forming as a pattern in his mind, and often Feigenbaum would try to lose him, and then ask Coombes to navigate them back to their street. He was getting quite good at it.

Every Sunday, weather permitting, that first Sunday's visit to the Rag Fair at Houndsditch was repeated, except that Feigenbaum varied their routine. As Coombes became more conversant with the area, they would sometimes approach the Petticoat Lane area separately, and when they ran into each other as planned, greet each other as friends. Another time, they would catch sight of, but not acknowledge the other.

Shiloh Coombes was wryly amused at himself; the way he seemed to just go along with what at times seemed the quite arbitrary directions of the old Jewish rag trader. Feigenbaum had explained what it was that he had in mind, but never in detail, always alluding to the plan in the making, for which he was training Coombes.

Feigenbaum made no bones of the fact that he sometimes involved himself in areas not strictly legal. He had at first thought that the old fellow had some nefarious scheme in which he'd wanted to involve him, but as time went on, Coombes had begun to think otherwise.

The strange thing was, it was as if he did not care. He had placed himself, and his trust, in this most unlikely saviour. At a time when he had felt himself at the lowest ebb, with no prospect in sight of a meaningful future, he had had been taken in by this man. Well so be it.

A curious fatalism had overtaken him, and he had simply decided to see how things panned out. To do as the old man asked. He had got to quite enjoy this game, of passing himself as a man of the East London mean streets. On the whole, though he could not exactly say that he was happy, he couldn't say that he was unhappy – content for the while, perhaps. His old opium compulsion seemed almost to have left him. He understood that it had been his only prop at a time of hopelessness and misery. Nevertheless, at odd times it would stab at him like a knife, as the urge still surfaced unasked, unwished for.

One Sunday morning Coombes was walking alone along Petticoat Lane, when he was accosted by a man, an acquaintance to whom Feigenbaum had introduced him as Sam. Now when in this

41

area of the great market, Coombes had begun to subtly change the way he spoke, and Feigenbaum had readily agreed it was a good practice.

'Always take on local color, my boy. You don't have to speak Yiddish, a lot of these London Jews don't any more, they are becoming integrated. A couple of words here and there, the manner – hey you get the drift, nu?'

This fellow though, had greeted him as Sam, and after some exchange of pleasantries, had asked Coombes to accompany him to the Synagogue in Bevis Marks Street. He had managed to convey to the man, a Mr. Greenberg, that he had an appointment to meet his relative, Feigenbaum. Greenberg had shaken his head sorrowfully: 'Ach weh, a good man you cousin, but I fear he has lost his way with God.'

Later, Feigenbaum had roared with laughter as Coombes had recounted his story, and his discomfort. 'You see my boy, you were too good a Jew! You will have to either learn more, or put it around that you have lost faith, like me,' he patted his young friend upon the shoulder, 'you did well though, and old Greenberg was not offended. Good; he is a decent old skin.' He learnt back, regarding his protégée with a critical eye.

'There is a germ of an idea there though - perhaps we shall have to present you as one of the old London Jews, one of the Sephardic following. They were here long before us Ashkenazim started to come over from Europe.' He laughed, 'you look bemused; I suppose you don't know much about all that eh?' One Jew is the same as the other, eh, isn't it?' Although his tone was jocular, there was a tinge of bitterness there. Just then their coffee arrived, and they spoke of other things.

It was not until they were making their way back towards the house of Feigenbaum when Shiloh Coombes again broached the subject.

'What is actually meant by those terms you spoke of back there; Sephardim, and Ashkenazim? If I'm to be able to sometimes carry off impersonating a Jew, perhaps I'd better get a bit *au faire* with some of this.' Feigenbaum regarded him, unsure where to begin. This young man, intelligent and all as he was, brought up as a thoroughly upper middle class English gentleman – what could he possibly know…

He chuckled, 'It's a long story, my boy; a long story.'

'Well at least give me a potted history, a bit of background. I can't always expect to be able to wing it like I did with Mr. Greenberg, can I?' And so began a conversation which occupied them the whole way back.

'I suppose we shall have to go back to when the Romans drove out the tribes of Israel from the Holy Land. To cut that long story short, some went west, into the Arabic lands, into North Africa. Eventually a lot of them settled in Moorish Spain, and in Portugal. It was something of a golden age for those wandering Jews, in that tolerant Moorish melting pot. Amongst themselves they even developed a sort of language called Ladino.

But then when the Catholic Christians drove out the Moors, they also made it uncomfortable for these Jews, the so-called Marranos. The Christians tried to get them to give up their Judaism, and if they didn't, they were persecuted. You probably know something about that bit, the Inquisition and all that, eh?' Coombes indicated for him to continue.

'Well, cutting it short again, some of these lot eventually settled into places like England, where it was a more tolerant situation. These are what we call the Sephardim. The Sephardic Jews.' He looked long again at his companion.

'Many have been long integrated into general society, of course. You possibly aren't aware that our Mr. Disraeli for example, the politician, is descended from these folk. A lot of the old families have been here in England for centuries. Follow all this so far? Good, now for our lot, the Ashkenazi Jews.

These people are descended from those who wandered north from the Holy Land, and on up into Eastern Europe, and from there some of us have finished up here in London as well.' His look was sardonic as he continued: 'Funny isn't it – we Jews all set off in different directions, and when we meet up again a thousand years later, we couldn't understand each other. Neither could speak the old Hebrew; still the formal language of the religion of course, but it was like Latin, a dead language.

All over central and eastern Europe, see, the Ashkenazim came to speak amongst themselves in a mixture of German with a sprinkling of Hebrew, with some Slavic words thrown in; this is what we call Yiddish.' Feigenbaum left off talking for a while, for Coombes to assimilate all this.

When he began again, it was to pose a question himself. 'Why is it like this;– we Jews, we wander all over the place, no real home, the goyim, the gentiles – pardon me, but the truth is, they tolerate us at best. When will it all end, eh?' The question didn't require an answer, it was rhetorical, nevertheless Coombes caught a glimpse into the existential melancholy of the eternal wanderer. They were silent for a while as they walked on. Eventually Coombes spoke.

'Actually I haven't seen you going off to the Synagogue, Mr. Feigenbaum, and from your philosophical discussion, I don't believe you have any more attachment to religion than I do myself, say. And yet you identify yourself as Jewish. Given the fact that as you say, Jews are always being persecuted, why is that? Why don't you just give it all over?' Feigenbaum gave him a sharp look out of the corner of his eye, snorting meanwhile.

Then in what was such a typical gesture of his, he tapped the side of his nose. Unexpectedly, he laughed, lightening the mood.

'Well it's this hooter, for one. I can't hide from it. As for the rest, you are quite right, I'm not all caught up in all that; all that - God said this, and God said that - carry on. As you yourself are also aware, all that blather is usually a vehicle of control by priests of all kinds, and that includes Rabbis.' He went on, 'as a matter of fact, I'm a great admirer of that Frenchie Voltaire, who wanted as his epitaph this aphorism: *Mankind will only be free, when the last king is strangled with the gizzards of the last priest...* ' When they had both finished laughing, Feigenbaum continued.

'No it's more a cultural thing with me; - I don't mean racial, but a shared heritage, a shared Diaspora.' His grin was mischievous, as he continued, 'and as you have so perceptively observed, it is also for me a disguise. I am not only a Jew, but I *play* the Jew, eh? Laughing again, he linked arms with Coombes. 'Having said that, I think that one day soon you and I might toddle around to the Bevis Marks Synagogue. You should find it interesting.'

The next week Shiloh Coombes saw little of the old rag man; Feigenbaum was often up and away straight after breakfast. He himself continued at his work in the rag laundry. Coombes wanted to prove himself, he felt that the old man was still testing him.. He wanted to show he was daunted neither by the work, nor the conditions, but he had to admit to himself that he was beginning to find it a drudgery. One day one of the Irish washerwomen though had put things in perspective for him. As they spooned down their midday soup, they fell to talking.

She was grateful she said, just for the chance to be able to feed her children and pay the rent on her one room. Her husband 'that feckless gobshite' as she described him, had taken off without so much as a goodbye or thank you, as she said.

Mrs. Flanagan was a formidable biddy, with a fierce unforgiving eye; privately Coombes thought that perhaps her erstwhile husband had been wise not to make an effort at any farewells. Nevertheless, as she said, the consequences for her would be very dire without the work she did here for the 'auld skin,' her appellation for Feigenbaum.

At first they had all been very suspicious of Coombes, but he had gradually won their confidence. He spoke now quite freely with the Irish women, they loved a bit of bawdy banter. He'd applied himself to their way of talking, and was always keen to pick up their expressions, try on their accents. Soon he felt confident that if the occasion warranted it, he could carry himself off as an Irishman; not perfect but passable in short conversations. He was starting to believe that he was near to that goal set him by Feigenbaum – to become invisible in the East End of London.

CHAPTER THREE

The day promised to be fine. It had rained in the early morning, a sharp shower, but the weather was now rapidly clearing, quite unlike the usual London grey, the drizzle from lowering leaden clouds. The cobbles were still slick and shiny, puddles there for the unwary, but the sudden appearance of a blue sky had brought an unusual amount of people out into the streets. Early spring, but although still nippy, there was promise of warmer weather in the air.

As Coombes and Feigenbaum strode along, children were everywhere, dodging amongst the horse drawn traffic. Their cries of childish delight as they ran and splashed through puddles mixed with the calls of the food vendors, plying their trade:- *'Fish fish fishooo...Fresh bread, fresh bread ladies – penny a loaf...Milko, Milko now, straight from the cow...Eggs I got, eggs I got – nice and fresh nah, eggs I got...'* bringing the housewives running out in their aprons to buy.

'Cheers everbody up, don't it', observed Feigenbaum, furling his umbrella at last.

'Yes indeed; I must say I quite feel in holiday mood, myself,' came back Coombes, 'the street urchins are all about eh – oh I say! Take a look at that swine over there.' Just as they had been enjoying the cheerful business of the street life, it was marred by the scene unfolding up ahead.

Out of a house doorway which exited straight onto the street, a man had rushed out, trousers only half done up, his braces down and with only a torn greyish undershirt covering his torso. He seized hold of a young boy by the collar who'd been skylarking with others in the roadway, and begun to thrash him with a broad leather belt. As he hit the boy, he shouted angrily at him. The other children with whom the boy had been joining in their fun, stood now silently watching.

'You rotten little barstid, I told you not to wake me, eh, didn't I ? Nah your for it proper. ' As the boy began crying out, a woman also came out from the same house. She was a slight person, and the man much larger, but she launched herself at the man, trying to take hold of his arm wielding the leather strap. With a backward swing of his arm, he swept her off her feet, so that she fell into the roadway.

'Keep out of it – ' but Feigenbaum was too late. In swift strides, his companion had reached the scene, where he also grabbed the raging man by the arm. This time the result was different. Ducking under a wild swinging fist which if it had connected would have finished the confrontation forthwith, Feigenbaum watched as his young friend ripped in two swift blows to the mans midriff, whereupon he collapsed wheezing, winded in a heap. The other boys still gathered around gave a ragged cheer, and then took to their heels. The boy helped his mother up, and they disappeared into their house, slamming the door.

The man was on his knees now, still trying to catch his breath, glowering up at Coombes, who stood over him, watchful.

''You'd better watch aht - I'll fix you for this you fuckun' sod, mark my words,' he finally managed.

'No - you watch aht; I warn you that if I 'ears that you are ever behavin' like you did 'ere, I will come around and sort you aht right and proper, you dog's arse.' For emphasis, he bent and twisted the man's ear quite savagely, causing him to squeal. The bully's bravado had deserted him; he offered no retaliation but remained kneeling, rubbing his sore ear.

At that moment, a window above screeched open, and the woman's head showed.

Without further ado various items of clothing was thrown in the direction of the man on the ground, followed by a pair of boots, on of which hit him on his upraised arm. Before he could voice complaint, the window was banged shut. Coombes and Feigenbaum stood by watching as the now completely cowed man hastily gathered his belongings and slunk off, to jeers and catcalls from neighbours.

As the two were themselves quitting the scene, the door

opened narrowly and the woman's face was framed in aperture. He face was white but resolute, as she spoke with some bitterness.

'I don't know 'oo you are, but I 'ave to thank you, I 'spose; that dosser was not my hubby. 'E's dead, aint 'e. In the war like. She jerked her thumb contemptuously, 'that'n weren't a patch on my Jim, not a bloody patch.' She looked without blinking at Coombes, 'but don't you dare judge me; Oh yes, I'm glad the mongrel's gone, but 'e 'elped me pay the rent, see - 'oos goin' to 'elp me now, eh?' and the door closed in his face.

Fairly taken aback at the result of his spontaneous actions, Coombes walked on for some minutes without a word: Feigenbaum thought it wise to keep his own mouth firmly shut. Finally he though it safe to venture an opinion.

'There is a saying; for every action a reaction. Sometimes the reaction is not quite the expected one.' Coombes glancing sharply at his friend, only snorted in reply.

'Oh come now my dear; we must always look upon such occurrences strategically.

Indeed I took several positives out of the outcome of your impetuous behaviour.' Again nothing but the sharp glance from the unmollified Coombes. Undaunted, Feigenbaum continued with his evaluation, 'firstly, you stayed entirely in character all the while. I particularly liked the bit about calling him a dog's arse.' Coombes had to laugh at this, despite himself.

'Thank you Feigenbaum. I thought it quite original myself,' turning an enquiring eye now to his companion, 'any thing else?' Feigenbaum punched him playfully on the arm.

'Well you did surprise me with your pugilistic skills; I was impressed. Very good my son, very good. I would bet that you have had a bit of training in the noble art, eh, eh?'

Coombes was soon restored to his usual temperament, as they chatted thus along the way.

'Well as a matter of fact I have. When I first came down from Cambridge I ran into an acquaintance from my old school, and he took me around to the West London Boxing Club. They meet regularly at the Bedford Head Pub, in Maiden lane, off the Strand. I dare say I picked up a few useful hints, apart from the occasional blood nose or black eye.'

'Well it certainly came in useful today. On the other hand, try to remember this – here in the East End, its best to mind one's own business, see. There is domestic strife and such carryings on all over the manor, and you aren't going to fix things –' his hand went up. 'I know, I know, you felt like you had to do something, right? But in the end, like the poor woman said, did it really help?' His grin softened the sting of the criticism.

'Now you probably think you are obligated to go back around there tomorrow and give her a bob or two – am I right?'

A discomforted Coombes shrugged, hands in pockets. Feigenbaum continued, 'I'm willing to bet that if you do, the door will be answered by that same gentleman you just now sorted out.' Coombes had to acknowledge that Feigenbaum was probably right in his assessment. He was beginning to realize that he had been a little impetuous, and his look was crestfallen. His companion clapped him upon the back, hoping to cheer him up.

'On the other hand, I could send a lad round tomorrow, 'e can suss out the situation, see. If she wants, I'll offer her job in the laundry; that or her lad could make himself useful about the place, alright?' Coombes had to admit his mentor's reading of the situation was probably very close to the truth, and they continued their constitutional without more ado. After calling in at a coffee house for refreshments, they made their way homewards.

As the day began to wane, with evening coming on, the two were once more were abroad. They were heading on towards their goal; they were going to listen to a political speech by a Mr. Robert Owen, a leading socialist. They had learned of it earlier, upon reading a poster they had come across. Feigenbaum had read it intently, and announced himself very keen to attend this meeting. The meeting was to be held in the Temperance Society Hall in

Whitechapel. Coombes had been intrigued by this unusual invitation from Feigenbaum; this seemed to be just one more side to his complex friend.

'You seem to have developed an interest in politics', he spoke said, his voice without inflexion.

'On the contrary, my dear chap,' he gave back tartly in reply to Coombes veiled amusement, 'I've always had an interest in all, although I tend to keep my ideas under my hat these days. I have always been interested in the human condition, often to my detriment I must say.' Feigenbaum was suddenly very serious as they walked along.

'As a matter of fact, that's the reason I had to flee the old country as a very young man. My youthful political opinions were perceived as too radical in some quarters, you see. I had to scarper, like quite a few others here in London. A fellow named Karl Marx, for one; he's still active in politics, he should be there today, together with some other interesting folk, along with every ratbag in London, spies and probably some gentlemen from Scotland Yard. He grinned suddenly: 'It should be quite entertaining.'

'Who are these gentlemen from Scotland Yard you spoke of, Feigenbaum?'

'You haven't heard? For this enterprise of ours I have in mind, you will need to know all about 'em. These are the people our Mr. Birtles was complaining to me about the other day. The days of his lot the Bow Street runners being the main thief takers in London is about over, you see. Early on the runners was meant only to be serving writs from the Bow Street magistrates courts, but then over time they was being asked to bring any reluctant miscreants before the courts. It was all getting a bit out of hand, see. Mr. Birtles might be open to a bit of freelance work, but some of his colleagues have been more than a bit free with the law, at times. Taking bribes, turning a blind eye to someone they was supposed to be bringing in, that sort of thing. No doubt you must have read some of it . There's been a lot of grumbling about it in the papers and talk in the parliament, so as a result we now have this new lot out of Scotland Yard. It's been a right hobby-horse of the Home Secretary, Sir Robert Peel. ' He laughed a short bark, 'that s why the call 'em bobbies, or peelers, see – 'ere, watch out for that horse shit –' They both laughed as Coombes nimbly hurdled the steaming pile.

'Old peel was always on about the rising crime rate, wasn't he, and so now they have these constables, or bobbies, getting about the streets with helmets on, uniform and all. Of course he sez they aren't military, don't he, but they certainly look it. Oh you have seen them then? They don't carry firearms, but they do have bloody great truncheons, and they like to use them. Mr. Birtles hates'em, he does, but that's only professional jealousy I sez to him. Anyhow, we have got our own fish to fry, and I'm sure Mr. Birtles will come in right handy, as we proceed.' They had now arrived at their destination, the Whitechapel Temperance Hall, the venue for the anticipated meeting. And anticipated it certainly seemed to be.

Although the doors of the Temperance hall were yet to open, quite a number of people, mostly men, were already gathered on the pavement and even spilling onto the roadway.

From their position across the street from the hall, the scene, lit only by a single gaslight, was of a surging shoving dark mass, white faces only briefly to be seen in the obscure light.

This growing crowd, some spilling out onto the roadway, was beginning to cause a hindrance to the normal horse drawn traffic. From what Shiloh could make out, there seemed to be several altercations going on at once. He turned t his companion for some explanation.

'What is all this then; the meeting has not even begun-' Feigenbaum seemed merely amused at the melee, as with a grin he turned to answer his friend.

'Well my dear, this isn't your Cambridge debating society, the rules are a bit loose, but It does seem as how the meeting has already gone into preliminaries; if they don't open up soon – there they go, its open,' and he darted forward across the road to join the crowd now shouldering their way into the hall.

Luckily Coombes pulled him back just in time out of the roadway as two teams of horses pulling wagons thundered into the street, pulling up just up from the Temperance Hall. One wagon carried some sort of machinery, all handles and polished copper fittings. Seated upon the second were a number of sturdy men in uniform, wearing tall shining brass helmets after the style of French cavalrymen. Although causing many to jump hurriedly back, their arrival was greeted with a good-humoured cheer from the crowd.

Feigenbaum explained. 'These are some of Captain Shaw's finest – the fire fighters. The Insurance companies pay for them to turn up at suchlike rallies; they fear that fiery speeches may set alight to the building, you see,' eyes glinting, he chuckled: 'what fun eh?' as he rubbed his hands. As the main push for the doors abated, Coombes and Feigenbaum made their way into the meeting hall.

Shiloh noticed with some surprise that there was to quite a distinct group of well-dressed people, both men and women, towards the back of the hall. Seeing his interest, Feigenbaum explained. 'Some toffs always turn up at these meetings; some are do-gooders, mind you, but most come to watch the fun. It's the sort that used to go out to Tyburn Hill for a picnic and watch the hangings. For them its like watching boxing matches, or dog fighting. Blood sports.'

Shiloh told himself that if not exactly fun, the event certainly promised to be diverting. After a lot of shoving and pushing, much calling out, the meeting was eventually brought to order by a stout man who resolutely retained his bowler hat inside the hall, no doubt to indicate his authority. This was born out by his veritable fog-horn of a voice with which he settled the unruly members of the audience.

When the noise had abated to a low rumbling hum, the man in the bowler bellowed his introduction to the evenings speaker, the Welsh socialist Robert Owen. He was received with a roaring ovation from a large section of the audience, and a vociferous booing from a smaller group right at the back of the hall.

'Those rowdy buggers right over the back there, they are professional agitators mostly', indicated Feigenbaum, 'they are always trying to disrupt such meetings.' Coombes looked about; these men seemed to be a tough looking bunch, nevertheless they appeared to be well outnumbered. He also observed standing all down along one side of the hall, the helmeted bobbies they had seen outside.

'Don't the Scotland Yard people prevent them from causing trouble?' he asked. Feigenbaum cocked a scornful eyebrow at him, 'prevent them? Lordy me no; some believe that they actually pay 'em to turn up.' As Robert Owen began to speak, they turned their attention to him.

Shiloh was a little surprised at the man's appearance. Given Owen's reputation as a fiery socialist firebrand, he had expected a more robust figure than this almost frail person speaking before this unruly crowd. His voice was also unexpected; although obviously Welsh by his intonation, he spoke in educated tones. Owen spoke with some eloquence, urging his audience to form some sort of organization - a union of like- minded men, he called it, to advance the cause of the working men of England. Coombes soon came to the conclusion that the man spoke a great deal of sense, not at all the ferocious radical as he had been described in the Tory press. He experienced a twinge of guilty unease; up until this meeting he had himself unquestionably shared that opinion.

But as Mr. Owen began to get into his stride, uproar broke out amongst the toughs at the back of the hall. They began cat-calling, whistling, stomping and calling out any rude rejoinder which came to mind, no matter that it was all non sequitur – 'Fuckorf aht of it, you Taffy bleeder – should be tarred and feathered,' and such like, some of them breaking into God save the Queen. This was followed by a rousing chorus of Rule Britannia. Then began much shouting from both sides, as tempers began to fray.

'Come on, we're best of out of it,' hissed Feigenbaum, as the meeting began to break up into scuffles, and those around Mr. Owen

gathered close about him as they forced their way to the front exit. '
No n , not that way, called Feigenbaum over his shoulder to Shiloh,
as he made off swiftly towards a darkened staircase leading to the
upper floor.

'Do come along, my dear fellow, this'll leads to a back way
out,' he continued to urge, as Coombes still hesitated. It had all
happened so quickly, he was not yet fully aware of what was going
on, in all the noise and confusion. His momentary hesitation was
broken when Feigenbaum ran back and grabbed his arm.

'The police will be making arrests, taking people's names –'
was as far as he got, and then had to himself to break into a run to
catch up with his younger friend.

Upon their return from the debacle at the Temperance hall
meeting in Whitechapel, Shiloh sat with Feigenbaum in the latter's
kitchen, drinking tea. They had returned from Whitechapel almost
without speaking, both apparently lost in their own thoughts.

'What I really don't understand, began Shiloh, ' is if as you
say, you fully expected a debacle, why on earth did we go to hear
Mr. Owen at all?' Feigenbaum put down his tea- cup, and leaning
with both elbows upon the table, he regarded his young friend.

'Well, see in the first place I wasn't really interested in Mr.
Owen or his speech, worthy man though he may be. I was on the
lookout for a certain person.'   'Ah, a bit of business, Mr.
Feigenbaum,' said Coombes, smiling. There was no answering smile
upon the face of his mentor.

'No, not just a piece of business, but a vital matter indeed.'
He sat still then, his eyes intent upon those of his young friend.
When he spoke again, Coombes was aware of a new gravity in the
old man's voice, as he got up from the table and began to pace about
the floor, hands behind his back.

'I don't rightly know whether it is any business of yours, I
certainly don't wish to involve you in it, but I will tell you something
of the matter as it might become necessary for you to know of it.'

He smiled then, but without mirth: 'forewarned is forearmed', he said then.

'I first ran into this fellow some years ago, you see, back in the old country. Very charming, liked by all who met him, or dealt with him.' Again the twisted grin; 'well almost all. My hooter here,' again tapping this generous organ,' my sixth sense, it told me he was perhaps other that what he seemed. Too glib, too good, I thought. But hey, what can you do?' Again his typical gesture, arms held out, palm up, 'what can you do with a feeling? Nothing but a certain distrust, some unease which you cannot put a name to?' Shiloh watched as the old man still paced the floor, seemingly needing this to bring coherence into what was obviously a difficult narrative. Coombes waited patiently. Although still obviously agitated, wringing his hands, eventually Feigenbaum marshalled his thoughts enough to begin.

'This fellow, his name is Adam Werth, though I don't know what he calls himself in this country. He uses many different aliases. He was from a Jewish family who immigrated to America, but he later returned to the old country.' He paused then in his narrative, and muttered, more to himself – 'and that was a great misfortune.' Suddenly weary, he turned and sat down heavily at the table. 'Ere, pour us a good dollop of port, there's a good chap. This tale is going to take a while.'

When he had finished his story, Feigenbaum sat silent, head bowed over his forgotten glass of port held still tight in both hands. Shiloh Coombes was also silent; he understood that the telling had left his mentor mentally and physically exhausted. It had indeed been a harrowing telling. Coombes turned aspects of the account over in his mind, before eventually speaking.

'So this fellow, this Werth, did you spot him there that night?' Feigenbaum lifted his head, seemingly restored to his usual self.. 'Oh no, I didn't really expect to,' he explained in a calmer voice, 'I was looking for another man, a friend. I'd had the word, see, that it was possible this Werth was set to do him harm. I wanted to warn him if possible.' Only then did he discover his untouched port, which he now sipped.

'He is one of us as well see, an émigré, and he once done me a great kindness.' He threw a sharp look towards his young companion. 'You probably think I'm a cynical old bugger, eh. I never forget a grudge, its true, but the rare good turns I've 'ad, I don't forget them neither.'

It was several days after these events when a singular occurrence took place. Feigenbaum and Shiloh Coombes were returning home from the Rag Fair, where Feigenbaum had not met with success. Nobody seemed to know anything of the whereabouts of the man he still sought. It was already far advanced into the evening, the air had a nip in it, though the weather had held good for those traders who made their living at the Sunday Rag Fair in Houndsditch.

They were talking animatedly as they came out of a covered way into a thoroughfare, so the two-horse open landau which came at them at a spanking pace nearly succeeded in skittling the both of them. The less nimble Feigenbaum had in fact lost his footing as he jumped back. Picking himself up, he was struck by the appearance his young companion. Coombes stood there, stock still, staring after the fast disappearing carriage. Feigenbaum had the fleeting impression that Coombes had seen an apparition. To somehow ameliorate the awkward moment, he said as much to Shiloh Coombes. At first It was as if the younger man hadn't heard the remark, but then after a pause, he turned to face Feigenbaum. He understood then that Shiloh has needed some time to compose both his countenance and his turbulent thoughts. The face of Coombes was deathly white, and set like stone. His eyes, glittered like broken glass. But when he finally spoke, his voice was steady, modulated.

'I beg your pardon, Feigenbaum; I didn't quite catch what you said.' Only a tic in his cheek betrayed his inner turmoil.

'Oh I say, Coombes, what is it ? I said you look like you have just seen a ghost.'

'I believe I have, my friend. I believe I have. A ghost of a delusion I once suffered.' Upon that , he nodded briefly and without a further word, hurried off into the gathering darkness, and was soon lost to the sight of his bewildered friend and mentor.

Assuming that his young friend needed some time on his own to reflect upon some disturbing private memory, Feigenbaum was not concerned when Coombes had not yet returned to the house by late evening. After sorting through some of his accounts, and dozing for a time before the fire, Feigenbaum ate a solitary supper of cold chicken, pickled onions and rye bread. Leaving a covered plate for the latecomer, the old man took himself off to bed.

The next morning, seeing Coombe's bed undisturbed, his supper untouched, Feigenbaum did begin to begin to worry. In the relatively short time of their acquaintance, he had become fond of Shiloh Coombes. A man of shrewd native intelligence himself, he had relished the conversations, the brilliant mind, of this strange young man. And he had plans for him.

But by the end of the week, having consulted with Birltles, and having sent out some youngsters to learn something of his whereabouts, he had discovered nothing. It was as if Coombes had disappeared from the face of the earth. Birtles had been pessimistic: 'it looks like e' don't want to be found, is my opinion. If he were dead, we would 'ave 'eard of it.' Feigenbaum had to admit defeat. Regretfully, he had to put Coombes from his mind. He had still greater concerns for his old benefactor, whom he feared to be in grave danger from the sinister Adam Werth. If Coombes had decided to disappear – well that was ultimately his business. More than anything though, Feigenbaum regretted that he had somehow failed to read the man's true character. He had thought that despite obviously having some private problems, Coombes was a man of integrity. To slink off like some cur… no, it was hard to fathom.

CHAPTER FOUR

The small compact figure marched with confident step down the corridor to which he had been directed. He knew exactly where he was going, only his innate circumspection allowed him to accept direction, as if he had never before been here - *Never let anyone figure you out, don't let them get the drop on you.* It was his ruling motto.

Although well below average height, he had about him a forceful, energetic appearance. Like many a short man, he tended to overcompensate. A patriotic Englishman, at a time when such sentiments were absolute, unconditional, he was also a secret admirer of a certain Corsican. Ned Birtles considered himself a self-made man. As such, he had constructed for himself a stern, even rigid code of conduct. *Always show a bold face* – another of his principles. In this instance, it required that his outwardly confident air masked an inner discomfort. For one thing, he'd always felt a little out of his depth in this forbidding building, this bastion of powerful secrets, and especially was he uncomfortable dealing with the man to whom he was about to make his report. . And this was not going to be good. The man whom he was to meet paid handsomely for his work, but did not react kindly to failure. Ned felt a trickle of sweat run down the back of his neck, which he endeavoured to mop with his kerchief.

In this long dark-panelled corridor, other than by number, no door was marked. The implication was clear; if one didn't know upon which door to knock – then one shouldn't be here. Using his reflection in the polished mahogany of one such door, Birtles adjusted his neck cloth. Squaring his shoulders, he knocked very firmly upon the door now before him. The deep rumbling voice, irritable, called; 'Come in man. You don't have to knock the bloody door down.'

The fat man sitting behind the desk before him looked him up and down in that cold manner of his - *rather like an undertaker, measuring up* - Birtles thought. He gazed thus for a second or two over his rimless pinz-nez, before jerking his head slightly, to indicate that the man before him might be seated. Choosing to ignore this meagre courtesy, Birtles however remained standing.

'So you *have* located him, your message said?', the fat man began without preliminaries, 'I told you not to come here unnecessarily; you'll get paid when I decide I have got my money's worth. Have you got anything else?' Here Birtle's facade of equanimity began to crumble. 'Well yes sir, I did find 'im wivvout too much trouble, like, but you see – ' 'What is it man, don't stand there mumbling. Come to the point.'

'Well sir, its like this; I've lost track of 'im, in a manner of speaking -' 'What on earth do you mean, man, in a manner of speaking. I told you to keep a close eye on him. Explain.'

Eventually escaping this uncomfortable interview, a chastened Ned Birtles went upon his way, still smarting from the abrasive cross-examination he had just endured. Nevertheless, when he took stock*:*

- Not too bad, not so bad at all, considering.

One thing that rankled; the fat man insisted upon calling him by his Christian name.. He must be aware that Birtles was not happy with this, Birtles detested the name his mother had bestowed upon him. He was known as Ned Birtles to all who knew him, having long since decided that Bryson was a poncy name, certainly not suitable for a man who had a certain image to maintain. Like a lot of short men, Birtles more than made up for his lack of height with a surfeit of aggression.

Watch art – 'ere comes Ned Birtles!

Despite that unpleasant scene, he was still employed on this job. He knew that although he had in fact failed to keep his mark under observation, his employer still considered him the best man for the job. But his sense of self worth, his pride in his abilities, had been hurt, far more than the caustic interview he had just withstood.

- hey, water off a duck's, if he still had the account -

Nevertheless, he really would now have to find the bugger – honour depended upon it. But where to on earth *had* that tosser Coombes disappeared? Having first regained a modicum of equanimity by smacking down the hand which an inopportune beggar had thrust at him, Birtles set off at a smart pace towards Horse Guards Gate, head up, arms akimbo. He *would* find the bugger, he would. And then this other business. The fat man, as Birtles always thought of him, had given him another thunderbolt. 'Birtles, just a moment, he'd said, as Ned reached the door to make his exit. The voice was now silky, polite. Ned feared this tone from the big man more than any shouting. Without speaking, Birtles stood foresquare, braced, awaiting what should come next. It was not good.

Seated by the drawing room window, the young doctor observed his patient at the bottom of the vegetable garden, busy with a hive of bees. Curiously, although he used a bee-keeper's smoke puffer, young man at the hives wore no protective clothing; he hadn't even availed himself of a net veil. The doctor shook his head slowly from side to side – part despair, part admiration.

Damn fellows mad, but he actually gets away with it

At dinner on the previous evening, his patient had loftily claimed that if one took the trouble to understand the psychology of bees, one should have no problem with them. The doctor snorted – *the psychology of the wee beasties indeed!* - After five years in India with the British army, he considered himself a bit more hard-headed than this admittedly fascinating but equally irritating patient. It was a little galling to watch the fellow prove himself right, as he picked out a piece of honey filled comb, and waved it at the doctor seated at his window. The most galling part; by his own admission, until two days before, the patient had known absolutely nothing about bee-keeping. There was something almost frightening about the way he seemed able to seize upon a subject. With his whole attention he would focus upon it, and absolutely within such a short time appear to know an enormous amount on the subject. The doctor had initially encouraged the patient's interest in apiary, with a view towards his recovery .

The man had effectively gone through the worst of the ordeal of breaking his opium habit, and he seemed to have improved markedly in health. But that had not been the full picture:- his mental condition had remained very low. During the first week under the doctor's care, his responses had been singularly unrewarding; he seemed sunk in heavy depression. In fact the doctor had consulted an older colleague, who had advanced the diagnosis of morbid melancholia, probably incurable and he'd strongly advised his junior colleague to have the patient transferred to the nearby lunatic asylum over at Hanwell.

It was difficult for the self-described hard-headed young ex-military doctor to put in to logical terms his reluctance to do so; his own instinct though suggested that here was a man who had gone through traumatic events; his refusal to open up, his depression, did not necessarily suggest a permanent clinical condition. So despite his vaunted hard-headedness, he had taken the patient on as his personal case. The fact that he'd observed several signs, some sudden glimpses of brilliance in the mysterious patient, had convinced the doctor to persevere. He believed that only time would tell, in such a case. He'd taken his patient completely under his wing, bringing him here to his uncle's secluded country house in Sussex.

This sudden intense interest in the bee-hives kept by the doctor's uncle in his back garden, he'd encouraged as a major step in his patient's eventual recovery. He just wished the fellow wasn't quite *so* single-minded about it.

As the doctor got to know this patient, he had more than once observed this amazing faculty of total focus. In writing up the case in his journal, the doctor was to liken it to a light focussed through a perfect diamond; cold, sharp and absolutely brilliant.

It appeared he was on the mend, but for now, this brilliant but enigmatic man needed for the most part rest and good care. Some country life, fresh air and fresh food could work wonders.

Invalided out of military service due to a stray Pathan bullet finding his shoulder, upon his return from India the doctor had been restless; he'd found the quotidian civilian practice of medicine very tame. Then of late he had found for himself a purpose; he's become more and more involved in doing pro bono work in the slum streets of East London.

It was during a late night call-out for a woman in difficulties with a breech birth that he'd first come into contact with his singular patient. In a squalid, dingey room, lit by the light of a single candle, the doctor had finished washing up after the difficult birth. He'd just begun addressing a few words of advice to the midwife when a knock came upon the door. Following a whispered conversation between the midwife and the visitor, she eventually deemed it prudent to allow this person to enter. He did so, dripping water everywhere as he did so. In the dim light afforded by the cheap candle, the doctor recognized the man. He was a Chinese Christian missionary with whom he'd had some contact in the course of work.

'Thanks to God I have found you doctor sir', he began without preliminaries, 'I would like to have your assistance if you could be so kind sir, to rescue a gentleman in distress.'

After a hasty conversation, it turned out that the missionary had been given the information from within the Chinese community that a certain opium den in Limehouse was holding a white man for ransom. Acording to this story, the man was kept drugged, and held without his cognisance. Although reluctant himself to get involved, the missionary was willing to lead the doctor to the vicinity of the opium den, and point it out. He was vehement that the information was reliable.

And so it had turned out. Initially reluctant to even admit to the existence of any such white man, the doctor had rapidly convinced the house's management that it would be better for them release their hostage, as they would certainly not wish to draw the attention of the constables. With the assistance of the waiting missionary, the doctor had taken the barely conscious man to a nearby church. From there eventually to have him carried to the doctor's private quarters in a hansom cab.

Still holding up his triumphant piece of honeycomb, Shiloh looked about him. The splendid morning, the joyous cries of birds all about; the beauty of the spacious gardens of his host – it all suddenly impinged upon his senses. It was as if the moment, so delicious, was frozen for a space of time. Breaking from the spell, so fragile as a bubble, he waved again to the doctor watching him through the window, and went on methodically removing more honey from the hive. The combs full of honey gleaming like gold in the sunlight. He said aloud the words which sprang to mind; 'the bounties of nature.'

He felt a great happiness, at peace with himself and the world.

'Well you certainly seem to have bounced back old boy, like an India rubber ball, I must say,' the doctor looked across the table with obvious pleasure, as he regarded his erstwhile patient, now so seemingly miraculously restored - not only to full sanity, but to a positive, lively outlook. His conversation now was in full flow, his sparkling intelligence one more fully engaged with the world. Curious about everything, he nevertheless already seemed to know a frightening amount of stuff about diverse subjects.

As he ate his breakfast kippers and toast, he had been quizzing the doctor in depth over the latest advances in medicine. Laughing, the doctor threw up his hands in mock surrender. 'You seem to know as much as I do, my friend, about medicine. I do believe you could pass the medical finals with the slightest amount of study.'

'Study you say? Where exactly does my weakness lie? I should have thought I would have no problem at all.' For the doctor, accustomed to the politesse of middle class etiquette - gentlemen always to pretend modesty with regard to their achievements - this man's blithely unselfconscious declaration of his competence was confronting, but at the same time the man's complete lack of any note of boasting mollified him. To be sure, there was arrogance there, but it was a trait that this man Shiloh Coombes was himself totally unaware of. Since his return from India, and very much as an outcome of his slum work, the young doctor had become increasingly interested in the study of mental aberration in it's various aspects. He had of late been reading up on the Viennese fellow Freud. One particular essay by Freud had caught his eye:- it dealt with the tendency towards obsessional neurosis, usually considered by Freud to indicate deep early childhood trauma. Freud had mentioned also in passing the name of a young psychological researcher named Asperger, who had not as yet published his theory on this subject.

There was much in the behaviour of this man - his obsessiveness, his frequent lack of empathy - to lead the doctor to believe that this diagnosis might well apply to his patient. In an attempt to get to the bottom of Coombe's problems, he broached the subject with Coombes.

By this time, the relationship between the two men had changed; it was no longer strictly one of doctor and patient, but had developed into an easy friendship. And it was in the relaxed spirit of this friendship that Shiloh now teased the doctor.

'Come come my dear sir, enough of this Viennese quackery. I very much resent you categorizing me as an asparagus, or some such – no no, I reject it - if I have any choice in the matter, I would prefer to be viewed as a perfectly good English carrot.' With that he leapt to his feet, and grabbing the doctor by the arm, propelled him towards the open door. 'I know you have a dicky leg, as well as your shoulder, but I am sure I can help you recover a better use of the leg at least, before you can turn me into a bloody vegetable, old boy.'

Initially, in the need to get Shiloh fit, and back in contact with the world at large, they had begun taking daily walks around the neighbouring country lanes. They had begun with Coombs still deep in depression, sitting in a bath chair. The doctor persisted; eventually for Coombes to walk under his own steam. Very soon, however, it was the doctor's leg that now slowed them down. Coombes had suggested to the somewhat sceptical doctor that with daily massage and long walks, he could get the stiffness out of the affected limb. They had been at it for only a few days, but already the doctor had to admit; his leg was decidedly improved. He still walked with the aid of a stout blackthorn stick, but more and more the stick was just for confidence.

'I must say, Coombes, I really do owe you thanks for my old leg, you know.' They had walked on a pace before Shiloh stopped and turned. He regarded his companion for a moment or two. 'You have rescued me on several counts, my dear doctor. One, from that beastly opium den, second, from the grip of the addiction itself, and thirdly, from going down into a black abyss of madness. For you to thank me, you must understand, for any small thing I might do for you, fills me with embarrassment. I will ever be in your debt sir.' So saying, he put out his hand.

It was then that the doctor realized that it was not lack of empathy, but a reticence, a deep shyness and sensitivity of soul which had made the man seem aloof and uncommunicative. Coombes went on: 'You may have noted in your file on my case – here he grinned at the discomforted doctor – 'that I am secretive, and it is true I have told you almost nothing of my self; to be fair, I have asked you nothing of your life, either. It seemed to me, that things were best kept at a strictly doctor /patient level. However, it seems that we have become friends, and perhaps we should exchange notes, as it were.' He still held firm to the doctor's hand. 'For example; tell me, for I do not know it. What *is* your name?'

The rag trader Feigenbaum sat in his chair by the fire, but there was a chill in his heart which no fire could warm. He listened further to the report of his informant in silence. When the other fell silent, he glanced up sharply from his contemplation of the flames.

'What was that you said just then– does *he* have something to do with all this?'

'Well Izzie, its like this see. I do a bit of work for this gent in Whitehall – yes, a very important gent 'e is too – and anyhow in the course of my investigations, the name of this Adam Werth came up. As you 'ad already warned me about 'im, I 'ad already sniffed around real careful like.' Birtles looked gravely at the man by the fire, 'and you were right, my dear – he is a right bad lot indeed. We – that is my client at Whitehall believes, that he was directly involved in the assassination of your friend.' Feigenbaum groaned at hearing this definite news of his friend's death; a death he had been powerless to prevent. Birtle fell silent, gazing into his wine as Feigenbaum began to rock back and forth in grief: 'Ach weh, ach weh', he cried.

'You asked about your other friend, that young Coombes.' Despite the signs still of obvious grief, Birtles saw that he had Feigenbaum's full attention once more. 'Yes go on, go on tell me – nothing as yet on young Mr.Coombes?'

CHAPTER FIVE

It was a chilly morning, low mist still hanging about, but the day promised to be fine. The two friends stamped their feet and clapped their hands vigorously together to ward off the cold, breaths steaming white in the still morning air. They were waiting for the village diligence to carry Coombes to the nearby railway station. His friend the doctor waited to see him off, still making suggestions for the immediate future of his former patient.

'For Gods sake, old chap; stop fussing like an old hen – I shall be perfectly alright. I absolutely must go up to London to visit my friend Mr Feigenbaum. He must think I'm either dead or have taken off somewhere' - here he smiled to take any offence out of his initial remarks.

'Have no fear John; I make so few friends I shall absolutely haunt you from now on.' He glanced over his friend's shoulder – 'Here comes the dog cart now', and picking up the small carpet bag containing the clothes which his host had lent him, Coombes was away.

As the day drew on, the weather deteriorated. It was grey and raining over London, as the train made it's way through the built-up city outskirts. With nothing but the miserable back yards of dismal row after row of suburban houses to look out upon, Shiloh Coombes felt his newly recovered sense of optimism badly diminished. During the period of his rehabilitation, he had allowed himself to forget what a grim place London could be, on such a day as this.

The hustle and bustle of getting off the train at Victoria Station, the shouting of porters, the whistle bowing, all combined to shock Shiloh back into reality. Waving off a looming porter, he grabbed his slight luggage closer to him. He laughed to himself at his action;

- *It's all I've got in the world*

Of course it was not quite as drastic as all that. The good doctor had insisted on not only lending him two hundred pounds, but had also thrust upon him a letter of credit on the doctor's London bank. Embarrassed, Shiloh had been about to refuse when the doctor had stopped him:

'Beggars can't be choosers, old boy' and his benign smile had taken any sting from his words. For Coombes, the extraordinary help this affable young doctor had extended towards him, the friendship he has so openly extended, and then this trust in him, was the final medicine required for his recovery. If another could value his friendship, could show such trust in him, it gave him the impetus to rebuild his own sense of self worth.

- *For he had fallen far into that dark abyss of despair.*

Removing his bowler to make himself even smaller and inconspicuous, Ned Birtles silently congratulated himself: ' *Neddy boy, you are a bleedin' fuckin' marvel, you are* ', even as his head moved rapidly from side to side, his gimlet eyes never leaving the approaching figure of his mark. And Ned was right to congratulate himself. With nothing to go on, just a man who had completely disappeared - and now he had smoked him.

Actually he had to admit, it hadn't been as difficult as he would tell it when he reported to his employer in this case, the Fat Man over there in that anonymous building in Whitehall. Then there was this other player, who hearing that Birtles was after a certain man, had offered him another retainer - to inform him before any other party of any success. This person had wanted all the information he could extract from Birtles, but Ned was not taken in by the man. He had posed as a journalist, but Birtles had not believed it. Journalists did not offer such money about. Being a natural borne businessman, Birtles had accepted the retainer, but with private reservations. Although he felt no love for the Fat Man, nor any loyalty, this decision hinged entirely upon the practicalities; with the Fat Man, he had regular work.

70

In making his inquiries, he had got some information regarding a doctor who did charity work in the slums of East London, and many he met were full of praise for this lone crusader. Birtles was not overly impressed by this – *just another nosey ponce with a bad conscience* – but there had been one gem of information he'd garnered amongst all these sentimental effusions, as he called them. Apparently this doctor had gained the release of an unknown white gent who had fallen into the hands of the Chinese tongs. Sniffing something, the bloodhound Birtles had quickly sought after and found this doctor's place of residence and the address of his practice. It had not taken much to elicit from the doctor's housekeeper the doctor's present whereabouts.

The man he'd consequently dispatched down to Sussex to sniff about had struck gold. That very morning Birtles had received a telegram :

Expect our friend on 10.25 Victoria Stn.

And - *ah yes,* here he comes now. Absolutely bloody perfect. But then as Birtles watched, things began to go wrong. On the other side of the platform, off to his left, pushing through the moving crowd of passengers, came the very man who had approached him, the so-called journalist. He was a man well above average height, and stood out. Birtles saw it all in a split instant, understood everything. The intent look on the fellows face, the folded newspaper – folded in such a strange way, half hiding his right and, while the other hand supported the paper – was there something – glancing about him, Birtles slid from inside his coat a slim black leather cosh. A harmless seeming object, except that inside the smooth leather was lead pipe. In one swift motion he threw it at the head of the tall man who by now was opposite him.

Gotcha

It was all done so smoothly, so unobtrusively, that none of the hurrying passengers noticed anything except that a tall man seemed to have fainted in the crowd. So smooth indeed that when Shiloh Coombes passed by, he saw only a knot of people surrounding a prone figure upon the ground. A few paces more, and he heard the excited cry: 'Watch out- he's got a revolver!' Shiloh half hesitated, then a voice very close to his ear hissed: 'Come on, keep walkin', for Christ's sake', and he looked down in some surprise, at the tense face of Ned Birtles.

Taking note of the urgency in the man's voice, Shiloh Coombes offered no argument, but hurried through the crowd after the squat figure of the Bow Street runner. Birtles commandeered a waiting horse cab outside the station, and they set off through the rainy, sodden streets. His attempt to speak to Birtles was cut short by him – 'Lets just wait until we get to old Feigenbaum's gaff –' he peered hard at Coombes – 'I imagine you *was* wanting to visit the old gent?' and without waiting for any answer, turned to look out of the cab window.

They were seated at last in Feigenbaum's kitchen, their wet coats steaming by the fire. The Bow Street Runner sat silent by the fire, drying his sodden bowler. As Feigenbaum busied himself coaxing tea from his samovar, Coombes began to apologize for his disappearance, but he was cut short by the old man, who had earlier received him without restraint, embracing him and wishing him a hearty welcome.

' -Yes, well never mind all that for the moment. We'll go into all that later, if you don't mind my dear, but right now we have grave matters to discuss. Nodding his emphatic agreement, Birtles broke his silence.

'I'll say we have; we seem to be faced with a rum situation 'ere.' Birtles then stood up, laying his steaming bowler upon the table. Without more ado, he proceeded to recount all that he had found out during his search for the missing Coombes, followed by a brief, professionally concise summary of all that had transpired up until this moment. All this he told in a flat monotone, facing a blank wall, eyes seemingly out of focus, as he recalled and recounted the minutest of details. Only twice during this account, did he have recourse to his notebook, to verify certain points.

Listening, Coombes was in awe. Feigenbaum had once intimated to him that he had much to learn from this squat pit-bull of a man, a type for whom he felt an instinctive dislike. He had dismissed the idea that he and this man might have something in common as some sardonic joke from Feigenbaum. Now he knew better. Birtle's attention to the tiniest details most would not even notice, his extraordinary recall; he was a marvel.

Shiloh's musing was rudely interrupted by that same marvel as he completed his report. Birtles now bent suddenly, so that his face was level with and no more than two inches away from the startled Coombes.

'That's me done; now if you don't mind, I want to hear from yourself in your own words, squire, just what 'ave you got to do wiv all this.' The words Birtles spoke were civil, indeed polite, but the tone held a heavy menace. Birtles then sat down across the table from Shiloh Coombes, from where he regarded him with unblinking eyes.

Coombes looked at the two men before him; where to begin? It was a complex story, one he had not as yet got straight in his own mind.

'My last few weeks – it is a convoluted tale, I'm afraid, and I promise you will hear it. For now, I think the main point is this; I haven't the faintest idea of just what is going on. Mr.Birtles seems to think that man at the station was about to shoot me. He seems to believe that I must know something of all this. I'm sorry but I cannot think Mr. Birtles, what that something might be'. Birtles sat impassive.

'Just tell us everything you can remember.'

Shiloh did his best to emulate the detailed account of Birtles, but as he tried to make a coherent account of his movements and whereabouts over the last fortnight or so, it became apparent that quite a lot of these past days had passed by him in a daze, and he had to be prompted by both Birtles and Feigenbaum.

Finally he came to a stop, feeling that they had extracted about all they could from him, short of draining his blood. The two across the table seemed to agree, as they sat for a while in thoughtful silence. He looked from one to the other, sitting silent at the table. Then Coombes addressed himself to Ned Birtles.

'As I said earlier, Birtles, I am completely in the dark here, but if I may ask one question; who set you out after me?'

For a long moment the squat Bow Street Runner stared at him, and Shiloh was about to conclude he would receive no answer. Finally Birtles spoke, and it was clear that he had been wondering how he should answer the question just put to him.

'Well sir, though I understand your interest, I regret that I am not at liberty to divulge.'

And the thin trap-like mouth once more snapped shut. Coombes regarded the man for a second or two through hooded eyes, but asked no further question. He spoke again to both men;

. 'Please don't think I am not grateful, indeed l I am indebted. I really must thank you both for taking the trouble – ' to be cut off once more by Ned Birtles, 'it wasn't our friend 'ere who got me after you, if that is what you are thinking – anyhow, I am not permitted to tell you who did, except to say that he is a werry important man, and that 'e didn't seem to wish you any 'arm, like. But the other one – 'im at the station – I got the distinct impression that he did intend you some grievous harm.' And he sat back, smug, sure in the belief that he had given nothing away. Feigenbaum however noticed the quick gleam of triumph, the flicker of a smile upon the lips of Coombes.

Having headed off this awkward line of questioning, Birtles began to elaborate on his contact with the other player in the unfolding drama. He recounted how this fellow had approached him, upon learning of Birtle's enquiries.

'The thing is, this other cove - I 'adn't told 'im nothin'see – 'e must have follered me, the cunning swine.' Ned Birtles didn't take kindly to being hoodwinked, he didn't, and he made this clear as he glared around the table. ' 'E was the one at the station all right.'

'You did well, Ned my dear, very well indeed, didn't he Coombes?' soothed Feigenbaum, and Birtles was soon mollified by their responses.

Feigenbaum poured out another tea, together with a tot of rum all round, and got up to pace the floor. 'You see, Coombes, much has occurred since you disappeared – yes later my dear, later – and we shall have to make plans.' His face was very grave, as they listened to what he had to say.

'Since you were here, I have had word that my friend, the one I wanted to warn, has met an unfortunate end. The people from Scotland Yard –' here a snort from Mr. Birtles – 'say it was suicide, but I don't for a minute believe it; I believe he was done to death by that evil scoundrel Werth himself. Mr. Birtles has verified my suspicion.' The memory of this tragic event overcame Feigenbaum for a moment; words failed him, and he turned away, loudly blowing his nose.

'No no my boy, it had nothing to do with you – at least I thought so until this very morning, but my friend was apparently already dead by the time you went missing.' He looked sharply at Coombes. 'But from what Ned has just told us, and judging from his description, it was that same Adam Werth who was out to kill you, right there on Victoria station.' He was still looking intently at the younger man. 'Can you not tell us *nothing* at all about this connection?'

It was an odd secluded spot, a narrow ledge of stone behind an old warehouse, overlooking the Thames. Sprouting moss, with a few weeds poking up through the cracks, it was clearly a place rarely accessed. The haunt mostly of alley cats, it now held a human figure. His long legs dangling over the edge of the coping, Shiloh Coombes sat deep in thought, his head wreathed in the fragrant tobacco he was puffing so furiously in his pipe. It was a habit of his to take solace in his pipe, when confronting some problem. His head had been full of confusion, his thoughts seemed to go only in circles; in short, despite that long session in Feigenbaum's kitchen, he'd been at a complete loss as to any conclusions.

In an endeavour to clear his head, he'd left Feigenbaum and Birtles to their endless conjectures, their own often conflicting theories. They were in the dark as much as he.

Only by thus sequestering himself here in this hideaway, did he feel he could bring all of his powers of reason to bear. For a man who had in recent times much stripped from him - family, financial security, not to mention his personal honour, Shiloh Coombes still had faith in his own intelligence. He knew nevertheless that to solve some of the mysteries presented, he would need to bring all of his faculties to bear, without distraction. When he felt the full calming effects of the tobacco in his pipe, Shiloh cleared his mind of all other things, and bore down on this present situation. Who on earth would want to kill him? There seemed much that was perplexing about this whole business. His relationship with Feigenbaum, perhaps, was that the key?

As Birtles had demanded, Coombes had given as much a detailed account of his circumstances over the last several weeks as he could recall. Pride drove him to be as meticulous at least as the seasoned Bow Street Runner had been when giving of his deposition. Birtles had presented his dossier as he had done many times in a court of law. And it had been like a courtroom, the kitchen of Feigenbaum; very formal, and to the point. Feigenbaum himself had sat at the end of the table, saying not much, enigmatic, but missing nothing.

In his endeavour to show himself to be at least as good an observer as the man Birtles, Shiloh recounted as much as he could remember that had occurred since he had last seem the old rag merchant. Well almost all. He had felt that the reasons behind his appalling lapse were his private business, and to disclose them would only be construed as some pitiful excuse. As it often the way with young men of high ideals, Shiloh Coombes could sometimes be very hard upon himself. As he tried to make sense of it all, Shiloh recalled his own words.

' – regrettably, I must confess I had been tempted to try once more the soporific effect of the opium pipe. Having found myself in an opium house, I found it difficult to leave. In fact I seem to have been continuously drugged, a prisoner in a torpor. Apparently they entertained hopes of extracting some sort of ransom from my family.'

Here he remembered that he had had snorted derisively – 'they were on a forlorn hope there' – but catching a quick exchange of looks between the other two, he had not followed that line, but had gone on to describe his convalescence and budding friendship with the young doctor who had in effect rescued him. 'I believe the doctor literally save my life,' he concluded.

Birtles had nodded vigorously in agreement here.

'If no money was forthcomin', those Chinks never would 'ave let you go – they would've dumped you in the Thames quick smart.' After discussing points raised by both accounts, the three had been reduced to putting forth various theories. First, as Birtles had put to him, was there possibly some other reason for Shiloh to have been detained against his will? Second, why had Adam Werth set out to kill him in broad daylight, on the platform at Victoria Station? Taking all of their conjectures into account, Shiloh had now begun to formulate a few questions of his own.

When he had first arrived, seeking a quiet spot for some serious thinking, the tide had still been running high; the greasy scummy surface of the river was scattered here and there with its daily burden of raw sewerage and rubbish, dead cats and even worse. Shiloh had barely noticed it. He now observed however that the tide was on the ebb, creating a different surface.

As Shiloh watched, the roiling river now had an oily metallic sheen, as it slid towards the distant sea. Knocking out his pipe, he was about to get up and leave, when he heard a familiar voice.

'Ther you are then, squire! The old geezer said you'd be along the river some'ow.' Turning he recognised one of Feigenbaum's street urchins, Young Sparrow, as he was known. 'I was moochin' along, nearly missed yer, when I got a whiff of your pipe tobacco, see.' The youth grinned with pleasure when Shiloh congratulated him for his sharp nose.

'E sez could you get on back, as Mr. Birtles 'as already gorn off 'ome,' as with a grimy finger he explored that same commended nose.

CHAPTER SIX

It was still dark as Shiloh Coombes set off with Feigenbaum around to the latter's workshop. This was the morning of the weekly 'day of reckoning', as Feigenbaum liked to call it; dealing with his perennial sparring partner, the hard bargaining rag merchant.

As was his custom, Feigenbaum had the material ready baled and weighed , all done the evening before. Coombes did not as a rule accompany the older man, but this morning he had insisted, saying that they should cover each other's back as much as possible.

'Yes well if you put it like that, of course I agree - yes, you are quite right. As a matter of fact though, since it's known all around the manor that I am always doing this, you know, carrying home a fair piece of dosh, sooner or later some goniff is going tho try his luck – so hey, I don't go unprepared' To Coombes astonishment, opening his great kaftan, Feigenbaum revealed a massive old horse pistol.

'I just hope you never have call to fire that monster – it would just as likely back-fire upon you.' Fastening his caftan once more against the morning chill, Feigenbaum chuckled: 'Yes well you see my dear, that's why it's never loaded – I rely upon it to create fright.' He was still smiling, 'I made it my business to also have it known around the traps that I carry it.' Patting his breast, he set off.

There was a faint glimmering in the sky; it hinted at the coming of the day but the sombre early light did nothing relieve the bleak ugliness of the scenes revealed to them as they made their way through the mean East London streets.

The dismal pre-dawn only gave enough illumination to point out their miserable surroundings. It was a bleak unkind light, serving only to pick out the shabbiness of the houses and the dreariness of these streets. There appeared to be nobody else stirring in that quarter of the city; the windows of the houses were all closely shut; the streets through which they passed, were noiseless, so silent one could imagine them to be empty of people.

'Why do you stay here Mr. Feigenbaum, if I may ask?' Affected by his depressing surroundings, the question had sprung unpremeditated to the lips of Shiloh Coombes, 'it's just so dreadful here.' The older man, who had been trudging along silently, his head sunk deep into the collar of his great kaftan, now glanced sharply up at his companion.

'I sometimes forget that you are one of us who is entirely ignorant of the Jewish dilemma. London you see, is one place where a person of the Jewish faith can live in relative safely.' Here he grinned sardonically, ' -as long as he keeps to his place. For us Yids in London, it's the east end; Whitechapel, round about here.' He chuckled, though without mirth, 'you might think its terrible, but after I done a scarper from that bloody Tasmania, I came straight back here. Do I love it here? No I don't, but for old Feigenbaum, this is home sweet home see.' His eye was suddenly fierce as he concluded; 'Here is where I'm at – there is no other place for people like me to go. I don't know what his game is, but if that swine Werth thinks I might be frightened off, he has another think coming.' Pulling up his collar, he strode off once more, leaving Coombes to catch up, feeling somehow chastened.

It was later that morning. As they sat eating breakfast, Feigenbaum and Coombes had a long conversation, during which much was revealed, conclusions reached, and some startling revelations were laid bare. As they drank tea, Coombes suddenly began.

'Mr. Feigenbaum, there are several points I have been mulling over, and wish to put to you. Firstly, with regard to that business on the platform at Victoria station; I have come to the conclusion that things were not perhaps as our admirable Mr. Birtles had concluded.' Feigenbaum looked at him with suddenly bright inquisitive eyes, his cup suspended between table and mouth.

'Oh yes, oh yes, now we are coming to it,' was his only remark, as he waited for the younger man to continue.

'You see I cannot imagine why this man Werth you speak of, would wish to attack me. There are several possibilities as I see it.' Coombes spoke in an intense voice, his piercing gaze held the eye of Feigenbaum, as if he saw scenes enacted therein. . Feigenbaum saw that Shiloh was totally focussed upon what he was saying and thinking, and wisely didn't interrupt. He had long been aware that this young man possessed a powerful, coldly logical intellect, and he wished to see it now in full flow. He remained silent as Coombes spoke on.

'The possibility occurred to me that he may have seen you and I together, perhaps at that political meeting we attended. That is not at all implausible. He may perhaps have intuited the truth, that you and I are somehow connected, perhaps working together, and this was a chance to attack those whom he regarded as enemies.' 'He's not wrong in my case', the old man growled, but Shiloh continued as if he hadn't heard.

'However I dismiss this whole line of conclusion. By your own description, Werth is ruthless, unscrupulous, but very intelligent. From what you have told me, I certainly believe he would regard you as his enemy. It is entirely feasible he might attempt to do you harm. I cannot imagine however that he would take this great risk to eliminate someone – myself - he can only regard as a minor problem.' His intense gaze now switched to face Feigenbaum, his hooded falcon eyes glowing.

'And then there is this small article I read in the Times.' He took from an inside waist-coat pocket a small piece of newsprint, and handed it across the table. 'Read it.' Feigenbaum rummaged in his carry bag for his spectacles and did as bid.

The article was small, the editor obviously did not consider it important news but Feigenbaum found it's contents interesting indeed. It merely noted that according to information received by one of his journalists, the Kronprinz Adalbert of B. would be travelling up from Brighton, after paying a visit to his second cousin the Prince of Wales. Carefully folding his spectacles, Feigenbaum glanced up; he was impressed. Despite the story being relegated to the social pages, Coombes had not missed it, nor it's import. The date of the newspaper gave the item significance – it was dated the same day that Shiloh had also arrived on that same train. Peering over his spectacles Feigenbaum looked up at Shiloh Coombes, 'Nu – and?' His hands spread in query. Shiloh continued.

'The fact that the man we believe to be Werth made enquiries about me, would indicate that he wasn't at all sure who I was. His predatory curiosity had been aroused - that our man Birtles was seeking a white man, supposedly a toff from the other end of town, here in the East End.' Shiloh smiled briefly, a rueful downturn of his mouth. 'It is possible he thought it could be someone of importance, perhaps a situation he could turn to his own advantage. No, it has to be this Prince that he was stalking.' Feigenbaum poured another two cups of tea, steaming hot from his battered old samovar, standing as always at the end of the table. It allowed him to think over what his young protégée had said. If Combes was correct, this was turning into something big. He was still stirring in the sugar when his eyes came up to meet again those of the waiting Shiloh.

'Yes, very good, very good. I like the way you looked for a back-story, not just what *seemed* to be the story. In my experience, things are rarely what they seem. The nobility, the petty princelings of *Mittel Europa* do seem to be fair game these days. As you suggest, it is entirely possible that Werth has been contracted, to be paid a lot of money to assassinate this particular cousin of the Prince of Wales. We must certainly take possibility that into account.' He pondered over this new thesis for a moment or two, before continuing, 'What bothers me though, is the way he went about it. Werth's presence on the railway platform seemed rash, unpremeditated. I know him of old; he is certainly not some political zealot, careless of his own life, willing to die for some cause – oh no' he paused then for effect;

'You must always keep this in mind. Werth has only one cause – himself. He is very intelligent, a brilliant mathematician in fact, but a criminal of the most vicious and depraved type.

He is what that young Freud in Vienna would categorize as a psychopath.' Calmly he passed a cup of tea to Shiloh, 'this is a very dangerous man we are dealing with. We shall have to be looking very sharp here,' Feigenbaum's expression was unusually grave; 'we are not even certain that your theory *is* correct; it could still be you he sought with murderous intent at the railway station. Just the fact that he was not sure just who you are, would be enough for this man to strike. Killing for him is commonplace; he is a monster and has murdered many. Now he has done for my friend; an honourable man, a man of goodwill to all mankind. I was his enemy before, now I intend to be a very vengeful enemy.' Again he paused, looked directly at Shiloh.

'I am glad that you have returned, but now I must warn you that I am out to stop this evil bastar, once and for all. Things may get dangerous, and I will not hold it against you if you decide this path is not for you.' For a moment there was silence between them, but then Shiloh's answer gladdened the heart of the old man. He has listened to the impassioned speech of Feigenbaum, but as his mentor had begun to give him permission to withdraw from what might lie ahead, Coombes had held up his hand, face out.

He did not in fact refer to the offer, but said only;- ' 'If this man is intent on doing either of us harm, we must get busy – first to know why, then devise some plan as to how we may outwit him.' Coombes stood up: 'But for now I suggest we get an early night, and face this afresh on the morrow'.

Although the night was still young, beneath the bridge arches it was nevertheless obscure enough – sufficient for such a meeting now unfolding.

The tall man waited until the other finished his rambling defensive account. The fellow before him was a sorry looking specimen, all too typical of the denizens of these slum streets. He had offered the man money to do a specific task, fairly simple, and now the creature was making his pitiful excuses. No matter how he phrased it, it was obvious the fellow had failed his task.

Nevertheless he was stood patient, as the tale of incompetence wound to an end. Although he stood back in the shadows, enough of his face was visible to be able to remark it's noteworthy features. The height of his brow was amazing, a truly lofty dome. Small sharp beak of a nose, mouth nothing but a slit. His slate grey eyes were as lacking in emotion and as cold as the northern sea. Although he had not spoken a word, and had stood silent as he'd listened to the lame report, the man before him had trembled with fear. Adam Werth was a name that had spread rapidly through the dark rat-runs of the city,every thieve's den in the East End had heard the name – but only ever in whispers. This man of the shadows was Adam Werth. He was inclined to simply dismiss this idiot, who was so obviously incompetent.

But perhaps emboldened by the other's silence, the pimp changed his tone. He began to demand to be paid something at least; 'Come on, guv'nor, I reckon I should get something for me trouble. C'mon, shell out. Give us a bit of dosh. You gotta pay sumfing for me trouble.'

At first he'd weedled, but gaining heart from the continuing silence of the man in the shadows, he began to hector; ' Listen, I spent hours out in the weather – ' he was cut short; surprise widening his eyes, moments before he fell in a heap at the other man's feet. He was dead almost before he hit the ground, the carotid artery in his neck severed.

The tall man stood over his victim then for a moment; to savour again that most exquisite of pleasures:- to snatch a man's life from him. The power of it intoxicated him.

Werth bent, wiped the blade of his open razor with meticulous care upon the dead man's clothing before calmly folding it and placing it into an inner coat pocket. He called over his shoulder to the bulky figure lurking back under the archway of the bridge. 'Well look lively man - into the river with him,' as he walked away.

As soon as he rounded the next corner, his unhurried gait changed to a soft -footed stooping run, surprisingly swift for a man so tall as he doubled back around the bridge pier to the river. He was just in time to see his burly accomplice heave the body into the river, before the dense smog roiling in from the river enveloped the scene. Satisfied, he drew the collar of his heavy mantle up so as to conceal his face, before taking himself off. The brute had done as told in the past, but Werth trusted no one. He has killed that useless fellow back there without compunction - the man had proved untrustworthy, therefore dangerous. *And to have the effrontery...!*

Anyone Werth perceived as a danger to himself, he always sought to eliminate. Safer that way, and killing them served other purposes. it was to serve as a warning to his hulking brute of an accomplice - fear was as good as anything to ensure loyalty - implicating him in the murder, thus binding him ever closer. But there was another motive; to tighten his grip of fear over the underworld of London.

Word would get out – they must obey him, or face the consequences. He was fairly new to London, but he'd soon realised that he and the East End slums were made for each other. This was a crime-ridden, violent world and he wished to dominate it, and to do so, he must be seen as the most ruthless and violent of all. Werth had ambitious plans ; he would gain full ascendency over this criminal sub-world. London, English society itself, would be his to plunder.

And then there was his Contract; If he pulled that one off, he stood to receive a princely sum – for a princely task. It presented many difficulties, of course, and may even not be achievable – meanwhile, this program to dominate all criminal activity in this rich city offered rich pickings if the main game didn't come off. He was brilliant; with a restless mind, and a rapacious personality. Unhindered by common considerations of morality, in every direction he looked, Werth saw advantage.

Satisfied with the way the evening had panned out, Werth

cleared his mind of what had transpired, his musings upon the consequences of his actions. By the time he strode away from the scene of murder, he had all but forgotten the incident. His thoughts turned now to a supper of beef pie and a couple of pints of landlord's best. Luckily he failed to detect the presence of the terrified young lad, who had been fishing for eels beneath the bridge.

Sometimes, just very occasionally, fate deals a surprise hand...

The pair had risen early, snatched a hasty breakfast before going out. Feigenbaum worked his way around the Whitechapel area, talking to acquaintances, listening to gossip. Shiloh Coombes, disguised in the rough working clothing of a dock -worker, had spent the day listening to the talk, in and around the many drinking establishments in the nearby docks area. As arranged they met in the mid afternoon at Feigenbaum's house. They had little to tell each other.

'A couple of times I tried to lead the conversation around to some of the murders happening about the East End,' Feigenbaum began, 'but each time men would just clam up, make an excuse to take off, sudden like'. Coombes also had little to offer.

'I didn't try to ask anything, just listened. I went about a few pubs in the area, even bought a drink or two, with no result. But the very fact that nobody, not one single old bar gossip, mentioned anything about the murders at all, tells me something: everybody is shit scared.'

Once more they had sat around the kitchen table, talking the situation around and around; they'd still not managed to come to any real conclusions. They had to admit that they were no closer to being able to fathom either the motives nor any clue as to Adam Werth's possible next move. Nor had they been able to formulate a plan of action. They could only agree that they must not remain like sitting ducks, but somehow fight back.

But how to fight back; with no clue as to the man's

whereabouts, nor even if he were still to be found here in London. Tired, dispirited, they'd finally run out of theories. Utterly bereft of ideas, they sat looking at each other across the table. For the time being, they were stymied. Abruptly Shiloh had leapt to his feet, snatched up his cap grabbed a coat, and gone out. He needed to walk, to refresh his body, to clear his mind.

'Ahoy boatman – I say you there, boatman,' Shiloh called, for once dropping his accustomed cover of East End street argot. He was perched in his usual spot, where he often went to quietly smoke a pipe, and think things through. This derelict hidden ledge, visited only by himself, was where he could best think uninterrupted.

But now something had caught his attention. Shiloh knew that the boatman he had glimpsed through the yellowish fog rising off the river, would be more likely to respond to an authoritive sounding voice. Only half -seen, wraithlike, but there had been something odd about this seeming apparition, of the boatman and his boat - some extraneous factor that had caught the keen eye of Shiloh Coombes. But the answer to his hail when it came, was anything but obsequious.

'Who the fuck are you', answered the boatman, wary.

'Come closer. I wish to speak with you,' Shiloh held up a silver shilling, twisting it so as to catch any stray light. 'This is yours if you tell me what it is you are towing behind your boat.' The oarsman sat for a moment silent, his oars moving only enough to hold his position against the ebb tide. He could see no threat from this lone figure sitting along the riverbank.

'Orlright. I'll kedge 'er a bit closer, but mind, no funny business, or you're in the drink, see.' With a few swift pulls upon his oars, he came alongside. A rope across his stern transom was attached to something low in the water. It was this unusual circumstance that had engaged the attention of Coombes. As the boat approached, he became aware of a vile stench. Shiloh already knew the answer to his question before he asked it;

'What have you there, boatman. What is it you are towing?'

'The way I see it, Mr.Feigenbaum, this string of similar murders –nobody willing to even discuss it - the man seems set on instilling fear into the underworld; he is creating his own myth. Now you've heard from our Mr. Birtles that he killed a man again just yesterday, slit his throat and threw him into the river. The point was, as Birtles understood it, Werth had more or less let it be made public. He wants people to know who is responsible - he probably started the rumour himself. Now this boatman, he told me that today's find was the third pulled out of the river in a week, not all by himself - one of his fellows found the other two. They are the river scavengers, you see, gathering flotsam for possible sale – firewood, lost dinghies, anything they can find, really. They also bring in the corpses, you see, apparently they get a bonus from the river authorities, who are responsible for keeping the river navigable and at least somewhat presentable.' Fegenbaum, who had been listening intently to this, suddenly burst out laughing. He saw Coombes looking at him somewhat askance: 'Well it's like fishing a drowned rat out of the sewer, to keep it tidy, eh. But go on, do go on.'

Rapidly Coombes relayed to Feigenbaum all that he had been able to learn. 'I asked the fellow if I might look at the corpse; I must say at that juncture he probably thought me mad – I tell you Feigenbaum, it gave off a dreadful stench'. He shuddered, then went on, 'after giving the boatman the extra shilling he demanded, I wrapped my nose and mouth as best I could, then set about investigating. It was obvious that this could well be another victim of Werth; the throat cut with one mighty slash, down and across the carotid artery – almost instant death. And I did notice this:- that diagonal downward slash, across the left side of the victim's neck, would have to be the work of a left-handed man, reasonably tall and quite strong.' He paused then, to watch for Feigenbaum's reaction.

'Well', he began again, '*is* our man left- handed?' Slowly the old man lifted his head from where he had been staring at the table-top, concentrating his thoughts.

'Oh yes, oh yes indeed he is. I saw him at a political meeting once years ago, writing, and as it always does to a right handed - person, it looked quite odd. 'Yes, I remember quite well. That was just before he turned us over to the Secret Police.' Feigenbaum was animated, stood up to pace the floor. He stopped after a turn or two. 'Nevertheless, there probably are quite a few left handed men, fitting your description wandering about the parish.'

'Then again, how many of these left-handers is prepared to slit throats? No, this is the work of Werth, and I intend to find out why. There's some factor here we have overlooked, some pieces of the jigsaw are missing'

The next morning, Shiloh lay in his bed much later than was his wont – he lay staring out of the window, eyes not really registering what he saw, so engrossed was he with his thoughts. Gradually Shiloh came out of his deep introspection. As he returned to the physical world, he began to notice the small buds of green that had appeared on the gaunt bare tree outside the window. He sat up then, and crossed to the window to have a closer look. These first harbingers absorbed his attention, until his cold feet reminded him that he stood slipperless upon the uncarpeted floor.

Suddenly galvanized, flinging off his night attire he began dressing with great haste. The early morning's intense concentration upon all aspects of the baffling situation had clarified Coombes's mind. He had decided upon a course of action; a long shot, but worth a try. Although feeling by now more than a little peckish, he made the reluctant decision to forego breakfast, so as to go about his self- appointed task without delay.

'- I say Feigenbaum, I'm going out for a bit, might be some time, called Coombes as he took up his hat, preparatory to leaving. Feigenbaum, still in dressing gown and striped woollen night cap, called him back from the kitchen. He seemed ill at ease, undecided how to broach an unpleasant subject. Finally he decided that the frontal approach was best.

'Of course it is none of my business, and I am embarrassed to bring it up dear boy, but I am relying on you, and if you intend further - how shall I say, experimentations of a chemical nature, you really should forewarn me.' Having spoken his mind, Feigenbaum stood silent, looking more than a little embarrassed. Swiftly Coombes went over to him, taking him by the hand.

'My dear friend, it is I who should apologize, not you. You needn't concern yourself about that. I fell prey to my own weakness, but rest assured, no further such incident shall occur. You have my word.' He released his grip upon the hand of his benefactor.

'I have learnt my lesson regarding opium houses', his smile sardonic, 'and anyhow my miserable self pity is only set aside momentarily, by opium dreams.' Shiloh took up his hat, turning as he went to leave the room.

'So an end to all that. On the contrary, old chap, I intend some scholarly research at the British Museum Reading Rooms. I may be away for most of the day.'

Leaving Feigenbaum, harrumphing to himself – 'Old chap, indeed' – but his smile contradicted his utterance

It was in fact quite late when Coombes returned. Finding Feigenbaum not yet at home, he hastened towards the laundry, hoping to find him there. The old dealer was in his dingy office, adding figures with the aid of an abacus. He turned In some astonishment as the door was flung open.

. Feigenbaum signed for his young friend to wait a while until he finished; stll panting from having run at least part of the way, Coombes waited with ill-disguised impatience. The return of his young protégée was in stark contrast to the cool young gentleman who had left the house earlier. The face of Shiloh Coombes was flushed with obvious excitement, as well as by exertion. He stood in fact for a moment or two, unable to speak as he attempted to catch his breath as Feigenbaum waited for some explanation.

'I've got it,' he cried, still panting, 'We have had it wrong all along. We've been assuming that for some unknown reason it was myself whom this fellow Werth was after.' His voice carried strong conviction, and Feigenbaum sat silent for a moment, digesting this new perspective. Closing his heavy accounts book, he bound it securely with a leather strap before sliding it into his satchel. 'Come on, lets hear the rest as we walk.' Soon out onto the street, and Shiloh went on;

'Well my research has changed things, if not clarified them. At the British Museum I spent some time studying the Almanac de Gotha, the stud book, as it were, of European nobility. I tell you there are thousands of them, some grand, but many not so grand. It took hours to plough through them. ' Coombes enjoyed the blank look he got from his friend, as he recounted this news.

'Nu. And?' was his sole comment .

'Well you see I wanted to check up on this fellow, you remember, this Kronprinz Adelbert of Bohemia that I believe Werth was intent upon assassinating.' Coombes paused to deliver his dramatic punch line: 'He doesn't exist, you see.'

CHAPTER SEVEN

The two of them had set off after lunch to track down a possible lead. Feigenbaum led them into what for Shiloh was still uncharted territory. Their way took them through the busy sprawling mayhem of Spitalfields market, after which they turned north as they headed towards Hackney. The streets became increasingly meaner, finally running into a maze of lanes and alleys. Feigenbaum paused in his stride, sniffing the air. 'Orrible, innit,' his accompanying laugh was without humour. 'They call this hereabouts the Old Nichol. The Nichol Street rookery. Come on, we are going down here.' They turned into an alleyway that led in turn to a small open courtyard. It was in a deplorable condition; refuse of all kinds is piled up against one wall. Shiloh was appalled by the dilapidated conditions of the premises all about. One entire brick wall had collapsed, revealing the interior, with plaster fallen from the walls and ceilings. The narrow staircase looking rotten and shaky, the pervading color a dingy smoky black, with glimpsed of leprous looking brickwork and broken laths.

Feigenbaum hesitated a moment or two, but then spied the entrance to a covered alleyway, even narrower than the one they had left. Gesturing that Shiloh should follow, he disappeared into it. So low in height was it that Shiloh had to stoop to avoid hitting his head upon the rotten looking beams above his head; underfoot the uneven cobbles almost obliterated by impacted filth. The sharp ammoniac smell, the stink of shit heavy upon the air indicated it's use as an impromptu 'place of ease' for anyone passing by. Although fast becoming inured to such conditions, after the time he had spent in the East End, Shiloh was nevertheless still capable of being shocked, By the time they reached the street towards which they had been heading, they had spent much time ducking into similar noisome passages. To Coombes the whole area resembled nothing less than some sort of giant fetid rats nest. It didn't seem possible that such a place had been designed by people. And even more unbelievable, designed for people to inhabit.   As they walked, he now broached this with his companion.

'Oh yes my son, this is really the worst slum of the East End; I agree, absolutely appalling.' But there was a note of mockery in his voice, which caused Shiloh to look sharply at him. Taking his cue, Feigenbaum went on, 'well you see, its like this. Every sort of do-gooder, bible bashers, politicians, journalists – they all comes down to such slums as this, and then they go away and fulminate about it. They write about it, the make speeches about how intolerable it is, they go on in the pulpit of churches about it. All that fulminating is good for the soul, and probably gives a man a good appetite. But other than make themselves feel better, and having demonstrated their compassion – they can in all good conscience put it all out of mind.' He looked up challengingly at Coombes, 'well that's the way Feigenbaum sees it.'   Coombes looked at him searchingly, 'you are cynical – and rightly so. But surely some good will come out of public agitation? Surely the Church – ' Feigenbaum cut in, 'Oh No, don't invoke the church! Hey, I'm just an old Yid, far be it for me to mention the church, let alone criticize – ' here he tapped the side of his nose, in that typical gesture of his, - 'but I will tell you something which I happen to know is true. The so-called Ecclesiastical Commission of the Church of England is the biggest slum landlord in the east end of London.'   Shiloh looked at his companion with unbelief, but Feigenbaum had walked on.

'But Mr Feigenbaum, surely you are not suggesting that the Bishop of London or whoever, is responsible for these outrageous conditions?' Feigenbaum smiled then,' Oh no not at all, not at all. He is no doubt a good kind Christian gentleman, with nice clean soft hands. No,but you see his commissioners though; they likes to run at a profit, and pity help the poor sod what can't pay his rent. Not that the commissioners, Gord bless 'em - would hurt a fly, good Christians all. But they do employ some very tough bailiffs for such work.' Although he spoke almost jestingly, Coombes sensed to anger beneath these words. As they walked along, he thought about what his companion had said, it's implications.

'If that's true - it is, isn't it? This means that the church is..*Is* it true?' but Feigenbaum gave no answer, only an ironical lift of the eyebrow, 'Nu? And so what? This world is a vale of tears. Come along; we have much searching before us if we wish to find this fellow.'

Evening was falling when they finally located the house they had been seeking. It stood at the end of a crooked lane, leading into an ill-favoured cul de sac, so obscure that they had actually passed it's entrance twice, due to the fading light. The street along which they had been walking, was but meagrely served by gaslight. The house appeared well-suited to it's miserable surrounds. Like those others about it, it hung perilously out over the narrow rough cobbled way, each decrepit building leaning upon it's neighbours for support. Feigenbaum looked back along the way they had come, taking the arm of his companion.

'Keep a sharp eye, my son. This is a right manky sort of place. Keep a sharp lookout.' He looked about. 'They call this hereabouts the Old Nichol. I reckon that this here is a real remnant, a piece of the ye olde London before the Great Fire, eh.' Coombes looked about him as directed. All was silent at this late chill hour, all were indoors. Nevertheless he felt an almost palpable sense of menace about this grim place.

' What a good thing that fire was after all, eh'. Chuckling, but without real mirth, Feigenbaum stepped forward, rapping sharply upon the unprepossessing front door, from which almost all trace of paint had long disappeared.

They were following up a long shot - or so Feigenbaum had called it, and he had fallen to grumbling as the search for this obscure address had taken up the afternoon. But Shiloh had been insistent that they at least check it out.

'I cannot give you the logic of it this time, old friend, but I do believe I am developing something of a sixth sense – it is indeed a strange piece of information our Mr. Birtles had given us, but as you have often remarked, the man has an extraordinary eye for casting about over the information, and spotting anything which stands out. He doesn't necessarily put it all together – that's our job, but I must say I believe we should always take note of his observations.'

.

Just that morning their informant had arrived - all puffed up like a pouter pigeon with self-importance, as Feigenbaum described him, as he departed.

So he'd been somewhat deflated at the response to his information from Feigenbaum.

Just the usual taciturn :- 'Nu? And?' But Shilow Coombes, entering just in time to hear what he had reported, showed far more interest.

'A brilliant student you said – oh yes, good morning to yourself Mr. Birtles – a brilliant student who reportedly took in his elocution lessons very quickly, you said? How interesting. Did you get the address? Good man, good man!'

Now they stood upon the threshold, awaiting the result of their knock.

'Come through to the parlour gentlemen, come through, the rotund little red headed man who had opened the door to them, having cast a quick appraising eye over them, invited them without ado to enter. He bustled ahead, thrusting aside pieces of random furniture, kicking out at various unidentified bundles and what appeared to be children's clothing littering the shabby rooms. As he went he apologised profusely, albeit with obvious insincerity, for the mess and confusion all about.

'Mrs Pugsley you see, that is my dear wife, my companion in life, has taken off with our offspring - to visit her sister in Yarmouth, would you believe.' He glanced back, to acertain as to whether his visitors could believe such a thing. Not receiving any encouraging remarks, he dropped the subject and opened the door into a room surprisingly tidier than the other. Here he presented himself as the expansive host, even to offering his visitors a drink.

'I do have some good whiskey in the house, as it happens.' Glancing across to where the man stood at a low table, ready to pour them a drink, Coombes noted that apart from several bottles of ordinary gin, there stood an almost full bottle of single malt from Islay - good whiskey indeed. He was reminded of Birtle's dictum:- anything unusual is interesting

– how come this cheap quack, in these dreadful surroundings, had such good whiskey –

Of which he now accepted a glass.

As Feigenbaum was also availing himself of their host's surprising hospitality, Coombes took a rapid glance around the room, his keen vision missing nothing. His eye fell upon a stack of printed posters of the kind that were plastered up in public places, advertising various products and wares. Seeing doctor Pugsley engaged still with Feigenbaum, he crossed swiftly to the table, and took one up. It was a pamphlet disclaiming the virtues of various patent medicines and general panaceas, with the usual style of florid grandiloquence.

Dear Gentlefolk, rest assured

YOU that have a Mind to preserve your own and your Families Health, may here, at the Expense of a mere Two-pennies, furnish yourselves with a Packet, which contains several Things of great Use, and wonderful Operation in human Bodies against all Distempers whatsoever.

Gentle women folk – I pray - please avert your eyes and go on about your domestic routines.

Gentlemen, before I go on, and I speak here not to the ladies for fear of offence, I wish to declare that I am not to be mistaken for some Upstart barber, nor a common boil lancer or some Glister-pipe Bum-peeping Apothecary - no, Gentlemen,

I am no such person.

I am a regular Physician, and have traveled vastly. Among Heathen, at no little physical Peril to myself, and to many Kingdoms of the Continent. In these Endeavors I suffered, but learnt much, purely to do my Country good. I am not a Person to fill your Ears with hard Words and Fear.

No! I bring Hope. I do not wish to discombobulate, to create anxiety, in telling you the Nature of *Turpet Mineral, Mercurii Dulcis, Balsamum Capiviet, Astringents, Laxation Harboundations, Circulations, Vibrations, Salivations, Excoriations, Scaldations,* or *Urinations.* These Quacks who do so, may fitly be called thus, because they prescribe only one Sort of Physick for all Distempers.

Now, Gentlemen, having given you a short Account of my credentials, and well-meant warning against the spurious, that Race of Quacks and Charlatans, I present you with my Cordial Pills. These being namely the Tincture of the Sun, having Dominion from the same Light, giving Relief and Comfort to all Mankind: They cause all Complexions to laugh or smile, in the very taking them; they presently cure all Dizziness, Dullness in the Head, and incidentally have even been accounted beneficial in cases of the Scurvy.

In the next Place, I recommend to you my incomparable Balsam, which heals all Sores, Cuts, Ulcers, new and old. Also good for Burns, Scalds, Swellings, Bruises, Strains, Aches, Weakness in the Joints and Limbs, &c. it cures the King's-Evil, is soothing for sore Breasts, and may be taken inwardly for a Cough, Consumption, short Breath, Weakness of the Back, or various inward Hurt.

The next Medicine contained within my Packet, is an admirable Electuary, celebrated throughout all *England, Scotland,*

France, and *Ireland*, Dominion of *Wales*, most particularly in the Town of *Berwick* upon *Tweed*. It cures most if not all curable Diseases, by very easy and gentle purging; further it encourages Appetite, dispels all Distempers in the Eyes, Face, swell'd Lips; and opens the Stoppage of the Liver and Spleen, &c.

The next I present you with, is my Specifick, which has been claimed, tho' not by myself, to alleviate all Agues in a Minute.

The next is my red special Plaister, which radically ameliorates if not cures the most inveterate Rheumatism and Gout within a few Days.

.Last, but not least Gentlemen, indeed the most useful Medicine prepared throughout the whole World, is this, my *Pulvis Catharticus*: Its Virtues are such, it will expel the rankest Poison; 'tis a perfect, safe, and speedy Cure, for all Venereal Maladies, of what Degree soever, and fortifies the Heart against all Fainting.

I do assure you Country Folk, as I do also assure my City clients, these Medicines are as good as any Physician can make, or Patient take; their Virtues are too well known, to say any more; so I shall leave you to experience them. I wish you to be my judge, as I wish you Health and Happiness. But do not I pray, delay. I shall be here at the present address for a only short time, as I shall soon be resuming my Travels in search of further Miraculous Cures. For treatment, advice upon these various medicaments, please call at my present lodgings (as advertised) between the hours of nine and six.

Dr. (emeritus) W. H. Pugsley

Coombes read all this through with growing amusement, then as the aforesaid Pugsley and Feigenbaum had now joined him,he handed a copy across to Feigenbaum, and addressed himself to Dr. Pugsley. The indignant gentleman was about to protest at this liberty, but Coombes' words calmed him.

'What a magnificent piece of writing, sir! How lucidly composed, erudite - such flowing prose! I must congratulate you sir!' As he took the delighted Pugsley by the hand; this gentleman was by now positively glowing with delight.

Feigenbaum, who by now had got the gist of the pamphlet, watched amazed. Following quickly upon his initial surprise at this undeserved fulsome praise for the shoddy document, he saw the truth: Coombes had completely won over their man, who two short minutes before had been somewhat wary, and would soon have him eating out of his hand. He shook his head;

the poor schmuck would be wagging his tail, if he had one –

'Well it looks like you were right – its definitely our man. And you did well back there; very subtle. I believe you got all the information we needed, without asking him any really direct question – he volunteered everything himself, didn't he?' The two were making their way back from their visit to the patent medicine man Pugsley. So pleased at the praise Coombes had piled upon him, Mr.Pugsley had been almost reluctant to let them leave, pressing upon them a good storm lantern to light their way, it being now quite late. 'Oh just send it back with a lad on the morrow', he had insisted, 'or indeed gentlemen, do call again yourselves, always welcome, always welcome' as he'd waved them on from his doorstep

.As his companion strode alongside him, silent, seemingly in a thoughtful frame of mind, Feigenbaum observed him, thinking back over their recent interview. The way he had lead that mountebank quack back there:- to tell them so much, without even knowing that he was being quizzed – bloody marvellous. He glanced anew at his young companion, face still set in deep concentration.

- he's come a long way in a few months. He's even better than I hoped for…

Following his blatant stroking of the ebullient Pugsley, it had been Pugsley himself who had volunteered the information that he did in fact take in some 'private' pupils, who wanted to take elocution lessons.

'Oh yes you see, that is my real profession. I did in fact travel abroad; I have been more than once tutor in English at various courts throughout the continent. This obvious inflation of the truth Coombes allowed to slide by, in fact it enabled him to lead the conversation towards this teaching of elocution.

'A man of undoubted talents sir, Yet you tuck yourself away in this obscure part of the city, a pity clients could not have easier access to you. Do you still take many clients?' Mr. Pugsley looked a little crestfallen . 'Well sir, as like many unfortunates, I have some pressing debts, and so at present I prefer the quiet life.' Coombes murmured suitable expressions of sympathy. Soon however the irrepressible Pugsley's spirit rose; he could not repress the boast.

'Actually, now that you mention it I did have had one particular client for a while, quite recently in fact – very remunerative he was. As a token of his appreciation – and for my discretion – told me not to mention him to any snooping narks. Even bought me that Scotch whiskey we enjoyed together' He stopped to savor the memory; a blissful far-away look upon his chubby, roseate countenance. But he soon came back to earth.

'Course my dear lady didn't take to him at all, put on an awful to-do about the aforesaid gent. But as I said to her, money doesn't grow on trees,' he posed the question to his guests;' Am I right or am I right?' to which they had both agreed - he was indeed right. Coombes was quick. 'But your dear lady took a dislike to him, you say? Jolly Inconvenient for you that, I suppose?' he remarked, conversationally.

'You are not wrong, not wrong there at all.' Pugsley in his excitement was fast becoming tipsy, Feigenbaum noted to himself. He hastened to recount this petty family drama. He'd soon become excited at the conversation, tossing off several nips of whiskey, while urging his guests to do the same. Coombes had indeed matched him drink for drink, but Feigenbaum had detected no influence of this upon his friend. He showed now just how little he had allowed the whiskey to interfere with his remarkable powers of concentration and memory, revealing that he remembered almost verbatim all that Pugsley had said.

'As soon as he mentioned his wife's animosity towards his elocution client, I had thought perhaps the man had committed some indiscretion towards the lady of the house. But when he said 'no, nothing untoward, nothing that the man had done, merely that 'she didn't like him one bit, not since she set eyes on him.' Then she'd told Pugsley, he's got the evil eye, he has - I knew he was our man.' He turned to his companion, a look of amusement upon his customary sombre features.

'I have to say old friend, that woman seems to have had a sharp nose, and a good eye. It would appear that even a man steeped in evil such as he, cunning, resourceful and ruthless, cannot escape that sixth sense that women especially seem to possess.'

'Yes, I got that same impression myself – she took one look, recognized evil, grabbed her offspring and 'went on holiday'. I think I would have to agree with you. But what does all that give us?'

'Ah well my friend, it gives us quite a lot, I should have

thought.' Coombes was in a heightened mood, and Feigenbaum was keen to hear what construction his young friend would put upon the admittedly rambling conversation. 'Firstly of course, we know he is in London – at least he was until last week, when he parted company with our man Pugsley. Second, I believe we know that he intends to remain for some time, hence the elocution lessons.' 'Hah!'' From that fat reprobate,' broke in Feigenbaum, only to have Combes disagree. 'Your distain for our Mr. Pugsley doesn't allow you to see that he does have some talents. For example that poster – the man is a marvel, Shakespeare himself could not have done better!' he laughed, 'the man is a comic genius!' and he was off laughing again, leaving the old rag trader a bit nonplussed. 'Nu. And?' he shrugged, unimpressed with Mr Pugsley's talents. He was also a bit peeved that he had been obliged to buy several packets of the quack's nostrums, to cover for their visit. Coombes stopped in his tracks, turning to Feigenbaum.

'As Pugsley himself admitted, in the short time he had, he couldn't give his client a perfect English accent, but he was able to get him up to a working Irish accent, as from an Irishman long abroad. Not bad, I'd say, and something you yourself could probably have managed.' Well? Was it not you who taught me to disguise my own accent, and to adopt the East End argot?'

'Alright, possible yes; nu - what else?' Feigenbaum wanted to give the impression that he was still not impressed with what it was they had achieved. He was always wanting to push this brilliant mind, to test it's possibilities.

'Ah well now. You want more. I must say I take a leap from logical reason here, to fly something of a kite.' Coombes stared away into the night, unseeing, but nevertheless comprehending. 'I believe he is about setting up an empire of crime here in London, the richest city in the world. I also think that this may not have been his original intention; that had to do with that failed assassination attempt on Victoria Station.' Wordlessly Feigenbaum nodded for him to continue.

' My guess is that he had accepted a large commission for the execution of that crime. Having failed, and thereby alerting the authorities, he now would not wish to return, neither himself in person, nor whatever money he had originally received. I wonder did he also had a contract on your unfortunate friend, or was that just vicious revenge? By your own account Werth had burnt a few bridges on the continent. Suddenly London was fresh pastures for him. He needed to make his accent less noticeable, and needs to stay somewhere near to here – the East End. Anywhere else he might be spotted as a fake, but here, people don't ask questions.' No, I'm sure of it; we don't know where he has been lurking, but he must soon seek out some sort of reasonable accommodation for a front, still around this area, probably within the borough. He's got to be near.' As they walked, Coombes went on with his prognosis,

'He's been building this reputation all around the manor for ruthlessness. To maintain his reign of fear amongst the low-life, he has to be seen around. If I am right, that might be his mistake - your admirable bloodhound Mr.Birtles will track him to his lair.' Coombes fell silent once more, staring down at the footpath; he was trying to put himself into the role of this man, to plumb his motives. 'It is like stalking a dangerous beast; he sees himself as a creature apart, a raptor, feeding at will upon the human race.' He lifted his face, looking directly at his friend. 'You are right - we must stop him'.

Over breakfast the very next morning, Feigenbaum and Coombes were again sifting over their conversation with Mr.Wilfred Pugsley, to see if anything more could be gleaned from the meeting. As Feigenbaum remarked, it had certainly been revealing, but what next?

'Yes well my dear sir, as you say, although helpful, Mr. Pugsley wasn't able to give a us any direction as to the whereabouts of Werth, but he did present us with a possible course of action, don't you see?' On observing that Feigenbaum did in fact *not* see, Coombes began his prognosis.

'First of all, we now know that he is building a profile for himself, as an Irishman returned after long abroad – perhaps in the New World somewhere. To do so, I deduce he will make a point of introducing himself around as Irish,' a swift smile, then on he went, 'Something for Birtles to get his teeth into, there, I should think.' Coombes paused, taking out his pipe, he gave his attention to the serious task of filling it with tobacco. With this done to his satisfaction, he continued.

'But we cannot leave it all to Birtles. We must take the fight to the enemy.' Feigenbaum saw the quick gleam in his friend's eye. In that instant Coombes appeared more like a bird of prey that ever; one which has first sighted it's prey.

'It is of course well-known that a fox is cunning, and hard to find. Instead of seeking, perhaps we might set a trap for our fox.' Shiloh turned his attention to cleaning his pipe. He glanced then over to his colleague, who still looked somewhat non-plussed.

'Oh don't you see; if he has remained in the area, he should return to his lessons from Mr. Pugsley, sooner or later. You have remarked upon Werth's obsession with detail, his obsess personality - he will want to work upon his accent.

Could you arrange for a constant look-out in the vicinity of Pugsley's house – make it clear to your lads that they mustn't approach him, but get back to us with the information. When we get the word, we must go armed, and if possible have the admirable Mr. Birtles with us.' Feigenbaum was nodding now in agreement. 'Yes, I think you have something there. It is as you say, our first chance of taking control of the situation.' The old man sat very still and somber, as he asked: 'One question - what do we do with him?'

To begin with, Birtles had been finding this meeting with his client the 'fat man' much easier than the last. Summoned only this very morning to meet his mysterious employer, he'd made it his business to be punctual – the fat man liked that, it seemed to put him in a good mood.

For starters, somewhat to Birtles surprise , he had been offered a seat – not the usual hard-backed affair, but a comfortable club chair. Usually Birtles elected to stand when meeting with this client, but the offer had been made so affably...

It was a mistake., he realized straight away. Not only did he lose what Birtles perceived as a psychological advantage, but the big man got ponderously up from his own seat and came around the desk. Birtles felt overwhelmed.

'Now Bryson Birtles,' began the fat man in a purring voice, 'I want you to tell me everything, leave out no detail, about what seems to be going on.' He stood now slightly behind Birtles; Birtles resisted the desire to turn and face the man. Obviously this was to be a serious interrogation, and he wished to appear calm. He leant back, hands behind his head, and deliberately allowed himself to relax. Despite this outward show, he was inwardly trying to calculate just how much he could report. He didn't wish for his employer to know that he was in fact working for two parties – the other being Feigenbaum. 'Well sir,I 'ave been carrying out your instructions – ' It was as if the big man could read his brain -

'Don't waffle man, get to it. And by the way, I'm aware that

105

you have some arrangements with this fellow Feigenbaum. And it is not my concern.' Suddenly he stood in front of Birtles: 'So tell me all.'

By the end of his recital he had been so thoroughly drained of information Birtles felt like a wrung out dish-rag. Leaning over him, the man had repeatedly gone over his account, asking Birtles to think back over seemingly unimportant areas, to elucidate upon the smallest of points. Finally satisfied that he had extracted all he could from his informant, he now sat down, elbows on the desk as he regarded Birtles with sombre eyes. Finally he grunted; 'You are indeed an observant man – well done.'

Still seated in this pose, again he began to speak. 'As you may have gathered from my interest in all this, there are elements of this business you have got into' – he waved down Birtles protest – 'There are dimensions to this business which involve the security of the nation. I must ask you to be very discreet as to what I am about to say. This man Werth is not only a master criminal as you have discovered, but a known political assassin. He is believed to be very dangerous.

Some time ago the German Secret Service warned us that he was believed to be heading our way. My investigations having confirmed that he had indeed entered Britain, I hired you Mr. Birtles to keep track of him.' He paused, to allow Birtles to assimilate what he had said. Suddenly he chuckled, a deep rumbling sound: 'They also warned about your chum Mr. Feigenbaum – oh you haven't to worry, he is not of concern to us, something about his political activities as a youth in Prussia. The fat man returned behind his desk, the interview over. As Birtles made for the door, his client called; 'Keep an eye on that fellow Coombes.though- I want to keep track of his doings.'

Birtles left the building; as he did he glanced up, he half

imagined a face hastily withdrawn from a window.

- fair gives me the creeps - like the eye of God 'e is -

The interview with his enigmatic client had seriously rattled him. That the Fat Man had managed to find out that he had a connection with old Feigenbaum, was uncanny. And the information that this Werth was perhaps a bigger fish that he had thought, was very sobering. Birtles considered himself a stout fellow, brave even, but he would right now walk away from the whole business…Except that the Fat Man had ever so obliquely threatened him, if he tried to pull out.

'Sometimes I believe you operate in how shall we say, grey waters, Bryson. I could suggest to you that it is probably only due to my protection that Scotland Yard keeps it's distance.' His smile had been fatherly, he'd even laid a heavy paw on the shoulder of Birtles. 'I hope we maintain our good working relationship, don't you?'

So Birtles made his way back to the East End, all the while mulling over the situation so far. And so far, the shadowy Werth remained just that – a shadow. He was going to have a serious talk with Feigenbaum. They would have to decide whether Coombes could be trusted. And if not… He would have to talk to Feigenbaum.

CHAPTER EIGHT

'Well its like this, isn't it. I got shopped – oh yes, well and truly shopped. There was this journalist see, a young fellow named Diggins or something like that, all fired up with his 'crusade'; save the poor downtrodden people of the slums, all that stuff. Oh yes I know, all very worthy of course, but when a man like that gets the bitt between his teeth, he don't care whether something is right or wrong, only if it fits his neat story.' Turning away he took up an enamel pitcher of water. Shiloh waited patiently as Feigenbaum fussed over the big samovar in the corner of the kitchen. He knew it was the older man's way of gathering his thoughts, of calming himself before continuing with his tale. To which he now returned.

'I had one of the lads bring in a stray one day, see – a wandering lad, an orphan it turns out, who has made his escape from some dreadful cruel orphanage. He had taken off, no idea where to go, just away, poor little bugger. I didn't really want to take the responsibility for him, but the other boys kept on to me about it – cut a long story short, I said alright, but he has got to earn his keep, like the rest of you.' He took a turn or two of the room then, Shiloh saw that his friend was becoming more and more agitated as he got into the story. Shiloh kept quiet.

'See, I was a street kid myself once, and I had taken on a few lost lads like him; nobody wanted them, nobody cared. So I used to give 'em odd jobs - as you know, I still do. I also took it upon myself to teach them a few survival skills, one of which was picking pockets. I used to be a right dab hand, in my day.' His grin was fierce - glancing up, he'd noticed Shiloh's frown of disapproval.

'Oh yes, oh yes, and unlike you, I don't have any bourgeois middle class conscience over it, not one bit.' Shiloh shook his head in denial, but the old man kept on.

'What do those bleeding hearts over there in the West End, in Mayfair think they should do, these lads, eh? Tell me that. Take up basket weaving or something? I tell you what lies in store for street urchins like them, with no skills at all.

They finish up having to sell their arse for sixpence, to rich toffs who hang around Piccadilly, that's what.' His look was fierce, as Shiloh met it. 'And you have been long enough out on the streets to know I am right. Am I right?' Dumbly, Shiloh nodded. He did know that this was most probably the truth of it; nevertheless it shocked him to hear it so plainly put.

'Anyhow', went on Feigenbaum, 'one day this kid gets isself caught, didn't he, lifting a wallet. Like I always told 'em, if you get grabbed, throw a faint. Then when you get revived, tell them you are starving hungry. Sometimes it works, and they might buy you a pie or something. Worst case, you might get a kick up the bum. Most people aren't going to bother dragging some filthy squirming little gutter -snipe around, looking for a constable, Eh?' Coombes nodded, more to indicate that his friend should go on with the story, than any actual agreement. He was confused – he didn't quite know what to think; all this about going to prison, teaching children to steal... Feigenbaum, having drawn tea from the now steaming samovar, then resumed speaking.

'Anyhow, This old codger grabs him, see, and the nipper does as I told him, and falls down in a faint. The long shot is, this old geezer, he grabs up the lad and takes 'im off home with him.'

Feigenbaum darts up a quick look at Coombes. The look is sardonic; his face wears a smile, but there is no humour in it. 'Oh yes, he is all very nice, gives the lad cake, would you believe, has him take a bath, all very nice indeed. Then when this young'un comes back into his fancy drawing room, the old gent speaks to him very kind, very kind indeed. Then he asks him to come and sit on his knee.' The look upon the storyteller's face is now even sharper, as he continues on, obviously affected still by the events he recounts.

Feigenbaum took a long pause then, as much as to regain his composure, as to regard his companion. After a long thoughtful look towards the darkened window, he recovers himself and continues. 'See, every street kid know the difference; sitting on one knee ain't the same as sitting on another, if you see what I mean. The kid plays clever, plays shy, and after a couple of days manages to do a bolt – you know, escape from the dirty old bugger.' Feigenbaum then fell silent, staring once more out of the window. Not knowing whether he meant to go on, Coombes himself spoke;

'Well what happened after all that? How does this lead to prison in Tasmania? ' The old man seemingly shook himself loose from dark memories, and went on with his account.

'Well that's it, isn't it – this dirty old sod tracks the boy down, helped by this journalist tosser. The old geezer's told him what the boy had said to him – about me and the other lads an all that. So the journalist wrote up a big story, all about this evil Jewish criminal mastermind, corrupting innocent young lives – hey, and I'm the first to admit there was a tinge of the truth there, but blown way out of scale, of proportion. There was a tide of public indignation, and I finished up arrested, tried and sentenced.'

His face broke into a wide grin suddenly – he seemed relieved to have unburdened himself.

He rubbed his hands together, in that typical gesture of his. 'I'm not complaining, mind, not really – I was originally set to hang, see, but it got commuted. Actually I heard later that that journalist, Deakins, or whatever his name was, developed something of a bad conscience. Later he'd had misgivings about it all, especially regarding the old gent's version of the story. I heard it was him who used some influence to get me commuted.' He grinned again, 'but if he ever thought I might want to go around and thank him, he's got another think coming.'

It had been a truly awful day, weatherwise. Not the usual London drizzle, but an almost tropical downpour. This time it seemed the heavens have indeed opened up. Other than a quick trip together down to the laundry, for Feigenbaum to post a notice - CLOSED FOR THE DAY for any hardy soul who might venture out into it. By the time they had returned, Coombes was thoroughly drenched, despite the use of Feigenbaum's umbrella. Feigenbaum himself, as always in his heavy Russian felt kaftan and what appeared to be a cod fisherman's shiny black waterproof hat, was derisive of his young friends complaints.

'Well it was your idea to come along, can't complain now.' With the ever-present danger of some move against them, Coombes had insisted that neither of them should go out alone, and preferably not at night..

Shiloh Coombes stood hands in pockets, moodily looking out of Feigenbaum's sitting- room window. The drawn back curtains revealed a grey and miserable outlook, the weather had abated not the slightest. There was no movement of any kind in this usually jostling, busy way-fare. It was as if they were alone in an empty city.

After they had dried out, they had played a couple of games of chess, but Shiloh had been too restless , continually jumping up, pacing about , going again and again to the windows. They had spent the rest of the day indoors, and he felt imprisoned – not just by the weather, but by the situation in which they now found themselves. They could do nothing constructive until they heard again from Birtles, but they had tacitly accepted that even the redoubtable Birtles would stay indoors.

'For the love of Abraham, Coombes; go into the kitchen and smoke a pipe – blow the smoke up the chimney.' For a second or two, Feigenbaum thought his tense young friend might have taken offence, as he glowered by the window. Then grabbing up his pipe and tobacco, he hurried out To Feigenbaums kitchen, muttering only in passing – 'I wish Mr. Feigenbaum you would not encourage me in this despicable habit,' to following laughter from Feigenbaum.

Night had fallen, Coombes and Feigenbaum sat talking at the kitchen table.

'From your account of last night I know you have had many hardships – grievous hardships, yet you seem unaffected by it all, in fact you seem to be mostly a man of sanguine outlook.' Coombes cocked an inquisitive eyebrow at Feigenbaum. 'How is that, do you think, when I, who has had a much easier life, am not. You see, I sometimes feel a great despair, a sense of inner emptiness. I don't think I have ever felt part of things, - oh you know, the usual trappings of ones class, the group assumptions, the social mores – I don't even like cricket very much!' He saw the amused smile flit across the face of the old man, -   'I know this may sound silly to you. I do not wish to sound sorry for myself, but I have felt like some kind of outsider – oh yes I know, I went to a Public School, all of that - but always this inner sense of isolation. All of my life, I have had a feeling of not belonging, on the outside looking in- almost as if I were an impostor; is this making sense?' As Coombes had unburdened himself of these inner demons, Feigenbaum had sat silent, listening with an intense look upon his countenance. He now spoke.

'Since we first met, I have puzzled over several matters concerning yourself, your antecedents. I have never broached the subject with you; after all it is somewhat delicate, it relates to your personal history, and I didn't feel that I had the right to pry. Time has however worked to consolidate my initial belief, and after what you have just said, I believe the time might be right to bring my theory into the open. Since knowing you I have entertained some ideas as to your ultimate origins. You know me well enough now, to know that I would not willingly say anything to hurt your feelings. However, I fear I might shock you with my conclusions.' Coombes remained standing by the window, his face in shadow. Only his perfect stillness indicating his attention to the words of the old rag merchant. The briefest of nods indicated that Feigenbaum should continue.

'You speak of your brother, yet he is not actually your brother, is he?' Shiloh was taken aback by the question. 'What do you mean? 'Of course he is my brother - well the fact is, we are of the same mother, but different fathers. What made you ask? Feigenbaum looked at him a moment, as he considered how he should proceed.

'The reason I wished to clarify this point, you see, is that according to Birtles you do not seem to resemble your brother in any way –' He smiled briefly. 'Other than the fact that you are both highly intelligent men. –oh yes, Birtles knows him - I hasten to say I do not ask this question lightly, and if you do not wish to carry this conversation further-'

'No, do go on, I am interested. I believe that you may be able to help me in resolving some things which have long puzzled me. What more do you need to know?'

.''Perhaps it would help clarify things for me if you were first to tell me all that you know of your parents, their families, and so on.' Coombes looked at him in silence for a long few seconds. These were matters he had never discussed with anybody, certainly not his brother, his only living relative. But in the short time he had known him, this old Jewish trader had become not just his benefactor, his mentor - he'd become his friend. Shiloh had come to trust this man like this no other. But still he stood silent.

Feigenbaum busied himself, fussing about his samovar, in reality to give Coombes time to marshal his thoughts. He realized that this request, to in fact unburden his heart, would be difficult for this withdrawn young man. He then took another several minutes to rake the fire in the grate, putting in fresh coal. Eventually Feigenbaum returned to the table, having managed to extract tea for them both. He began again, speaking very gently:

"If I am to help you, think it's best if you tell me in your own words what you know of your life, your background, even seemingly unconnected scraps. Don't try to analyse as you go – just tell it. You cannot but be somewhat subjective – it's your life, after all.' His broad smile took some of the tension out of the air. 'But together with whatever objectivity I might muster, taking into account my own theory – why then we should be able to fill in some areas you are not too sure about.' Feigenbaum threw wide his arms :- 'Nu?'

Coombes nodded his agreement. The older man seemed to

know something he did not. He stepped from the shadows, and without ado began his account. Feigenbaum listened intently, his chin cupped in his hands, elbows upon the table, his tea forgotten. This could be a long story. Shiloh Coombes was however very succinct, as he sketched out what he knew, snatches of memory, of his early family life.

Shiloh went on to reveal that he and his brother were from different fathers, as Feigenbaum had indeed earlier surmised, and the tragic circumstance by which this had come about..

Their mother Constance had while still very young married Sir Magnus Mycroft, Bart, a widowed gentleman some years her elder. They had a son, my brother, but while his son was still a young boy, sir Magnus met his death - thrown from a horse, as I recall it.' Coombes stopped his reminiscing for a moment - 'I believe it was not all that tragic an event for dear mater – from odd remarks she made, I don't think there was by that time much affection between them.' He threw Feigenbaum a wry grin – 'or is that just my subjective view?' But Feigenbaum only nodded, for Shiloh to continue his story.

Sir Magnus' bachelor brother, by now Sir Rupert Mycroft, inherited the family title, but not the estate. The proviso was that he take on responsibility for his nephew. The boy was set to inherit the estate from his father, and the title only after the demise of his uncle Rupert. Here Feigenbaum interrupted the account:- 'How was it that you didn't really become acquainted with your brother.?'

'Oh, his uncle Sir Rupert made sure of that. I gather that he really resented the proviso in his brother's will – it more or less hinged upon his satisfactory guardianship of my brother, as to whether he continued to himself remain as interim beneficiary.' His tone was bitter, as he continued, 'Sir Magnus knew his brother all to well.' Feigenbaum waited patiently, giving Coombes time to marshall his thoughts. After a moment or two, Coombes once more took up the account.

'He Interpreted this proviso in his brother's will, you see, as permitting him to take full control of his nephew's upbringing and education – and incidentally, his finances. I must say Sir Rupert managed this with great zeal – and severity. With the connivance of his lawyers, he eventually had himself appointed the boy's guardian. To his credit, I suppose, he has apparently enlarged the family fortune.' Shiloh's smile was thin: 'An up-side to his natural miserliness.'

' As my brother was at boarding school during my early life, we had very little to do with each other – we had little opportunity. Relations between my mother and Sir Rupert being as they were, my brother had never been allowed to visit mother at home.' Coombes' took a turn around the room, hands behind his back, before continuing.

'I was aware that she visited him sometimes at his school, but to my shame I could remember only feelings of resentment over these visits. I didn't wish to share his mother's affection with anybody.

After the funeral of Sir Magnus, what with all the attendant stress, my mother had suffered some kind of emotional collapse. As a consequence she spent much of the period of mourning re-cooperating in Bournemouth. I now know that it was during this period that Sir Rupert arranged for his guardianship of his brother's eventual heir, apparently on the grounds of his sister-in-law's insanity. During this time her expenses were met from her dead husband's estate, but I gather the purse-strings were fairly tight drawn.' Here Shiloh came to a full stop.

Feigenbaum saw how these recollections, delving into an unhappy past, were taking a toll. The younger man looked exhausted. 'Let us stop for the while, suggested Feigenbaum, 'It is late and we should get some sleep'.

Over breakfast next morning, without prompting Shiloh Coombes took up the story once more.

'I must say, that after all her troubles, I am glad that at least my poor mother found some happiness. She had never been close to her own family – rather nasty father apparently – so she spent much of that period in Bournemouth very much alone. It was there she met my father – very romantic, he was painting a sea-scape. They fell to talking, and that was the beginning of their relationship. Under the circumstances, she would have been very vulnerable. It was inevitable that eventually she should find someone to love. They quite quickly decided to marry; this time she married for love. Her second husband was the artist Edward Coombes. Their life together was alas all too short – Edward - that is my pa, also died prematurely. Sadly, he was carried off during that big flu epidemic.' Coombes shrugged, gave his sardonic grin: 'I never actually knew him, you know. Funny, but I just saw something we have in common, my father and I. He also had become estranged from his family because of his actions – in his case, his choice of career – he was a dedicated artist, according to my mother, possibly even brilliant but unfortunately not a successful one. So when my pa died still a struggling artist, he left mother in a desperate situation as you can imagine. She sold off the remainder of his work one by one, of course. There she was with me, the infant Shiloh still in arms, a few memories – and a burden of debt.' Coombes was silent for quite a few minutes, the scene vivid in his mind's eye. Gathering himself once more, he continued.

'My mother was always a rather delicate woman, apparently; she just could not cope. Her constant money worries, together with ill -nourishment, fatally weakened her, I believe. It was only a matter of time before she herself fell ill; it was only a very short time thereafter that she succumbed to galloping consumption.

I'm well aware of course, of the proper medical name of this disease – pulmonary tuberculosis - however I prefer our ancient name for It - galloping consumption – it's a very accurate description of the monstrous thing...' He appeared to drift of into some sort of private state of mind, turning to look out of the darkened window. Although neither man had finished their tea, Feigenbaum busied himself again with the samovar to allow the younger man time to

116

once more gain his equilibrium. After preparing the fresh tea, he gently urged Coombes to continue.

'Well where was I – oh yes, mother dies, what was to become of little Shiloh, eh?'

Absurd that I should wish to weep now for my parents – after all, I never knew my father of course, and even my memories of my mother are faint and disjointed. I only recollect bits, vignettes; a sunny day, laughing, strolling together with her, on a sea-side promenade somewhere. I don't even remember at which. Strange, such persistent memory.'

'Ah yes; perhaps that is why you feel to weep. A *mensch* should not be ashamed to weep. We Jews certainly have had plenty to weep about. But do go on.'

'You know I must tell you about my brother; he is a very distant man, a veritable sphinx. He always seemed locked into himself, very secretive, really.' As he spoke, he stared ahead, eyes out of focus. Feigenbaum understood that he was explaining his inscrutable brother to himself, as much as to his companion. Coombes shook his head, as if to clear it from unwonted images.

'The funny thing is, although he loathes anything smacking of sentiment, of brotherly warmth, I understand that in his own peculiar way, he concerns himself about me. Funny isn't it; I believe he does have affection me, but cannot possibly admit it – either to himself or me.'

He looked towards Feigenbaum then, suddenly very animated, stood and began to pace back and forth. 'I think I have just understood – all along I had thought that I was the unfortunate brother, but I suddenly see that he must have felt abandoned by our mother, left alone in that gloomy great house, with only his uncle and his household people.' He stopped his restless pacing:

'But you see, despite his ambivalent feelings, it was he who apparently insisted his guardian – his uncle, but not mine you see, to take me in and give me an education.' Truth is, it would have been hard work, the old boy is a bit dour – and a skinflint.' Shiloh's smile was sardonic,

'Sir Rupert didn't initially accept that he had any responsibility for my fate, as my mother had re-married. That fact seemed to have further alienated any feelings he might have had for his brother's widow. He continued payment of her an allowance as before, but it was quite a bit less, hardly adequate. Much later it was my brother who told me of this, and of the blazing row he had with his uncle when he happened to discover this piece of miserliness. My brother is somewhat older that me, and we never really bonded, but I shall always treasure that he stood up to his uncle over that allowance, and also my own situation after she had passed away.

- Oh yes, it was the workhouse for me, no doubt on it. But apparently my brother stuck to his guns, and I was taken in. I never saw him much even then, as he was already up at Oxford. Never saw much of the old uncle either – it was sort of tacitly understood that I keep out of his way as much as possible. When in the house, I mostly ate in the kitchen with the housekeeper – I must say Mrs. Mumford was better company than uncle Rupert.

- It was rather lonely in that gloomy household, but I did make one friend, and I believe, one friend is enough to banish all loneliness.' He smiled at the recollection.

'She was the daughter of the neighbouring family, the Truscotts. During the whole of my schooldays, she was the one bright spot to look forward to, during the school term holidays. Olivia, for that is her name, was also a lonely child. Her family seem to have been typical of the class, self-centred, distant from their children. I wonder that they have them.' Shiloh was bitter as he continued, 'My mother was poor, but I remember the warmth of her love. Mostly the Truscotts employed tutors for their daughter's education. As a matter of fact, the parents seemed to be mostly abroad, swanning about in Paris or Italy somewhere.

So Olivia was like me in that respect; we seem to have been brought up by housekeepers. As neighbours, inevitably we were inevitably drawn together. We were situated out in the country a bit, so we had to entertain one another. We would roam in the woods, have clandestine picnics, and so on. She was a very imaginative, headstrong girl and bossy with it, but I of course thought her marvellous.

As for my brother, we would sort of meet during school breaks, he would inquire after my progress at school, that sort of thing, all very formal. Usually fairly awkward occasions for him, I don't wonder.' Shiloh's face cracked then, in a genuine smile; 'I tended to gush my gratitude, of course, and he would say things like; - Oh do get a grip Shiloh, or, - if you blub I will not endure it. - I rather idolized him though.' Shiloh's face then lost it's animation, as another, darker memory came to him.

He stood facing the window, hands behind his back, when he next spoke, 'And I let him down, you see.'

CHAPTER NINE

Olivia didn't at first notice his entrance into the room, and Charles Warner took a moment to observe her unawares. She stood before the large windows, looking out over the garden below. Her half profile, a dark ringlet against her perfect skin, the plain grey dress, sweeping graciously down to the floor, but fitted close to her bodice, revealing her perfect figure - *stop* - he must keep in mind the commitment he had made to his mother. Mother had been insistent: he must break off any relationship with Olivia Truscott. Not that Charles believed he *had* a relationship with the lady, actually. Oh yes they were friends, for his part – yes, he adored her. Yet he'd never dared indicate that he would like to have a deeper relationship. There had been occasions when Charles had sensed things could so easily become serious between them. Despite his self-imposed restraint, once he had almost inadvertently kissed her. Luckily Olivia had danced away, laughing off the awkward moment. So as far as Charles knew, for her it remained plain and simple a friendship. Against his strongest instincts, Charles told himself that it was better so.

Of course it was natural that he had become infatuated with her; how could he not have. He'd returned from the Crimea a miserable wreck, one leg gone, his spirits at a very low ebb - and then he had met her. In response to the war-time emergency, Olivia Truscott had returned home from a stay in Paris to do volunteer nursing amongst the numerous war wounded taken into her family's large country house.

Olivia had been marvellous. For a young woman with a privileged and sheltered upbringing, it seemed she was born to the task, cheerfully taking on the most menial or unpleasant tasks.

Fired by the stirring endeavours of Florence Nightingale, the

Truscotts had in a froth of patriotic fervour turned over their large house and grounds as an emergency rehabilitation haven for war wounded. The reality of it however had driven them to flee to Italy for a prolonged stay. So it was left to their young daughter Olivia to carry the family standard.

On her return from Paris, Olivia had plunged into the situation, losing her self, her own problems in the work. She was adored by all of her patients, of course, but somehow Charles felt it was he who seemed to get special attention. She had been so kind and sweet to him; she'd nursed only his physical condition, but by her presence alone, restored his zest for life.

During his rehabilitation, they had formed the habit of strolling through the grounds arm in arm, as he slowly became accustomed to his wooden leg. They had laughed a lot together; even after he was declared fit to leave, they had remained friends. Fortunately Charles lived within reasonable distance.

He would often arrive to take her for tea and scones whenever she was off duty. Charles soon became her willing slave, prepared to take her wherever she wished. He was one-legged, but a horse and buggy was not beyond him. At times in an unguarded moment, he'd observed in her a fleeting melancholy, a reflection of some inner sadness, but if asked, Olivia would make light of his concern. Suddenly her mood would lift; on a whim she might opt to visit some old pub to drink cider and share a few laughs with the locals; for a respectably brought up young lady, there was something of a wild streak in her. Once when they had met up in London, Charles had hired a small equipage and taken her at her insistence to visit some radical political meeting, which to his dismay had ended in a riot.

Charles had been concerned for Olivia's safety, She'd been afraid, of course she had been, but he'd seen that Olivia had also found it exciting, and had been in high spirits all the way back to her hotel. At such times, all things seemed possible; Charles felt he had never been happier in his life.

But now he had to come to terms with the cold reality of the situation; he had this painful duty to perform. Charles was finding this meeting very difficult, not only emotionally - it involved a certain element of deceit.

'Look here Olivia, I tried to explain to mother that we were just good friends, but she insisted that it would not be fair to you, what with my leg and all, to monopolise your time - oh you know, make it difficult for you to attract a husband – '

'What upon earth gives you or your mother the right to assume that I am seeking a husband?' She literally stamped her foot in annoyance. 'What presumption – and you may tell her that from me. I think you should leave now, Charles, don't you? Go on, run back to mummy's apron strings,' slamming the door on her way out, she left him alone in the room with his miserable thoughts.

His mother had been very definite about it. 'I have seen you making moon-eyes over that Truscott girl. Believe me my son, I would be the last to want to hurt you, but I had better tell you now, before things ever get serious,' wringing her hands as she spoke, 'better I tell you rather than someone else.' She was not one for gossip, his mother, and what she now recounted, had the finality of truth about it.

'It's not just me darling, don't you see? It seems to be common knowledge. She will have to move right away from here, if she is to ever live it down.' He tried to ague that this was all malicious hearsay, but his mother interrupted him – 'Darling, its all over town. It seems your Miss Truscott had to have an abortion. At least three busybodies have made it their business to inform me. I just don't want you to' –

'Mother, say not another word – no not one more word please. The young lady is someone who has treated me so well – it will be painful, but I bow to your wishes. I will arrange to distance myself from Miss Truscott.'

Snatching up his walking stick, Charles limped away. At the door he'd turned, 'I would at least like to allow her to think that it is she who is breaking off our relationship.'

- - Ah well; at least he had managed that -

The truth was, Charles Hamilton was not exactly heart-broken. More sad, really. Before hearing from his mother of the scandal surrounding poor Olivia, he had already come to the conclusion that any possibility, any hope of a relationship was doomed. He had been unable to find a pretext, until now. He was still full of gratitude - of course he was, always would be, for all of her many kindnesses towards him. And in his heart he adored her still. But in his heart he also knew that it had been all a bit of a dream; he had been enjoying her company so much, but it was foolish to think that he, still not fully healed and a wooden leg – not to mention the other complications - the idea of trying to make love with a wooden leg – or even worse, without it...It brought him out in a sweat. Nobody appeared to show him out the door, as he slowly made his way over to his waiting buggy.

From behind a curtain on the upper floor, Olivia watched him go. What a cruel charade that had been – she knew well enough what it had all been about. Poor Charles, he had been at such pains to give her the opening, to allow her to feign outrage.

At first upset, bewildered, Olivia tried to order her thoughts, the questions racing through her head – was it because he thought that the lack of a leg would make him ineligible as a possible spouse? She had only known Charles since he'd lost it. If only he knew, she had been as emotionally damaged as he. They had given each other so much! As she went over the painful scene with Charles, Olivia's thoughts turned bitter. The most hurtful of it had been even worse than the stiffness of his tone - that certain note of falseness.

She'd known of course of his infatuation with her, and she had always enjoyed his company. She had a great affection for Charles, and had even considered that if he did ask her, she would have accepted an offer of marriage.

Of course she would have had to tell him; no knowing how that would go. Funnily enough, she began to realise, Charles' leg hadn't been a consideration. Her instinct told her there was more than Charles's wooden leg behind this. She must accept that somehow her sordid secret was out. Olivia squared her shoulders. She'd believed she had been making progress...

This trouble would not go away, she knew it now. Some people would never let it go - it would probably blight her whole life.

– *And that perfect swine Mathieson* –

With an effort of will, she put him firmly from her mind. Memory of him always put her in such a fury. More of immediate concern was the whereabouts of Shiloh. Her best friend Shiloh Coombes, to whom she had turned in her desperate need, who had suffered so much over all this –

who now seemed to have disappeared into thin air.

The day broke, clear and fresh; the constant rain of the past days now come to an end. Feigenbaum had risen early to prepare his samovar for tea; glancing from his window, he observed that his young lodger had risen even earlier. Clad only in trousers and undershirt, Coombes was exercising vigorously out in the small yard behind the house with his Indian clubs, a recent enthusiasm. Soon he came bounding in, all gloomy introspection now set aside, in this brilliant new morning.

'Heres a thing,' he began, 'one of your lads - the one you call sparrow - was here just now watching me drill. He said he wanted to talk to 'the ole gaffer' and was rather secretive about it – didn't want to talk to me. Just you.'

'Ach, probably just wanted to scrounge an advance,' Feigenbaum was dismissive.

'No, I got the impression he felt it was something important. I told him to get back here in half an hour.'

When the lad eventually returned, his story turned out to be very important. So much so, it earned him a shilling from Feigenbaum. 'Keep sharp young sparrow - this cove is really dangerous, know what I mean?' as the sparrow took off, coin clutched tight. The sparrow had told them of this younger boy, who had watched unseen the slitting of a man's throat, and his body being dumped in the river. By great luck, the terrified lad had recognized one of the killers – the one who had dumped the body. The other he had not seen before, but upon hearing the description relayed by the sparrow, Coombes and Feigenbaum had glanced at each other. It was him, all right. Werth still lurked somewhere in the East End. Feigenbaum urged Sparrow to locate the boy in question, and get the frightened lad to call on him. 'Tell 'im there's a couple a bob in it for 'im if 'is story is kosher.'

With their informant gone, they reviewed the situation. 'As we now know the name of his henchman, we might proceed along that line of inquiry,' suggested Feigenbaum. Coombes was staring into the distance, eyes out of focus, considering their options. So intent was he, Feigenbaum was unsure as to whether he had been heard or not. Coombes lifted his head: 'Yes, we might but then we would probably only manage to nab the fellow himself. Werth is too cunning; he would not trust this fellow to know his whereabouts. The main thing is of course, we don't want Werth to know we are on the counter-attack.' He rose to pace about, puffing on an empty pipe. 'No, we don't need to have his henchman's place watched – at least nothing too close mind, casual, an occasional walk past will do the job. I believe it might be more urgent we re-visit Mr. Pugsley.

'Oh I don't know if that will be any use,' Feigenbaum demurred, 'You remember you suggested we get a couple of lads to hang about down there? Well the locals sussed 'em out, thought they were up to no good like. One young'n got hisself a right smacking. So instead I've sent a lad around a couple of times during the week, with the pretext of returning Mr. Pugsley's umbrella. At no time was he at home'. 'Perhaps the lad should have waited' – 'Oh he did, I told him that but he waited two hours and still no show.' Suddenly Coombes was alert: 'when was that last visit, do you recall?'

'Of course I do,' said Fegenbaum, ' It was just day before

yesterday, before the bloody rain set in.' Shiloh was on his feet, 'Come along my dear fellow; we must hurry there to Pugsley's house at all possible speed.'

'Hang on, hang on; if Mr. pugsley has come to some harm, it's already happened. We would be better served to approach his house after dark.' Coombes hesitated, his wish to act now tempered by the good sense in Feigenbaum's assessment. 'You are right, as usual. It will give us time to get a message to Mr. Birtles.. I'm going out, back later.' At the door he turned; 'Could you arrange to have a hackney cab at five thirty this evening? I will seek out some suitable attire. I must dress for the occasion,' and as he hastened off, '- Oh and don't forget a message for Mr. Birtles to meet us there, in that street nearest his cul de sa..'

With the cab already waiting at the door, Feigenbaum looked at his waist-coat watch; five thirty... Suddenly - seemingly out of nowhere - Coombes presented himself, announcing that he was ready to go. Feigenbaum was taken aback – his young colleague was quite transformed.

'I'll be blowed! Tell the truth Coombes, 'pon my word, I would not have recognized you in the street.' He walked around the man before him. What he saw standing before him was a very grubby fellow of the lowest sort. Filthy cap down over his brow, with a scarf all but covering the lower half of his face. The man slouched convincingly, hands in his pockets. 'Where on earth did you come by such a costume?' Coombes laughed, gratified at Feigenbaum's response to his disguise.

'Actually I have assembled this costume, as you call it, from the old rags coming into the laundry, helped with a bit of soot from the kitchen stove. I thought it might do the trick.' His loose grin even showed blackened teeth.

'Shall we go? I believe time is of the essence,' as he headed for the cab. To Coombes' delight, after casting a jaundiced eye over the appearance of Coombes, the driver insisted upon advance payment. They set off; as they already knew where Pugsley lived, it took them but a short while to arrive in the vicinity of his house.

As the hackney came up to the street off which Pugsley's cul-de sac led, Coombes spoke rapidly to his colleague. 'I shall slip out now, without the cab stopping. Could you then take the cab just up a ways, and remain in it. Tell the cabbie he may put his horses nose bag on, but to be ready to leave fairly quickly.' Before Feigenbaum could reply, Shiloh had slipped out of the off-side door and scuttled off into the shadows. He had no other recourse than to follow out Coombe's directions.

It was difficult for Feigenbaum to be patient, and despite his assurances to Birtles, doubts began to assail him. Although he had been successful in obtaining some information that might or might not be be useful to Birtles, he felt conflicted. Certainly they must explore every possibility, every snippet of information, but... Feigenbaum was uncomfortable; he felt he was betraying the trust of his young colleague.

That meeting with Birtles had discomforted Feigenbaum considerably. Birtles had come to him shortly after Shiloh had left the house, and Feigenbaum's suspicion that Birtles had been awaiting that exit was soon justified. Birtles had wished to speak with him, and him alone. He'd started right in:

'Look Izzie, I won't beat around the bush – I know you is fond of that young feller, be that as it may, but wot I 'ave got to say, I want you to 'ear me out. ' Feigenbaum was nonplussed, but nodded for him to continue.

'See, I 'ave been workin' for this other geezer, 'es somethin' to do with the government. Very secret, 'e is.' Birtle face was solemn. 'I shouldn't even be tellin' you this, but I reckon I 'as to.'

Feigenbaum's rising apprehension did not show, as he nodded again. 'Go on. You know that I keep stumm.'

'Well, on 'is orders I 'ave been investigating this same Werth feller as we was lookin' out for. I reckoned there was no conflict, and I didn't bother to tell him I was already on the case' –

'Not to mention getting another fee off this other gent,' teased

Feigenbaum. Birtles was ruffled; 'Look I didn't need to tell you that, did I ? Unlike some, I got a missus and three kids to look aht for.' Feigenbaum calmed him with a few soothing words. Mr. Birtles was an easy man to ruffle.

'Well anyhow, my principal, 'e's also asked me to keep an eye on young Mr. Coombes. 'E didn't say why, but wants me to keep 'im informed of 'is movements.' Feigenbaum regarded his informant for a while, his mind racing. 'Are you suggesting that Shiloh is somehow mixed up with – Werth?

'No Izzie – you is jumpin' to conclusements. 'E never said that - just keep an *eye* on 'im, 'e sez.'

'But you Ned Birtles; are you putting two and two together?'

'Not at all, Izzie, as God's me judge. All I'm sayin' is, all avenues must be explored. What I am suggesting, is that you see if you can find out more about 'is life 'istory. I mean, 'e is a bit of a mystery man, ain't 'e.' Just turned up one day on you doorstep like, didn't 'e?' Feigenbaum had never discussed with Birtles the dire circumstances in which he had found Coombes. He forbore to do so now. He decided he would try to be as objective as possible, and do as Birtles requested; - listen to what the man had to say. Birtles did nothing without solid reason.

As Feigenbaum sat mulling over all this earlier meeting, there was a soft tap tap on the side door of his cab, and the very object of his thoughts appeared at the window;

'I'm 'ere. What's doin'?'

'Evening Ned. Funny, I was just thinking about our conversation earlier. You know, about young Combes - '

'Yes well I've found out something further to all that, we have to talk about it later, but what are we doin' now, here?' he sounded aggrieved, 'it's way past my supper time.' The evening had advanced, a cold drizzle had set in. Not a good place to be.

They'd hardly had time to say a few words when a slouching figure came lurching down the street towards them. 'Watch aht – 'ere comes some drunk - 'Ere! Piss orf or I'll smack you one!'

pulling his blackjack from under his coat. The drunk leapt back with surprising agility, 'Good evening to you, Mr. Birtles,' said Coombes with a grin. He held up his hand, 'Before we get into any explanations, I think that as soon as possible we should enter Pugsley's house – yes, break in. I've had a look around, nobody there, and I think we must get inside. Pugsley may have got wind of our surveillance and made off, possibly to Yarmouth. It's been some time since anybody has seen the gentleman.'

Feigenbaum was in a sour mood. Against his protestations, the other two had insisted he remain with the hansom cab while they proceeded to carry out Shiloh's plan. Feigenbaum hauled out his big old turnip watch for the third time – 'dammit! Only five minutes all up?' giving the offending time-piece a vigorous shake.

-        *They were certainly taking there time about it –*

- The house stood silent and dark; the mean street in which it stood, empty of people. Although early, the dismal weather ensured the inhabitants of this mean cul-de-sac were all indoors. Coombes hissed, pointing out a dim window here, there a slim chink of light – but from this house before them, nothing. Birtles nodded, it did appear that nobody was at home here. He turned his face to Coombes.

- 'Well that's established; Now wot?' Without answering, Coombes was off at a cat like run, and Birtles was forced to follow as they went down the narrow garbage-littered lane alongside the house. It was very gloomy here, and Birtles had to tread carefully – suddenly he ran into the back of Coombes, who had come to a halt. There was a crash of falling barrels, followed by two cats dashing by them. Somewhere nearby, a dog began a furious barking.

- 'That's torn it – we better scarper, eh?' 'No. wait; see if anybody is roused. Even if it was heard, I don't expect anyone would come out to investigate,' Birtles saw Coombes grin, even in the dim light, 'its dangerous out here.' They waited in the shadow of the wall for a few minutes until the dog ceased its barking. Without speaking, Birtles indicated that they could in fact make use of those same barrels unbalanced by the cats. With as little noise as possible, two barrels were soon placed one upon the other against the back wall of the house. Both men understood what was to be done, as without words Coombes hoisted the diminitive Birtles until he could stand upright upon them, Coombes steadying the precarious barrels. At his utmost reach, Birtles managed to get both hands upon a small window ledge, high in the wall. With an agility that astonished Coombes, he swung himself up, so that he half stood upon the ledge. With one arm and his head wedged into the lintel above, he quickly slipped a thin blade into the side of the sash, and within seconds had disappeared without a sound.

Pausing for a moment at the alley mouth – still an empty street - Coombes made his way carefully around to the front of Pugsley's house. As he mounted the steps, the frond door opened silently, and Birtles beckoned him inside.

- With drapes on all windows, they found the inside of the house in stygian darkness, thick and impenetrable. As they hesitated, waiting for their eyes to adjust, Coombes switched on the small battery lamp he carried in his greatcoat pocket. An alarmed Mr.Birtles stood before him.

- 'Ere! ' his whisper was loud, 'we don't know if anybody is at home or not.'

- 'Oh yes, I believe we do. Look at this,' as he shone his light over a small scatter of mail before the front door. 'Come along Birtles. We must search this house from top to bottom. I believe our man may have taken off, but if not – his voice suddenly sombre – he must be here somewhere.'

- It hadn't taken long to find Mr. Pugsley. As soon as Birtles opened the cellar door, they knew the worst. It was immediate, almost overpowering. The smell of violent death; of excrement and fleshly decay.

- After an almost cursory look at the body of the unfortunate Pugsley, the overpowering stench made Coombes turn to leave the murder scene. something, a glint, made him bend and retrieve an object from the floor of the cellar.

- 'Come along, Birtles, I believe there is nothing more for us here; we should perhaps leave this to the Scotland Yard people.' Birtles snorted at mention of the Yard, but said nothing. He was as keen as Coombes to leave this gruesome place.

'Well sit down Ned, sit down with us for a bit and we'll have a good talk.' Feigenbaum busied himself with re-stoking the coal fire in the grate, and then lighting the spirit stove beneath his beloved samovar. Coombes and Birtles were taking off their outer garments preparatory to drying them by the now crackling fire.

On re-joining Feigenbaum in his hansom cab, Shiloh had quickly hushed his querulous complaints, cautioning him to say no more, as Birtles gave the driver a terse instruction. Feigenbaum remained silent, even when he heard Birtles direct the driver in the opposite direction to their own. Leaving the cab near a rank in the City itself, they had then taken another to Feigenbaum's house. Still he asked no questions; Feigenbaum knew how to keep stumm. He understood that something serious had occurred back there; serious enough to cause the drawn pale countenances of the two men sitting opposite him. So serious in fact, that Ned Birtles had felt it necessary to lay a false trail away from that silent dark house. The three rode all the way in silence. The old man knew that with patience, he would hear all.

The other two were still withdrawn, seemingly lost in their own thoughts, trying to get a calm grip on what they had seen, what it portended for their investigations.

'There you are then gents: a good hot cup of Indian tea,' as he placed two steaming cups upon the table.' Birtles had sat down, and now he lifted his eyes to Feigenbaum. 'Thank you Izzie, but I wonder if I could have a stiffener in it.' Other than raise an eyebrow, without a word Feigenbaum went over to his liquor cupboard and took out a bottle of gin. 'Yes, I think we all going to need one.'

Judging his two companions to have recovered at least some

composure, Feigenbaum put his cup onto the table, firmly enough to gain their attention. 'Now, is anybody going to tell me what happened back there?' Without interruptions, other than the occasional comment from Coombes who sat looking into the fire, Ned Birtles soon came to the end of his recital of events.

'Oh that poor man, groaned Feigenbaum, who expecting the worst ,was nevertheless horrified, 'it looks as if Werth has somehow got wind of our visit - no, more likely Pugsley mentioned it himself, and was punished so dreadfully for speaking –oh that poor little man.' Coombes turned to him; 'Yes, and more than just a punishment for Mr Pugsley; it was meant also as a warning to us'.

'Now this awful business this evening; it brings the whole thing to an even more personal level.' The others said nothing, waiting for him to speak. 'That poor Pugsley, that poor man died directly because he had talked to us, to Coombes here, and myself. We were careless, weren't we, and failed to protect him. From now on, we must be always on guard, we must be careful who we talk with, and we must know who we can trust.'

Having delivered himself of this, Feigenbaum looked directly at Shiloh Coombes. "and by this I mean, we can have no secrets here, nothing up the sleeve, as it were.' Coombes looked slightly nonplussed, but nodded slowly for the old man to continue. 'I'll be very blunt – Birtles here has come across some information which seems to indicate that you have not been entirely frank with us.' As Feigenbaum spoke, Ned Birtles stood and crossed to stand, arms folded, by the door. Coombes turned back to Feigenbaum – 'What? I don't think I know what you mean.'

Birtles spoke then, in his monotone as he recounted his misgivings, 'I don't know what it is about, and I am not at liberty to tell you the name of my informant,' he had been looking out over Shiloh's head, but now he fixed him with a stern look, 'but I would like some answers.' The face of Shiloh Coombes was impassive, only his eyes glittered as he met the implacable stare. His voice was calm, as he spoke, 'Well if I can help to elucidate, my dear Birtles, fire away.' Birtles continued his keen evaluating gaze for a moment or two more. 'I 'ave been very frank with Feigenbaum 'ere; I 'ave been contracted by a secret government agent to carry out investigations. As my interest also concerns this Werth, I felt I should come clean with Izzie. If we are to get this business sorted, we must pool our information. Nah then; it is my profession to be suspicious, Mr Coombes. It is my stock in trade, sir, suspicion is.' He glared around, 'when my employer – who shall remain nameless, asked me to keep a sharp eye on this Werth, he also asked me to keep an eye out for your good self. I think we are entitled to know your connection 'ere.' Coombes remained still, but a faint smile crossed his countenance. 'As you wish, of course your employer must remain secret. I know he rather likes that to be the case.' The smile had definitely broadened. Birtles was flustered – 'then you knew –'

'Well no I didn't, but you have given me enough clues.' He turned then to Feigenbaum, who had silently listened to all this. 'You see, Mr Feigenbaum, I believe Mr Birtle's employer to be non other than my brother'. He chuckled, at the astonishment on both faces. 'He has doubtless asked you to report back to him of my doings.' He was curt, 'We are estranged you see. He is no longer speaking to me, but he no doubt has his reasons for keeping informed of my whereabouts.' He stood up from the table, 'I hope that will satisfy you both.' He nodded to the others, ' we have much to do tomorrow, I believe a good night's sleep will prove advantageous. Good night.' Coombes stuck his head back around the door : 'Good work Birtles'.

Shiloh Coombes sat bolt upright – at first disoriented, he gradually recognized his surroundings in the dim pre-dawn light. He was in his bed, the familiar outlines of the room's furnishings quickly calmed him. Shiloh realized that he was in a sweat, his nightshirt quite damp. Slowly Shiloh disentangled himself from the last remnant tentacles of the nightmare from which he had just emerged. It had been extremely disturbing, various dire images had held him in terror, mixed with horror. The image of Pugsley, just as he had seen the poor man hanging from a hook in his own cellar - face dark purple, tongue and eyes nearly bursting from his head – Just remembering again this frightful image brought Coombes out in a fresh sweat. And then in the dream, the eyes, still bulging grotesquely, had turned slowly towards him. The look implored him, beseeched him; at the same time, there was reproach in that dreadful gaze. Shiloh got from his bed and drank from the water glass on the small bedside cupboard. Crossing in bare feet to the window, he stood shivering. He was looking out at nothing in particular, not wishing for the moment to risk falling back into that same dream. As he returned to full consciousness, Coombes began analysing the dream. That almost unbearable look of reproach, he understood, was something originating within himself.

He admitted to himself his deep remorse – Pugsley could have been killed for one thing only – he had spoken to Feigenbaum and himself about Werth. He recalled then another dream, seemingly unconnected with the other wherein he was running through a dark wood, made even more so by a thick low-lying mist. He ran on terrified, knowing only that he was being pursued by some dread Thing, some evil entity. He recalled a sensation of running, but with great effort, as if shin deep in some glutinous mud. Glancing back he saw a shrouded figure, at first he had the impression that it appeared to be like a monk, with a cowl covering it's features. The swirling mist obscured the apparition– suddenly he experienced a clear recall. He saw the face of his hunter – it was a tall man, just as had been described, with an unusually high forehead – and wearing glasses! Shiloh concentrated upon this image, not letting it fade. Somehow, he knew this to be the face of his enemy.

Still disturbed by this vision, Coombes shivered before the window. He dreaded falling back into that dark nightmare, and as a consequence was reluctant to return to his bed. Eventually succumbing to the cold night air, he returned to his bed and was soon fast asleep. As he awoke next morning, light streaming in through the window, Coombes fell once more to mulling over his strange dream. He then remembered he'd had a second dream, a much more pleasant experience, after his return to bed. He had been back with in the country, where he had stayed with the young doctor who had helped him so much. In the dream they were walking together along a country lane. The doctor pointed out a large owl sitting motionless in a nearby tree. 'He looks so solemn, doesn't he Shiloh. He looks like a stern schoolmaster, it even appears as if he wears spectacles.'

Suddenly Shiloh leapt from his bed; striding across to where he had left his greatcoat still drying before the fire, he began rummaging in its pockets. 'Aha! Still there!' In his hand he held a pair of spectacles, badly broken. Both lenses had been smashed. He recalled that he had been in a state of shock as he had picked them up from the floor of that cellar. He'd put them into his pocket, where they had remained, forgotten. Yet somehow, in some corner of his consciousness... His dreams had helped him to full recall.

CHAPTER TEN

She left early to catch the train up to London, telling Mrs. Billings the housekeeper that she would probably return late that evening. With her Olivia took her only one small piece of luggage. Since her parents had gone abroad, Olivia had become much more independent – far too much so, in the opinion of Mrs. Billings. She'd known the head-strong young lady since childhood, and although as housekeeper, she had no formal control over her, there was a strong tie of affection. As the trap driven by her husband set off for the station, Mr. Billings stood on the doorstep, her hands wringing her apron with worry. She would have worried even more if Olivia had told her that she had no intention of returning that evening. Or even that she might not return for days.

Jermyn Street, that same evening in London; a discreet and proper member of a solid and very proper club, received extraordinary news. The Diogenes Club doorman had just approached, coming up to where he sat by the fireside, reading his evening paper. 'I beg your pardon sir, but there's a young lady wishing to speak with you, sir.' In the sudden silence, he rose, albeit ponderously, put down is port and carefully folding his newspaper. About to go, he paused, looking around. 'I hope you gentlemen don't think it *too* amazing that a young lady wishes to converse with me.' The quip, followed by a murmur of amusement from his fellow members helped mask his discomfiture. It was considered bad form in general to have women calling at the club. Not *done*.

Just behind the club porter's booth, in the cheerless room used for that purpose, Olivia waited in nervous anticipation. For the first time since leaving home that morning she'd began to entertain doubts about this coming meeting. She had on previous occasions met the brother of Shiloh Coombes, but they had never had much to say to each other.

Not that the taciturn man had ever seemed to speak with anybody. He'd always been such an aloof, almost formidable presence; rooms fell silent as he entered. Shiloh would not hear a word against his brother but at the same time had always shied off discussing their relationship. So though Shiloh obviously held him in great esteem, paradoxically, the two brothers seemed like strangers. In the midst of these rather negative thoughts, the door opened, and the fat man himself entered.

Suddenly Olivia found herself tongue-tied, in the presence of this man, who stood now within the doorway, watching her impassively. He regarded her a while in silence; 'I imagine you've come out of concern for my brother.' Olivia was taken aback by this, but it allowed her to speak out,

'Oh, oh yes sir, I mean, oh I'm not beginning very well am I?' He nodded ponderously, before answering her in a rumbling deep voice, 'just calm yourself my dear. I am not surprised that you are concerned for your friend. I was just a little surprised that you had tracked me to my lair.' Moving across and seating himself ponderously upon a wooden bench along the wall, he indicated with his head: Please, won't you take a seat? Miss Truscott, isn't it?' Olivia relaxed, and sat down also. Shiloh's brother didn't seem quite as forbidding as she'd remembered. 'You see sir, I didn't know who else to consult. I 'm aware that you don't keep a close contact with your brother, but I have been so worried about him; you see he has completely disappeared.' To her surprise, and the fat man's consternation, she burst into tears.

When she had recovered her composure enough to continue, Olivia gave the fat man back his large white handkerchief which, blushing furiously, he had hastily thrust upon her. As she did so, it occurred to her that his seeming coldness was more due to his total lack of social ease than an unfeeling nature. He was just a very shy man. She laughed, albeit shakily, 'there; silly me. I'm sorry, it won't happen again', as he again regarded her gravely.

'I understand your concern for my brother, and it does you credit as his friend; I must commend you. As to Shiloh's present situation; I am aware of his approximate whereabouts, but I can only tell you that since his disgrace, he seems for the present to prefer not to have anything to do with old acquaintances.' He waved down her remonstration – 'I think we should perhaps respect his decision, don't you?'

Olivia felt herself once more close to tears, but managed to hold back, 'But that's just it , you see. About his so-called disgrace.' She took a deep breath: 'It is not his disgrace – but mine.' Her lip was trembling, but she refused to cry.

'Some time ago, I found myself in a very serious position. I had behaved very foolishly, and allowed a man whom I trusted to take advantage of my foolishness.' He sat silent, nodding only for her to continue. Only the sudden glint of light in his deep-set eyes indicated his interest. She took a full breath and continued. 'I should have been ruined absolutely, and in my distress I turned to Shiloh, my friend since childhood. He was so supportive, told me he would arrange to get some money, enough for me to -' here she gave a sob, unable to hold it back, –'for me to travel across to Paris and obtain an abortion.'

There was a hiatus, an almost breathless silence, as they both felt the impact of the words Olivia had just uttered. Men and women in their strata of society never spoke to one other of such things. She looked defiantly into his eyes, but saw no look of censure, or of distaste. Instead the fat man blew out a great breath, and sat back against the wall. His gaze fixed high upon the opposite wall.

'Well well my dear; that was very brave. I am sorry for your trouble, I really am, and I feel quite honoured that you have entrusted me with such a painful personal piece of information.' He sat silent a moment or two.

'I am also gratified to hear that my brother is not such a black villain after all.' He turned to face her then, 'you must know of course how Shiloh obtained the money – Oh you don't? Instead of coming to me, the fool apparently took the money from my uncle's study, and allowed himself to be thrown out of the house in disgrace,

138

branded a thief.' He saw the stricken look upon the face of Olivia, but hastened on. He felt he owed her the plain unvarnished truth.

'I blame myself here; as you observed, we werenever close, we didn't share secrets. Shiloh was always so different to me; passionate, impetuous. But as for him being a thief, I never actually believed it.' The fat man got up, and began pacing about the room, as he bared his inner feelings as he had never done before.

As a matter of fact, I had suspicions of the whole scenario. I always believed that there was more to it than that. I had a theory that my uncle', here he glanced again at Olivia, 'I'm sure you are aware that my uncle is how shall we say, a difficult man – actually he's a bit of a swine.' Mycroft was amazed to hear himself; it was true, but he had never before admitted the fact to himself. 'I even had a theory that he concocted the whole thing to get rid of Shiloh, whom he detested for various reasons.' He stood before her now. 'You see, it's a bit complicated; Shiloh is my half brother, and my uncle is not his uncle, if you see what I mean.' Olivia sat silent; much of this was certainly news to her.

Mycroft began again, 'I was wrong, it appears, but then why on earth did my brother just disappear? I think that subconsciously, he wanted to be thrown out, to be done with having to skulk about, dodging uncle Rupert. I just wish we had been close enough for him to talk to me, it was our housekeeper Mrs. Mumford who finally took it upon herself to tell me something of the tension in the house. She also vehemently believed him innocent. ' He paused, a slight smile on his lips, 'She's rather a dear old thing, very good to myself as a boy, always cooking my favourite puddings, and doubtless she did the same for Shiloh as well. I thought it best to tell you all this; having pooled our information, perhaps now we together might be able to do something to set things to rights.'

Olivia felt a great sense of relief, mixed with mortification – obviously she was pleased to hear Shiloh was still alive and somewhere here in London. On the other hand, she felt absolutely miserable all over again. Her foolish shoddy affair had caused so much trouble for him. She smiled a tight smile, nodded for him to continue. 'First off, I understand of course that you cannot come forward – '

'Oh no sir, that is no longer true,' Olivia spoke with passion, 'After all that you have told me, I believe that I must bear the consequences of my own actions. Don't you see, Shiloh made me promise to tell nobody, but I honestly had no idea where the money came from. Now that I do know, all of my efforts shall be bent upon clearing Shiloh's name. I shall write to your uncle, and I shall tell him the exact truth.'

Slowly the fat man turned his head towards her; his response was ponderous, 'No Miss Truscott, that would not suit at all. I should think Shiloh would feel that his admirable intentions were all to no avail. It is evident that he wished to prevent your being engulfed in public scandal. He would take it amiss. I believe I know my brother at least well enough to say that.' Considering this for a moment or two, Olivia had to agree. She nodded for him to continue.

'You see dear lady, as I mentioned earlier, I believe that there are other dimensions at play here; undercurrents to which sadly I tended to turn a blind eye – anything for a quiet life, I suppose,' his face wore a rueful half smile, as he continued, 'until our Mrs.Mumford opened my eyes to the situation pertaining at Five Elms. This was a chance for Shiloh to show defiance, not only defiance but contempt.' Olivia nodded slowly, and he went on; 'Actually it brought a bad situation to a head. It's not the sort of thing one normally speaks about, a bit sordid really, family linen and all that, but when I learned of the true situation, I had a thundering row with uncle Rupert. For one thing as I told him, Shiloh was entitled to consideration at Five Elms, not only as my brother, but as the son of our mother.'

Olivia was aware that although he spoke in a very even voice, there was great passion there. 'My mother was widowed at the death of my father, through no fault of her own. Five Elms should have been her home. Listening to Mrs. Mumford, you see, I came to understand that my uncle had treated her abominably.' By now Olivia saw the gleam of unshead tears in his eyes. 'Worst of all, he prevented me from spending much time with her. The few fleeting visits I had from my own mother over those years when I was up at school, were all undertaken without his knowledge'. He stopped then, feeling somewhat embarrassed at what for him was an angry outburst, but the gentle hand upon his arm did much to ease his discomfort. 'Thank you for sharing such personal information. Whatever the outcome, sir, I am glad that we have come to trust one another.'

He looked long at Olivia without answering, then; 'Yes, and perhaps if we are to help Shiloh, it would be best if we put *all* of our cards upon the table.' She looked at him, slightly puzzled. 'Whatever do you mean?' Suddenly embarrassed all over again, he withdrew his arm from her reach. He wished to regain composure before posing the next few awkward questions; again he began to pace the floor. He walked, hands behind his back, until he came again to stand before Olivia. 'I'm sorry to be so blunt, but I must have all of the facts.' Her face had become very pale, but she was unflinching as she nodded for him to continue. 'You said earlier that you needed money to obtain an abortion in France. Did you in fact obtain that abortion?' She looked into his eyes, 'No. I did not.' 'Then if I may ask, what transpired?'

She knew she had no option but to tell the truth. 'Well you see sir. When told by the midwife in Paris that I was almost too far along with the pregnancy, I spent a whole day wandering about the Tuilleries, and finally came to a decision. I decided I would give birth to the baby, and see to it's adoption.' He looked at her keenly; 'And what happened then?' It was Olivia's turn to pace the floor, as she tried to get control of her emotions. 'Well you see, the moment I set eyes upon my baby, I knew I could never do such a thing. I weighed up all of the repercussions for myself – and I decided I would keep him, no matter what. He is cared for by a young French maid who lives in a small cottage quite close to our house, I can see him constantly.' Her look was defiant; 'I know I must tell my parents eventually, and I do cannot imagine what they might say. I have made my decision'- she smiled then, 'as they say, one makes one 's bed, one must lie in it.' He stood silent for a time, allowing himself to absorb this surprising development. Then he spoke.

'First of all my deepest apologies for prying into your private affairs. And I would like to say this: I admire your stand. I would doubtless have understood had you proceeded as planned, but I would have thought less of you. You are a young lady of courage and principal. I have only one more question, if you don't mind. Is my brother in any way responsible – but she broke in, somewhat to his surprise, with a laugh,

"Oh no sir, you have it all wrong! You thought Shiloh – no, it was another person – I will not call him a gentleman. As a matter of fact though, your brother did offer to marry me, purely out of the finest motives. He was my friend. However, I didn't think marriage between us was a good idea – I love him dearly, but oh you know how he is, all smoke and mirrors, a mind like quicksilver - I don't believe he could settle down to domestic bliss, do you?' He had to smile himself;

- *Shiloh, as pater familias...*

'But you see, he was quite prepared to saddle himself with me, so that is why I am so concerned for the truth to come out. '

The fat man mulled over this for a moment or two, then gave his opinion. 'Well that's all clear, and I applaud your stand, but I believe my brother would be disappointed. He would feel that all of his efforts to protect your good name were for nought, don't you see. Its not just all about you, its also about his standing up to my uncle. Let him be; he has made a stand, a quixotic self -sacrificing stand which will probably be the making of him. I believe he must be allowed to handle the fallout for such actions himself.'

Olivia looked at him, 'From that, I take it that you have decided not to tell me where I can at least find Shiloh.' But the fat man was immovable; he had made up his mind, 'Yes my dear, and I am sorry, but I think he is best left alone at this present time.' Responding to her look of distress, he finished, 'All I will say is that he is living in the East End of London, quite safe, and in answer to my inquiries, he seems to have gone into the rag trade.'

CHAPTER ELEVEN

Feigenbaum, in dressing gown and slippers, was busy at his usual task of preparing his beloved samovar for the day, as Shiloh entered the kitchen and placed the pair of smashed spectacles upon the kitchen table. Feigenbaum glanced at them, then at Coombes. 'You seem pleased with yourself, but I can't offer more that a couple of pence for the frame,' and he returned to coaxing forth his first cup of tea from the samovar. Glancing again towards his young colleague, he saw that Shiloh was not amused. He stood looking at Feigenbaum with an intense look. 'Oh I think you might value them more than that, when I tell you where I found them.'

'Nu; a pair of smashed specs. So what?' Shiloh smiled then suddenly, and sat down, 'I usually like to do my Indian club exercises first thing, but perhaps you might pour me a cup as well, and I will explain.' Shiloh Coombes then recounted how in the shock of their gruesome discovery in the house of the unfortunate Pugsley, he has seen the glasses upon the cellar floor. How he had picked them up at the time, but after pocketing the find, he'd simply forgotten them. 'The thing is, I remembered them this morning. And I also recall, that when Pugsley was reading his pamphlet with me, he used no eye-glasses.'

Feigenbaum leaned forward to examine the broken spectacles. His examination was brief, but his judgement incisive, 'I think can say with some certainty that by the style of the frame, these glasses are made in eastern Europe, perhaps Poland. They are both reading glasses and distance glasses. See here,' he pointed out to Shiloh, 'how the lens is polished in two facets. They call them bifocal. . And I can also say I remember that Werth used to appear with at least similar glasses,' he looked up from his examination, 'and what does that give us? Not much, even if they are his.' Shiloh thought about this for a moment or two, 'I hoped you might verify my suspicion, that they probably belonged to our man. He probably lost them, scuffling around in the dark, and trod upon them. So now he finds himself handicapped, both for reading and seeing at a distance. Don't you see – he *must* get himself a new pair, and soon.'

Feigenbaum leapt to his feet, rubbing his hands together with glee, he paced the floor. ' Yes yes, this may be just the bit of luck we have been waiting for,' he cried, ' We should be able to track down which optician he might go to. They are mostly Jewish, at least in the East End. What do you think?' but as he turned, he saw through the kitchen window that Shiloh Coombes had begun his exercises.

After breakfast Feigenbaum went off to attend to his business at the laundry. Shiloh Coombes, dressed and ready to go in his street disguise, sat awaiting the arrival of Birtles. Together they were to scour the East End for a spectacle maker who might be making a pair of spectacles. It promised to be a long day. With his feet up on Feigenbaum's kitchen table, Shiloh sat reading a day old newspaper. Suddenly he was alert, feet coming down from the table. A small paragraph in the social announcements had caught his eye. –

The Nabob of Mysore would be arriving on tomorrows' 10.30 mid-morning train from Brighton, where he had been on a visit to His Royal Highness the Prince of Wales.

Rushing to the front door of the house, Coombes flung it open, at the same time giving vent to a shrill whistle. Hurrying back inside, he was just finishing a hurriedly scribbled note when one of Feigenbaum's street urchins announced himself at the door. ''Ere lad –wait here till Mr. Birtles arrives, and give him this. Wot's the matter? You know Mr. Birtles don't you?' When the boy nodded, Shiloh hastily pulled a coin and thrust it into his hand. The lad still looked strangely at him. Coombes was pleased; even this sharp lad had not penetrated his disguise.

From the East End Coombes made his way across London as quickly as possible towards Victoria station. Dressed as he was, and very dirty with it, he did not attempt to take a hackney but did manage instead to jump onto the backs of several drays and lorries along the way. As these often took the less crowded back streets, Coombes found himself making good time. For this he had to thank the endless hours he had spent with the indefatigable Feigenbaum, learning to navigate through the maze of the East End. Shiloh now found the streets broadening, the way getting straighter. He still kept to a fast pace, not knowing if he would be on time or not.

Shiloh carried no watch, but as he darted on foot through a narrow lane filled with refuse, but definitely a short cut, a church bell gave him the time: ten o'clock, and the train expected in half an hour. Coombes slowed his pace; he was even now approaching the grand main entrance to Victoria station. As he had hoped, he was early. This would allow him to take up a vantage point and watch events unfold.

Feigenbaum was also having an eventful morning. The boy who had witnessed the murder under the bridge had been waiting for him on the steps down to the cellar laundry. Young Sparrow, who had first reported the lad's story, held him fast by the ear. The younger boy was snivelling, bent over with pain.

'Oi! Let go of 'is lug; go on, you got 'im 'ere, now you better scarper,' and he bent and peered at the trembling lad. 'First off, I'm sorry 'e was a bit tough on yer – look 'eres the dosh I promised,' as he took out several coins from his purse and slipped them into the boy's hand. 'Nah then, nice and easy like; what 'ave you got to tell me then my dear?' The poor frightened boy stood irresolute; his mother would really welcome this money, but she had warned him that very morning not to mention that 'orrible business' to anybody. 'Too many folks around 'ere talk too much, luvvie. Keep stumm, and live long, that's wot I say,' and she had sent him off to look along the river for firewood. He'd been there scrounging along the low tide mud flats when the older boy had collared him, and dragged him here to face this old gaffer. He stood there shivering half from fear and half from the cold; his ragged trousers were rolled up, his legs and bare feet still plastered with the stinking black mud of the Thames. He'd been forced to leave the few sodden sticks he had gathered – he knew others would swoop upon them. He had begged the boy Sparrow to let him go, that he didn't want to say anything but the bigger boy had been adamant. Sparrow had replied only that as he had already been paid to fetch him to Mr. Feigenbaum - to Mr. Feigenbaum he must go. His ear was still burning, gingerly he felt if it was in fact still on his head. He looked fearfully at Feigenbaum. 'I'm frightened mister, I don't want to say nuffink,' he still held the money, and was wondering if he could take a runner, when Feigenbaum spoke again, his voice gentle.

'I know you don't want to get into no trouble, my dear, but I promise that anythin' you tells me, stays with me. Look, If you still feel that you can't trust me, you can get along 'ome now; give that money to your mum, mind.' This unexpected generosity melted the boy's fears, and he thereupon recounted without prompting all that he had witnessed down under the bridge one night as he was fishing for eels, 'and mister, I recognised 'im - the one what tossed the stiff into the river; 'e is a cove wot sometimes calls on me mum.' His down-turned face told Feigenbaum all he needed to know about such visits.

Before making his way into the main platforms, Shiloh did a swift search along the small huts or booths outside the station, used by railway porters, carriers and hackney drivers to shelter from the weather. As it was a fine day, apart from a few men drinking tea, these were mostly empty. A quick manipulation with a thin bladed knife, and he had a door open. Luck was with him. Hanging on a hook, one dark blue jacket, and to complete his luck, an almost shapeless porters cap. Nobody took any special notice of the figure slouching through the station portals, hands in pockets.

Once inside the station, Shiloh Coombes made his way through the surging throngs of passengers, seeking the particular platform at which the Brighton train would arrive – he looked at the overhead clock – in about five minutes. He chose a viewpoint on the overhead pedestrian bridge across the platforms. The air up at that level was horrific, thick with the stench of coal smoke, but the overview of the whole platform made it necessary. The cap and coat had been useful in getting past the gate check at the entrance, but

Now looking around for the most suitable hiding place, Shiloh took off both and hid them. Several people had accosted him for service as a porter, each time he had managed to put them off , muttering something unintelligible.

He had not long to wait, the train arriving right on time. Shiloh had kept his eye upon two top-hatted gentleman waited back from the first melee of passengers, assuming them to be most likely there to receive the Nabob from the train. He felt entitled to be a bit pleased with himself, he thought; the dash across London - suddenly his theory fell apart as a similarly top-hatted gentleman stepped from the train, handing down a beautifully dressed lady. These two, to be warmly greeted by the waiting top-hatted party.

Scouring with gimlet eyes the now thinning concourse of passengers, Shiloh was spotted a portly dark-skinned gentleman dressed in a turban and robe dismounting from a rear carriage, indeed the very last wagon, followed only by the guard's van. Dashing down the stairway, Coombes unobtrusively retrieved his porter's disguise from where he had lodged it behind some rubbish bins. Donning it once more he hurried towards the rear of the train.

The going suddenly became difficult, as a new wave of passengers were disgorged from another train that had just pulled in, on the other side of the platform. As best he could, Coombes kept his eyes upon the bobbing turban coming slowly in his direction. He got to within ten feet of the turban's bearer, when Coombes caught sight of that face – the tall forehead, the raptor beak nose – then it was gone, but Shiloh could take no chances.

'Watch out! Man with a gun over there! And suddenly things got very chaotic. Several men jumped out of the crowd, forming in close about the Nabob; all around screaming, shouting broke out and before he could leave the scene, a firm grip settled about his arm. Glancing sharply at the offending hand, Shiloh saw that it belonged to a bulky tall figure. The man was soberly dressed, wearing a bowler hat, and on his face, a neat military moustache.

'Well, and who might you be then? What's all this callin'
out?' the voice was implacable, 'I'm from Scotland Yard, and I want
the whole story from you my lad,' as he led Shiloh Coombes back
out of the crowd. Dragged thus by the arm, Shiloh was still only half
distracted by this unwelcome attention, he still scanned the crowd for
sign of the face he thought he had caught a glimpse of. Seeing his
attention was still with the knot of people on the platform concourse,
the detective suddenly hissed at him; 'Who is it? Who are you
looking for? Is he you accomplice - come on my lad; I want
answers, and if I don't get 'em quickly, I shall be taking you into a
dark corner and beating the shitter out of you till you give me your
full story, squire. Do we understand each other?'

It was late afternoon before Shiloh Coombes made his way
back to the house of Feigenbaum, which he had left so precipitously
some hours before. . The old rag trader greeted him as he came
through the door. 'At last! Where have you been? I was beginning to
worry, my boy.' He was not angry, but anxious. Shiloh apologized
for causing this anxiety; he began to explain, but he was interrupted
– 'you look all in; before you start, sit down and I'll get you some tea
- have you eaten? you'd better have some of this madiera cake as
well.' As Feigenbum spoke, Coombes suddenly realized how tired
and hungry he was. He slumped into a chair, as Feigenbaum busied
himself around the kitchen.

At last, feeling much refreshed, Shiloh began his account of
the morning's activity. As usual, Feigenbaum sat silent as he
listened to him, absorbing the information. 'So, who was this geezer
at the station, the one that grabbed you?' What did he have to do
with anything?'

'I must admit you could have knocked me down with a feather
when he introduced himself. He was a detective from Scotland
Yard. He was pretty hard at first, but when I explained a few things,
he was more amenable. A formidable character though, and I must
admit I had some qualms about lying to him.'

'Feigenbaum looked at him, round eyed; 'Lied to him? I hope

he believed you; from what Birtles sez, these Scotland Yard people could prove a right nuisance if we get on the wrong side of them.'

'Yes I know, but I didn't think the truth would hold up. We have no proofs, and if I were to mention the murder of Pugsley, I believe he would have seen me as a suspect.' Feigenbaum got up to pace about, as he thought about this. 'You're right. Of course. What did you pitch him them?' Coombes smiled at this, 'Oh I gave him a good pitch all right; just enough of the truth for it to hold up, and enough embroidery for me to escape his clutches.' This broke the tension, and they grinned at each other, 'I was wearing this rail porter's cap and coat, you see, so I told him I had been working that day when there had been a scuffle on the platform a couple of weeks ago – yes, that day I arrived back from the country; Werth was there, when Birtles managed to fell him – I told the officer that I had seen this man with a revolver on that occasion, and today I thought I saw the same face of that man; I called out today to warn everybody.' Feigenbaum applauded;' You should be on the stage, my dear chap. Brilliant – and he swallowed it?' Shiloh Coombes laughed, 'Well not entirely, but I told him he could always reach me either working on the platforms or outside in the porter's huts. He accepted that, and let me go. I made sure to give him a good description of Werth though.' Once again Feigenbaum congratulated his protégée, but Coombes held up his hand.

'- Wait; there's more. When I took off for the station, after reading that piece in the Times about the Nabob of Mysore travelling up from Brighton, it was a sort of *déjà vu.* Then as I made my way along towards the station, the fact that the first princeling turned out to be non existent, made me think that the same might this time again be the case.' His grin was triumphant, 'And I was right. There is no Nabob of Mysore – there is of course the Maharaja of Mysore, a very important Indian Prince, but I felt sure that there was no Nabob of such. The man who did alight from the train, was indeed a dark skinned chap in a turban, but it is my opinion that he was a white man in disguise.' Here again the grin of triumph. 'And I believe I know who it was – and who it was the first time, impersonating a German nobleman.' He sat back, awaiting Feigenbaum's reaction. Knowing this, Feigenbaum instead rose once more and asked, 'Another cup of tea? You can tell me your theory as I stir up the old samovar.' Laughing to himself, Coombes sprung his bombshell; he had kept the best till the last, 'I have reason to believe that it was non other than the Prince of Wales himself.'

On taking leave of her missing friend Shiloh's older brother, Olivia Truscott stood for a minute or two on the pavement outside his club, in Jermyn Street. It had gone better than expected; Olivia had certainly learnt things – and although still rather astonished that she had done it, she had unburdened herself of her deepest secret to a man she hardly knew. And yet she was glad that she had. Thinking back over the meeting she had just had, Olivier found she had revised her opinion of him; he seemed to be not such a forbidding, cold man as she has always viewed him. He was certainly a very introverted and shy man, and this had perhaps tended to colour her girlhood opinion. Olivia was grateful at least to learn that Shiloh was all right, and even understood the reasons for the fat man's unwillingness to help her towards getting into contact with him. At least he had told her where Shiloh was apparently in hiding, down amongst the slums of east London. He had given of his opinion that Shiloh must be left to resolve his own life.

'I know you are his good friend, and I honour that,' he had begun. 'but you must also realize that there is something – oh I don't know how to say it without seeming to criticize my brother, but to be blunt there is still something about him, brilliant though he is, that is permanently immature.' As he spoke he'd looked at her pleadingly, almost begging her understanding. 'You do know what I mean, don't you?' Olivia nodded; She did understand. It had been what had always attracted her to Shiloh Coombes. His flashing wit, his keen intelligence, his often disconcerting lightning quicksilver change of mood.

Shiloh had always been a diverting companion, but she had always acknowledged that this restless brilliant mind was not to be kept up with, any more than one would try to keep up with some passing comet across the night sky. Immature was not quite the right word – perhaps it was more that he was an individual who did not easily fit into any category by which grown men are recognized. Despite his brother's misgivings, Olivia was still determined to locate her friend.

Musing thus, Olivia gradually became aware that she had been collecting curious glances; she realized that it was not done for young unaccompanied ladies to loiter on the sidewalk at this time of evening. Hurriedly she waved for a hansom and got in without clear idea of where she intended to go.

'Just take me up along St. James park, if you please driver,' as she settled back to think of her next move. To find Shiloh, Olivia would have to find some way of exploring the East End, a part of London rarely even spoken of within her level of society, let alone visited. She had just that once gone with Charles into Whitechapel, to see a political meeting, but it had broken out in a riot and they had left the scene in a hurry. What had begun as a bit of a lark, had turned into a frightening experience. Now she must find some way to do it alone. She thought of the hotel where she had last stayed in London; they might think it odd that she carried only a small overnight valise. Not accustomed to visiting London alone, Olivia began to keep a look out for some alternative hotel. Seeing one whose name she recognized, Olivia directed the driver to turn into the entrance driveway Regent Hotel. She remembered Charles had mentioned staying there. No sooner has the cab come to a halt than a hotel footman in a top hat and tails came to help her down, and ask for her luggage. He showed no surprise when she handed him her small carpet bag. Olivia was pleased she had resisted explaining her lack of luggage.

Earlier on that same day Charles Warner had just returned from his morning constitutional and was hanging his hat upon it's usual peg, together with the stout blackthorn walking stick he still carried. He was about to take off his greatcoat when he saw the letter addressed to him upon the hall table. Only whim made him pick it up – a small pile of unopened envelopes in the hall table drawer was indication of his unwillingness to deal with the outside world. Since that cruel conversation with Olivia – *oh dear Olivia* – he had been in a state of depression. Nevertheless he still took a daily hike, often across the fields. The battle to keep upright when his wooden leg sank beneath the surface was the only thing to take his mind from the sadness of his daily existence and the futility he foresaw as his future. Life had begun to feel like a burden.

In his misery, Charles had been sort of aware of his mother's concern, but it was not until he looked for his old service revolver – merely to clean it – and could not find it. Then it dawned; she had hidden it from him. An awful wave of shame swept over him, that he had caused her so much anxiety – he had sat down upon his bed and wept like baby.

His mother and he never discussed the revolver. From that time on though, Charles had by force of will begun to lift himself from the veritable trough of despond into which he had fallen.

As he sat down to a late breakfast, Charles remembered to letter he had stuffed into his pocket as he had come indoors. Fishing it out he smoothed the envelope upon the table, opened it and began to read. It was only a short note, and after reading it Charles sat holding the letter in one hand, staring before him, breakfast untouched.

'Don't you like it sir?' startled from his tumultuous thoughts, Charles turned; 'what? what was that?'

"Your kipper sir; don't you like it? Can I bring you something else?' The girl stepped back, half alarmed at the intensity with which the young master gazed at her,' Yes – I mean no; no nothing at all thank you,' he managed to utter, then getting from his chair as quickly as is possible with a stiff wooden leg, hurried out from the dining room towards the stairs. At the bottom he turned,' oh, could you get Wilson to get the trap ready to take me to the station.' He turned again,' - and ask Wilson to check the time for the next train to London.'

Birtles was blunt and to the point. 'That Scotland Yard detective whose notice you managed to attract, 'as enlisted my help to locate your good self. I warned you, Mr. Coombes; once they gets you in their clutches, once you name goes into their little black notebooks – why I reckon you never gets clear of 'em. Any'ow, 'e just wants to 'ave a bit of a talk wiv you, 'e sez. 'E didn't ask me if I knew where you was livin' or anyfing, but 'e seemed to think I knew you. I staved him off, of course, but if you want to avoid the geezer, I suggest you might want perhaps to lie low - get orf back down to your friend the doctor in the country for a bit.' His tone was non-committal, but Shiloh understood the implied criticism. Birtles had always made much of his policy of no cooperation with the detectives from the Yard; he had not forgiven their usurping of his former role.

'Thank you for the warning, Mr. Birtles, but as I am innocent of any wrong-doing – I even returned the porter's get-up - I see no harm in having a bit of a talk, as you put it, with the detective.' Birtles, still poker faced, shrugged and turned to leave. 'Alright – I 'ave delivered the message, and that's wot 'e paid me to do. And I *'ave* warned you.' He paused at the door, turning; 'If you must see 'im, mind you stick to the same story you told 'im. 'E will ask you over and over, always lookin' for some crack to break your story.' He almost smiled then, 'Izzie 'as told me your account to the detective regarding your presence at Victoria station; nice work, thinking' on your feet. Always go economical with the truth with these Scotland Yard geezers, I say – they are not used to too much of it, and they gets all suspicious,' Tipping his hat, Birtles took his leave.

Shiloh was still looking at the door after it had closed upon the exit of Ned Birtles. He felt a small satisfaction; Birtles had almost complimented him. He recalled Feigenbaum revealing that Birtles would refer to Shiloh sardonically as 'the toff'. Shiloh smiled to himself as he recalled his own nick-name for the dimunitive Birtles, coined after their first rather abrasive meeting; *the truculent runt.*

Shiloh had since come to grudgingly respect the man, but now for the first time Birtles had seemed almost amiable. He was grateful that Birtles had managed to deflect the Scotland Yard man, giving Shiloh the opportunity of avoiding him. Shiloh took the warning seriously, but nonetheless he fully intended to meet with the detective from Scotland Yard, and if possible to glean just how much the police knew about Werth. Despite Birtles misgivings, it might be time to share information – well some of it anyway. Leaving a note on the table to Feigenbaum, Shiloh Coombes picked up his hat and took himself off to the headquarters of the police in Whitehall Place.

Upon entering the office of the detective handling the case, Shiloh noted with amusement the surprise on the face of the detective as he rose from his desk. He had recognized Coombes, now in respectable street clothes. The detective examined the man before him with undisguised interest. Shiloh in turn used the opportunity to get a good look at the other man. Previously they had only met under tense circumstances, in a gloomy soot-begrimed corner of the railway station buildings. The man before him was tall, a little over six foot, and despite his military moustache, a rather melancholy face. Coombes fancied the detective had a sort of spaniel countenance, except for the eyes – inquisitive, unblinking.

'Well sir; come up in the world, have we? I wouldn't imagine a rail porter's pay – ' but Coombes raised is hand,' Actually sir, I have come to dispel some misunderstanding. For starters, I believe I mentioned that I was working on the station platform on the day of the first disturbance of which I was a witness. I didn't however wish to imply that I was there as a porter. Upon the second occasion, I was indeed in the guise of a rail porter, but it was not my intention to fool the police sir.' His interlocutor still regarded him, expressionless – apart from those sharp appraising eyes.

'I for my part wish to assure you that the police are not to be fooled – sir.' He continued his slow appraisal of the man before him, as he stepped closer,' and just what *was* your purpose in masquerading as a porter, if I may ask?' Coombes was beginning to see that this particular policeman was indeed not a man to be fooled with. Stifling the automatic urge to step backwards, Shiloh was therefore now almost toe to toe with the detective. Shiloh had correctly understood that the stepping into his space was meant to have caused him to step backwards, giving the other quite a psychological advantage. They stood thus for a long second, eyes locked, Shiloh noted a slight crinkle of amusement around those piercing dark eyes. At the same moment both men stepped ever so slightly back. Turning abruptly, the detective returned to his desk, from which he had arisen at Coombe's entrance. He sat now, hands clasped behind his head, relaxed, 'All in your own good time, squire, all in your own time,' his smile was wolfish as he waited for the reply.

Without being invited, Shiloh sat himself on the other side of the desk.

'Well as you asked so nicely, I shall tell you of my business, and my reason for being at the right place at the right time.' Shiloh then proceeded to tell the detective some of the truth about his relationship with Feigenbaum, though their plan of a private agency of detection he made out as more advanced than it was. His story was essentially the truth - as Feigenbaum had always reiterated, the truth is easier to stick to than a lie. It was however the bits left out which made the difference. Shiloh felt reasonably confident that his listener accepted his version of events. The detective had listened to him without comment, only asking Shiloh to pause while he took short notes. When Shiloh came to an end, the detective closed his notebook and stood up; 'Thank you Mr. Coombes – that is your correct name is it ? We'll be in touch sir.' He crossed to the door, which he opened. As Shiloh walked through the doorway, the detective with the sharp beady eyes called after him:- 'And any time you wish to actually tell me the whole story, sir, I'll be just as happy to listen,' as he quietly closed the door.

Charles Warner could hardly believe his eyes; it was as if he had conjured her up, the object of his thoughts but a moment past. He was seated in the lobby of his London hotel, ostensibly perusing a newspaper, but in reality wondering where he should begin his search. But suddenly here she was; Olivia Truscott in person. Unbelievable. He froze; he'd certainly not expected to see Olivia here, of all places. Although he had rushed to London to seek her out, Charles was so completely disconcerted, he has not worked out what he should say to her…

In something of a panic, Charles attempted to manoeuvre himself into a more unobtrusive position behind a convenient potted palm, but his wooden leg played him false. The end result was the exact opposite of what he had intended, as he sprawled head-long onto the polished floor, hitting his head a solid thump on a small table on the way down.

At the hotel booking desk, Olivia turned to see the whole undignified scenario unfold. But unlike Charles first horrified expectation as he lay half stunned on the floor, she did not look at him in distain, but instead within seconds found his head being cradled in Olivia's lap.

'Oh Charles – are you all right? Oh please god you are all right!' was as music in the ears of Charles Warner, who allowed himself to keep his eyes closed a little longer than strictly necessary. The two hot tears which had fallen upon his face were bliss; In those few moments, he knew that this has been a most serendipitous accident. He had the courage now ; the need for constructing awkward explanations, embarrassments were swept aside. The next minute of course the rush of several hotel staff to help their fallen guest put an end to his moment of bliss, but he would not forget it, nor the real anguish he had heard in her voice.

After some very solicitous first aid treatment insisted upon by the hotel staff, Charles made his way across the black and white marble floor of the hotel's palm court. Amidst the general to-do of his fall, he'd managed to ask Olivia to meet him here. Charles paused for a moment, looked about; it had been a favourite haunt of his this, in happier times. He'd come down from school, and meet his favourite aunt Violet here for tea and water-cress sandwiches. Those carefree days before he'd left for the Crimea - Charles shook his head to clear it of the whole jumble of disagreeable thoughts that had just flooded his memory. He found himself looking around in some distraction, before spotting Olivia across the room, seated beneath a group of palms. Charles hurried across to her, taking care however not to let himself slip. Oilvia could hold back no longer, as she leapt to her feet to guide Charles the last couple of yards.

'Oh Charles, I feared you might take another tumble – oh show me you poor head, its all plastered up, I didn't know you had gashed your head' - still holding the hand which she had extended to him, Charles gently took hold of the other.

'I would like to promise only this – whatever happens, I won't ever again let anything come between us – our friendship, I mean,' Charles was bright red by now, waiting for her reaction. Olivia looked deep into his eyes for a very serious moment, then simply leant forward and kissed his cheek. 'That would please me greatly,' she said, turning towards their table. Seated, they looked at each other – there was no tension in the air, only each waiting for the other to begin.

Olivia took a deep breath, slowly exhaling,' Charles, before we go any further, there is something in all fairness I must tell you.' It was as if he hadn't quite heard just what she had said: 'Well Olivia I have something which I must tell you – ' realizing that they had both said almost the same thing at the same time, both burst out laughing, so loudly that people at other tables were turning their way.

Charles was still wiping the tears of laughter from his eyes when he felt a not too gentle tug upon his ear. As he turned he knew who this could only be. The booming voice of his aunt Violet told him it was so. 'I knew I could tell that laugh anywhere.'

Managing it not too awkwardly, Charles stood to welcome her; 'Aunt Vi! What a coincidence; I haven't been here since, since I - well since I got back,' engulfed in a cloud of perfumed lace, Charles submitted to his aunt's exuberant embrace. Over her shoulder, he saw the raised eyebrows upon the face of Olivia. There had been a moment back there, a long drawn-out moment, when they appeared to tremble on the edge of something very serious..

CHAPTER TWELVE

Knees tucked up beneath his chin, Shiloh sat enjoying the unaccustomed sunlight. He was in his favourite spot on the blind ledge by the river, smoking and thinking one more time over small aspects of the situation, seeking some small clue he may have overlooked. He recognized the low whistle – just three descending notes – and moments later the grubby street-rat face of Young Sparrow peered around the corner.

'Ere; this young twerp want to talk wiv you,' and he indicated the boy he held firmly by the collar. The boy held both hands clasped to his ears, and Shiloh remembered Feigenbaum's account of Sparrow's method for leading young boys about. Swinging his long legs around, Coombes soon stood before the lad in question. 'Well come on Rolly bollicks, you wanted to talk', as he let go his grip just long enough to give the back of the boy's head a good clip.

'''Well done, Sparrah me lad, but off you toddle, the old gaffer should have some supper for you,' and Young Sparrow took the hint and left without ado. Shiloh studied the boy a moment or two, and then placed him. It was the boy he had once saved from a beating in the street, as he was walking along with Feigenbaum. The boy in turn studies the man before him; finally satisfied that Shiloh was indeed the one he sought, he began speaking. ' Me ma sez not to tell anyone 'cept you – I din't want to even tell you, but she said you are a proper gent , an' if I tole you, you might give me some money.' He looked up at the figure before him, but without too much hope. This man his ma had called a proper gent didn't look all that flash to Roley Lambert.

Shiloh Coombes was dressed in his street clothes, that is to say the clothes he normally wore about the streets of East London. Shapeless workman's grey trousers held up by a thick belt with large brass buckle, a shirt without collar, and a grubby red neck-cloth around his throat. To complete his attire, an old market porter's weskit topped off by a cheap cloth cap. Shiloh noted the boy's less than admiring assessment of his outfit, of which he himself was rather proud. He had in fact very carefully chosen every item as part of his blending in with the local dress code. Shiloh put out his hand, which the surprised boy looked at doubtfully, eventually shaking hands. Nobody had actually shaken his hand before, so he did it very energetically.

'How do you do, ' Shiloh spoke in his own voice, 'My name is Mr. Coombes, but you may call me Shiloh, if you wish.' He felt that the boy might trust him if he could present himself as a 'proper gent'.

'My name is Roland Lambert, but you can call me Roley,' gravely the boy gave back, seemingly heartened by Shiloh's *bona fides.* ' Well now Roley, what is it you have come to see me about?' The boy glanced about reflexively, in that time honoured slum gesture when about to share some information, 'My mam sez not to tell nuffing, best keep stumm, but I tole the old gaffer about wot I saw, didn't I. Well, I wasn't goin' to say anythin' else, but last night 'e came round late to our gaff , drunk as a pig 'e was, and before long 'e turned nasty and gave my poor mum an awful beltin'.' Shiloh intuited that he boy was probably used to violence vented upon his mother, but obviously this time he had decided to do something about it. There was barely controlled anger in his voice a he spoke now, 'Cholly Kypser is 'is name, the dog. Just before the sod took off, after kickin' the old girl about a bit, 'e sez somethin' about doin' for that nosey pal of the old Yid right and proper, 'e said.' The boy looked hard into Shiloh's eyes. Coombes saw a knowingness reflected there, way beyond his years.

'E means you, guv'nor, when 'e said that. Finish 'im right and proper, was what 'e said.' The boy looked about once more, before continuing, 'my mam said to warn you, and she don't want any money, she said' he looked up again – 'but if you can see your way clear, a few bob wouldn't go astray, coz she is pretty bad knocked abaht, and can't get out of bed.' He looked anxiously at the silent figure of Coombes, intent upon his words. Without any further discussion, Shiloh fished into his pocket, and gave the lad all of the silver in it. 'It's not much but get a doctor for your mother, and if its insufficient, come and tell me what it costs. Is that clear? Oh, and thank you for that interesting information. Tell me; did you ever see this man together with a very tall man – taller than me, with a high forehead – yes, you have? Lets walk along a bit, and you can tell me about it…'

Together with Ned Birtles, Shiloh Coombes had spent the best part of two days going about the East End, talking quietly to anyone in the spectacle trade. Eventually they had become dispirited at their total lack of success – nobody it seems had made a pair of spectacles for a man whom they'd described.

'I'll be off then,' was all Birtles said, as he pulled up his coat collar against the now steadily increasing rain. Apart from his usual taciturnity, he showed no sign that he thought this had been a waste of time. On impulse Coombes called after him; 'did you think this was a wild goose chase, Mr. Birtles.' Over his shoulder came the answer; 'worth a try guvnor, worth a try,' as the dimunitive figure turned the next corner. So Shiloh had made his way back to Feigenbaum's house, foot-weary, damp, and nothing to show for it. Nevertheless he smiled to himself – *Birtles had agreed with him, at least.* The problem was, they had nothing much else to go on, tracking down the elusive Werth. Even the slightest clue must be followed up.

It was a day later; the weather having cleared up, Shiloh Coombes had been down by the river. After his meeting with the young Rolly Lambert, Shiloh decided it was time for another meeting with Feigenbaum and Ned Birtles.

Shiloh felt that things were perhaps progressing - he now had the name of at least one of Werth's henchman, and knowing something of the fellow's behaviour pattern, it might be possible to either grab the man themselves, perhaps have him arrested for murder… Shiloh urgently needed to discuss their next move with the others.   Whatever, they had to take the initiative from their enemy – and soon.   Too many had died already at the hands of this ruthless man

.He sought out Sparrow, and soon found the youth hanging about near the local bakery at the corner.   Shiloh hoped to find him there, as the sparrow had admitted to a liking for the baker's plump young niece.   Unfortunately Mr. Frith the baker did not think the sparrow a good prospect for the girl, and privately Shiloh agreed with him.   Nevertheless, it made him easy to locate.

'Wotcha guv'nor', as with an irrepressible grin the youngster fell in with the passing Shiloh, who had signalled him with a jerk of the head.   'How goes it with the baker's girl?   Making any progress?' Sparrow darts a glance at Shiloh from the corner of his eye,' Oh I fink she likes me well enough – its 'er uncle wot hates my guts,' he grinned, 'actually she sometimes still manages to slip me a sugar bun, so I guess I'm goin' alright, eh?'   They both laughed, and then Shiloh asked him to locate Feigenbaum, who he'd last heard was going across to visit the Bevis Marks Synagogue, in Whitechapel.

'Before you go looking for him,' Shiloh told him, 'I want you to call in and leave a message for Mr. Birtles.   Tell him I'd like a talk with them both as soon as possible.'   Sparrow looked a trifle anxious, fiddling with his battered top-hat, in a futile attempt to bring it to a respectable shape.   Picking up on this sign of reluctance, Shiloh asked the reason.   'Well it's like this guvnor; once I couldn't resist - I lifted 'is wallet, see.   Nothin' in it mind, but it hurt 'is pride, like'. He glanced again at Shiloh, 'Perhaps I can get another lad for that one, eh?'   Neddy can be right vindictive, know wot I mean?'   As the spry young scamp took off, Shiloh had to laugh to himself;

- Lifted Ned Birtles purse, eh?   What effrontery!

There'd been no escaping it - His aunt Violet might present on the surface as yet another frivolous society matron, but Charles knew her better.   Beneath her fashionably gay manner, she was a woman of strong will.   Charles bowed to the inevitable, albeit with some feeling of relief ; whatever Olivia and he were about to say to one another was for the moment postponed. Judging by the alacrity with which she had accepted his aunt's invitation – insistence really – to lunch with her, Olivia seemed likewise relieved.

And now of course was not the time for any sort of declarations. The opportunity was lost, his confession to her would have to wait. Anyhow, Charles reminded himself, he had come up to London with the sole purpose to help her as a friend.

Initially as they had seated themselves for lunch, there had been was a moment or two of awkward silence, Charle's aunt took notice of the unspoken tension between the two young people. She rose to the situation; this was after all her forte. By the time they had began their meal Lady Violet had managed to get going a lively conversation. The young woman across the table soon won her approval – bright, intelligent and obviously well-bred.

it was a serious concern of the whole family that although Charles had seemingly recovered from his physical wounds, there were signs that he was still not emotionally well. Among other signs, he'd seemed to have lost all interest in the opposite sex, positively avoiding even those with whom he had previously been on good terms. Finding her nephew here in the Palm Court, in the company of this charming young lady therefore caught his aunt's immediate attention. She was trying to assess the possibility...

After some amusing family stories of Charle's childhood, mostly embarrassing to him but giving the two women much to laugh at, Lady Violet suddenly swooped; 'So you two, where did you get to know one another?' As the story unfolded of Charles recuperation and Olivia's role in his recovery, at first her hopes were if not dashed, at least dampened.

As the conversation continued, however, with both so keen to emphasise the professional nurse/patient relationship, Lady Violet began to observe the small things; quick glances at one another, blushing from both when the other intercepted such glances - all told her more than words. These two, although seemingly set upon denying it, were obviously more than just patient and nurse to each other. She determined to get to the bottom of this seeming mystery.

'So you have come up to London, Olivia, to try and seek out a friend who may be in some sort of trouble, and you nephew, have come to assist in this search.' She smiled at them benignly, 'very commendable, Charles. Of course you probably feel that you had a duty, that you owe your nurse some support.' She noted keenly his reply; 'well yes- I mean no, - and Olivia's hasty, 'oh Charles owes me nothing, I believe he has come out of the goodness of his heart,' meanwhile blushing furiously.

'Well that's established then; just good friends,' the two young people nodded emphatically, though both again appearing ill at ease; once more they fell into an awkward silence.

'So do you have a plan, or were you just going to lounge about taking tea in the Palm Court, hoping your missing friend might saunter by.' This had the intended effect, and they had to laugh, 'Well no Aunt Vi, in fact we had just run into each other when you came barging up.' He looked entreatingly at Olivia, 'and so I was about to offer my services – a quick grin – 'out of the goodness of my heart.'

'So here you are, all primed for action, with no plan at all. Typical youth. I must say this all sounds absolutely fascinating, playing detective – I have always wanted to do something exciting like this.' She beamed at the two before her, 'I have decided that I am going to help you,' as they glanced at one another with rising apprehension. Lady Vi became even more determined to ferret out this mystery.

'Well as you seem to have come up to London, Olivia, without a real plan as yet, why don't you allow me to offer you accommodation at least.' She smiled cheerfully at her nephew, ' Charles will tell you I'm sure that my house is large and rather empty – look, I absolutely insist,' sending her hapless nephew a stern look; 'I'm sure you Charles will be concerned for Miss Truscott's reputation –' turning then with a smile to Olivia, 'There, it's settled then. Can't have you living unchaperoned in hotels, my dear; I'm sure your mother would agree?' The two young people knew that there was no way open for them to refuse the invitation. 'Of course you will also stay with me Charles – I assume that was your intention?' He looked at his aunt, knowing she had out-maneouvred him, 'Well thank you aunt Vi, and for the very kind offer to Olivia.' He turned to her, 'Is that acceptable to you, Olivia?'

Returning home after receiving Coombe's message, Feigenbaum hung his umbrella and great kaftan in the entranceway, and proceeded with much grunting to remove his street boots, changing them for his comfortable *pantoffeln*. These noises attached to his return did not go unnoticed by Shiloh Coombes as he waited next to the kitchen stove, drinking tea. As his friend finally made his entrance, Coombes greeted him. 'Aha! Home at last – you have walked far, I believe, and you have unfortunately brought ill tidings,' as Feigenbaum stared at him, open-mouthed. 'How – ' but Shiloh cut in; 'elementary really - removing your boots seemed to take an arduously long time, you were obviously very tired. And from your frequent pauses, the deep sighs, I understood you to have brought bad news' Feigenbaum looked at him intently.

'You know Coombes, you continue to astonish me with the way you put together all the little bits and pieces; small observations, background sounds. Well done, well done'. Shiloh smiled at him. 'Of course my conclusions were confirmed when you didn't as usual call out if the tea was on…So, while I pour the tea, would you like to share your findings?' Feigenbaum seated himself with a sigh, but spoke only after he had drank deeply from his cup.

'Yes, I bring bad news. Very bad news indeed. After you and Birtles had no luck asking around after a spectacle maker around here, I went across to the Bevis Marks and spread a wider net. Lots of London's spectacle makers are Jewish, you see. Shiloh Coombes was filled with foreboding at the tone of his old friend. 'I asked a different question, and I got a different answer.' He looked up, his face set in planes and deep furrows. The old man suddenly seemed much older. Coombes leant forward, concerned, 'what is it? What have you heard?' Feigenbaum drained the rest of his cup, setting it down upon it's saucer with a clatter; his voice held a tremor, something Shiloh had never heard from this man before. 'Its terrible; we caused it, its down to us – I don't know, we were too careless or something. Somehow we always seem to underestimate our opponent. I can't - I just don't know what to do, anymore.' Both men sat in silence for some minutes, Feigenbaum sunk in despair, with Coombes impatient, but realising he must allow the distressed Feigenbaum to take his time, to marshal his thoughts. He waited as Feigenbaum took a couple of deep breaths. As he regained his equilibrium, he turned then to his young protégée.

'I asked around the synagogue, nothing direct, just oblique like, if anyone had heard something unusual going on. I chatted to lots of people, but got mostly gossip. Then I got lucky – if you can call it lucky. ' I don't know for unusual,' one old geezer tells me, but Manny Rosenfeld – he's retired now - he says, 'e got hisself strangled, didn't he. Sittin' in the outhouse, 'e was.' He stared into Shiloh's eyes, 'I knew old Manny; sure he was retired, but you guessed it – he used to be a spectacle lens grinder.'

Shiloh Coombes mind raced; he saw the unavoidable implication – their inquiry had lead directly to the murder of the old man. Obviously the man Rosenfeld had made up a pair of glasses for Werth – and when the chase got close, he was simply eliminated. Shiloh now spoke;

'Well for one thing, I refuse to accept that we killed this unfortunate man – it's *not* down to us. We were following a legitimate line of inquiry into several murders, I recall. We didn't cause this man's death -

the monster Werth did for him. We mustn't allow ourselves be deterred. We swore that we would not stop until we have him, no matter what. Agreed?' The old man stared at him, but then slowly nodded his head, 'Yes, perhaps you are right. I was taking this too personal.' His raised eyebrows indicated that Shiloh should continue.

'That is why I believe the best thing we can do now, the right thing, is to press on and at least do this unfortunate Mr. Rosenfeld the honour of tracking down his murderer.' The two were still staring at each other, when the doorbell rang.

'Ah; that will be Mr. Birtles – I'll let him in shall I?'

While Shiloh attended to the entry of Birtles, Feigenbaum busied himself with his beloved samovar. He'd said nothing, but the tea prepared by Shiloh had been a bit stewed. For Isidor Feigenbaum, who had spent much of is life a wandering, rootless man, the samovar was a comforting familiar thing. Long ago he'd formed the habit of turning to it whenever his mind was troubled. Not just the tea making, but attending to the water, the polishing of it's splendid brass and copper fittings was somehow a comfort.

When his affection for his samovar was remarked upon, he always recounted the story, that it was the only thing he had from his mother. This was not strictly true – he had always remembered her old samovar with affection, but this actual samovar he had bought over in Cheapside no more than ten years hence. It was the idea of samovar as a familiar comfort that he treasured.

'Well then Izzie, tea brewin', eh?' as Birtles entered, still wearing his leather top-coat, but having at least taken off his wet boots in the entrance. 'Aha, got the fire goin' as well, have we,' which decided him upon divesting himself of the wet overgarment. He nevertheless kept on his wet top hat, until it began to steam. Throwing it down upon the nearest chair, the diminutive detective placed himself squarely in front of the said fire, lifting his coat-tails to better warm his rear.

'Oh to be sure, and welcome my dear,' said Feigenbaum, 'and when your arse is sufficiently toasted, come and sit at the table and have some tea.' He had never seen the usually touchy Ned Birtles so ebullient. 'Well then,' began Birtles as he took his tea in both hands, blowing loudly upon it, 'I 'ave been summonsed, and here I be,' he cocked his eye at Shiloh Coombes, who had just entered.

'Yes Mr. Birtles, thank you for your promptness, and I am sorry for your soaking. The weather appeared clear at the time I sent off the lad with the message.' In a quick few terse words, he put Birttles in possession of the latest situation. 'It's getting very dangerous Mr. Birtles, and although Mr. Feigenbaum and I have determined to continue our hunt for this man, you should perhaps consider your own situation. Unlike ourselves, you are a married man, I believe, with considerations of family – '

'Gor bless you sir - considerations! It's a bleedin' millstone about my neck!' They all laughed, but then he became very serious.

'In the beginning, yes, I was working for Mr Feigenbaum 'ere. I also have my other principal to consider in all this,' he began, 'but I am beginning to take this 'orrible business very personal, very personal indeed.' He glanced about, at his truculent best. 'I don't believe any of us – including' my good self, is safe from this murderous bastard until 'e is either apprehended - here Birtles paused for emphasis – or 'e meets wiv an unfortunate accident.' He looked about, from one to the other of his listeners, 'not after this last murder of the old Yid – beggin' your pardon Izzie – dreadful business, eh. No gents, gloves off now- it's us or 'im.' Shiloh jumped up then, shaking Birtles by the hand. 'Handsomely said Birtles, I think I speak for Mr. Feigenbaum here, when I say we are very heartened to have your unstinting support. Now, given these latest developments, I think we should begin our next plan of action, don't you?'

169

CHAPTER THIRTEEN

The man sat in his room, curtains closed to keep out any glimmer of daylight. Just one solitary candle stood against the prevailing gloom. But that is how he preferred it. He suffered from a family weakness; the pupils of the eyes were always wide open, and did not contract on being exposed to light. With eyes so extremely light sensitive, by default he had become a creature of the night. It was his belief that this long habituation to the dark hours gave him advantage, much like a cat. Whatever, he certainly felt most at home in the darkness of the night.

There was other quality he fancied he shared with cats – both were superb nocturnal hunters. The termination of his connection with his eye-glass maker - regrettable but necessary – he had achieved with consummate skill. Sitting there in the half dark of his room, he reviewed it in his mind, savouring again the forensic skill of the operation.

The stalking: waiting silent and still for most of a wet cold evening.

The approach: A door opens, some light spills out, but his hat brim is held low, expecting this. His eyes were nevertheless a little dazzled but he had held his nerve. In dark clothes, standing perfectly still, he had let the old man shuffle past, not more than an arms-length away.

The finale: Waiting, feeling and counting pulse - spiked a little but almost immediately back to normal - the sound of newspaper tearing, the door whipped open, quarry head down – perfect timing – the piano wire garrotte immediately looped around the neck - pressure, tighter ... over all too soon, but what mastery of execution. Noiseless, no alarms raised, not even a dog barking. Away and walking down the road, clothing unruffled. Master of the night.

He took out of his pocket his garrotte, pulling at it to see that it was still held fast by it's wooden handles. After assuring himself

170

of it's continuing trustworthiness, he folded it carefully, and inserted into a concealed pocket inside of his coat sleeve.

If there was one thing which might excite his cold soul, it was such moments of supreme craftsmanship – no, artistry - of the highest kind. After thus re-living one more time this recent thrill, he took to polishing his fine new spectacles; the name of their maker already forgotten. His mind had turned once more to the business in hand, evaluating the various factors, the pros and cons of his grand plan. Things had gone almost without a hitch; this plump city of London was his for the picking. These people had never come up against anything like him.

His original reason for being here, the assassination, was for the moment on hold. The interference from the old Jew and his associate, this meddling young fellow Coombes, had seen to that. But if they thought that he was to be so easily deterred, they had some unpleasant surprises to come. It had been a revelation to him, that this wealthy city of London did not have anything quite like the Prussian Secret Police, with it's enormous powers of coercion, intimidation. The police, such as they were, seemed to be run by amateur gentlemen, as so much in this effete country seemed to be. He smiled to himself, thinking about this.

,He'd been very busy at first, arranging discreet quarters for himself, making preparations for the assassination attempt, but he'd not been in London very long before being struck by the enormous potential here for a truly masterful mind. His heart had soared; it had been moment of exultation - it was then that he had realized that here lay his destiny – to create in the world's richest city, a mighty criminal enterprise…

That interfering Coombes was proving difficult to eliminate – a trap; yes a trap, something to lure him in…

Although at first somewhat put out at meeting his aunt, on reflection Charles was beginning to realise it was perhaps not such a bad thing. For one thing, being alone just the two of them, seemed to create an almost unbearable tension between himself and Olivia. The meeting with his aunt also proved to be fortuitous, in that her impulsive invitation for them both to stay with her in her Knightsbridge house had at a stroke solved several of the problems which would have arisen – had he and Olivia had the opportunity to discuss them.

In fact it might work out rather well, he considered. The three were enjoying a fine breakfast together on the morning after their meeting at the Regent Hotel. Although now autumn, it was an exquisite morning, and his aunt had decided that they should eat out on the sun terrace. Charles had finished his breakfast; sitting back somewhat from the table so as to enjoy a small cigar with his coffee, he was observing his breakfast companions. Their animated conversation, the frequent laughter, told of the growing rapport between the two women. His aunt really surprised him - charmed by the younger woman, her usually imperious manner was nowhere in evidence. He took the opportunity to study Olivia; unaware of his regarding her how vivacious and witty she was – and beautiful. Her beauty he never had become accustomed to; instead of filling Charles with admiration, it had only fuelled his sense of bitter inadequacy.

- But now he had made a decision, and he meant to hold to it.

'When you have finished that cigar, Charles, you should join us so that we might begin to plan our campaign.' The quick shared look of alarm between Charles and Olivia was intercepted by Lady Violet, 'Now I won't be excluded Charles; I believe you will find me very resourceful. You two have rushed away up to London, full of energy, very admirable of course, but no plan; no Charles, listen to me.' Her guests had little choice but to do so, the imperious note back in her voice, aunt Vi was not to be denied. 'From what you have told me, Olivia, you have come seeking your friend, without the faintest idea where he might be in London – good lord, he may have run away to sea or something, as far as you know.' She turned a stern eye to her nephew.

'And you Charles, have out of the goodness of heart as you say, come galloping along like Sir Galahad' – 'actually, hobbling aunt – ' interjected her nephew, but this was swept aside with a gesture, '- all I am proposing is that you base yourself here with me, and I can help coordinate your search', she came to an end, waiting for their objections. As neither seemed to very enthusiastic over her announcement, Lady Violet began again, in an almost plaintive voice,

'Oh please let me help – it all seems so exciting, and I don't get much of that these days; life has been so utterly boring since your uncle died,' as she dabbed at her eyes with a lace handkerchief.

'My dear aunt Vi, you are so transparent, and I don't think this is to be taken as something for your amusement,' put in Charles, embarrassed at his aunt's blatant ploy, 'I have as you say come up to offer to help Olivia with her search, but I think it would be presumptious for you or I to insist upon helping her.' He turned to Olivia, 'as a matter of fact, I had not got to the point yesterday evening of offering my assistance,' his face was grave as he went on.

'But I would like to do so now. I place myself at your disposal'. Olivia's look was equally grave, as she nodded . 'Thank you Charles, and it is much appreciated.' She turned then to her hostess,

'Although we have just met, Lady Violet, I feel we shall become good friends – and yes thankyou, I do also accept your generous offer. I am going to need all the help I can get, I'm afraid,' impulsively grasping the other's hand, who clasped it firmly back. 'Let us make a plan' said lady Violet.

'Capital idea, but first off, I'd like to make the point that we are not beginning so completely in the dark – I have already discovered the general area of London in which Shiloh may be found, began Olivia, 'You see I did have a bit of a plan; straight from the railway station I went in search of Shiloh's older brother. All I knew is that he was some sort of Whitehall boffin. It turned out to be not so easy, however. I traipsed about to several government departments, but nobody had ever heard of -or didn't want to tell me –of his whereabouts. So you see, right at the beginning I almost fell at the first hurdle, so to speak. But just then, a bit of luck – one of the clerks had been giving me the eye – yes, the cheeky beast – so of course I smarmed him up shamelessly. He told me in all confidence that I might try another tack; it turns out you see, there is a directory of every gentlemen's club in London – and an annual list of their members.'

'Yes, quite correct, I know it well,' said Lady Violet, laughing' it's often consulted by wives seeking their husbands', again laughing, 'of course its completely useless, - club doormen will swear on their mother's graves that the 'named member' is anywhere the member wishes him to say; it's a major part of their job' both women were now laughing, as Charles feigned amazement, looking from one woman to the other.

'I swear, but I am beginning to realize just what cynical scheming creatures women are. Smarming up to clerks, indeed, not to mention you aunt – I hope you didn't ever check upon my uncle in this manner,' and all were laughing, the easy shared laughter seemed to suggest to Charles that perhaps they might , the three of them, be able to work together.

'Anyhow, Olivia, what was the result? By your smug look, I presume you met with some success' Charles teased her, and Olivia felt a tug of hope - *that they might yet get back to the happy relationship they had always enjoyed. She'd hated that stilted oh so formal conversation...'*

She also remembered anew, in that flash of a moment that she must tell Charles all, if they were to fully regain the warm friendship she knew they both treasured. His coming up to London to help her, had affected her much more than she had wished to show. It told her that despite his mother having warned him of rumours concerning her personal past, Charles had acted instinctively to rush to her assistance. Charles had shown her that he still considered the value of her friendship transcended the bounds of conventional morality. She also realised then how ardently she had wished for his approval – or at the very least, his acceptance. Briefly, Olivia recounted how she had tracked down the elusive brother of Shiloh Coombes.

'Well done old girl, well done' cried Charles. 'Yes bravo Olivia, –but go on dear,' added Aunt Violet, impatient. 'What happened then?' Olivia set about recounting all that had transpired that evening. How she had tracked Shiloh's brother to his lair, as she put it, and glossing over those personal confidences between them, Oliver nevertheless gave a true to the facts account of the conversation. The others agreed that she had done very well, but as Lady Violet then said, 'it's one thing to say, somewhere in the East End, but unless one has actually been into the area, it is impossible to conceive of. Despite all of the worthy do-gooders, I think one should only go down into the slums if forced to, really'.

'Oh well, Charles and I have been 'down there', as you put it ; some time ago we were both in London at the same time, and Charles had been taking me about London all week. He even hired a dashing Landau so we could gad about in style' – suddenly Olivia blushed;

     -   *here she was, recalling a happy time they had spent together, forgetting for a moment or two the fragile state of their present situation –*

Quickly she regained her equilibrium, 'I has mentioned I should like to see more of the city than the fashionable side of London. so this evening we went to see some public speech by this Welsh chap. There was a riot so Charles insisted on returning me to where I was staying with my cousins. It was all terribly exciting.' Lady Violet sat silent, though glancing up now and then, looking very thoughtful. Olivia hoped she had not offended their hostess by her account of their slumming excursion.

Charles watched as his aunt got up out of her chair then went in through the french doors and unlocked a drawer. Taking something from it, she came back out onto the terrace.

'I say steady on auntie' cried Charles, alarmed as his aunt approached; in her hand she held a revolver. Hastily he scrambled to his feet, ready for whatever was to transpire. Charles glanced across at Olivia; she sat still, seemingly frozen in place. Cursing his missing leg under his breath, he moved awkwardly to place himself in front of her. Surprisingly his aunt burst out laughing, and turning the revolver over, handed it to her surprised nephew.

'Goodness Charles, did you imagine I might be going to begin shooting? Really, you are a silly.' Lady Violet passed the incident off thus lightly, but she had noticed how her nephew had moved to stand in front of his young lady... *just good friends indeed*

Charles looked at the revolver in his hands, as he automatically broke open the chamber to check if the piece was loaded – it was not, but then he became doubly astonished; 'I say old girl, how did you come by this - this is my own service revolver-' the steady glance between nephew and aunt told him the answer; he remembered with shame and embarrassment his mother having removed it from his room. Obviously she had given it to her sister in law, for safe-keeping... Aunt Violet met his gaze unflinchingly;

'I believe you should perhaps carry it with you, my dear, if you are going to be dragging this young lady through the slums.'

Having discussed over the breakfast table their first foray into the East End, Lady Violet had insisted that Olivia accompany her to the Army and Navy Stores, to obtain suitable stout shoes and all weather clothing for what she termed their expedition.

Charles' sarcastic remark that they weren't actually going as far as Africa, she had waved aside. 'You should perhaps consider what attire you feel might be suitable for this enterprise; we ladies will do likewise, thank you very much', as she swept out, with a helpless Olivia in tow. He had to admit, she had a point. After first obtaining a horse-cab for the departing ladies, Charles waved them off from pavement at the front of the house. As soon as they had left, Charles called for Thompson, his aunt's long serving butler cum general factotum. Thompson had in fact been his uncle's batman all through the Crimea campaign, and Charles had known him for a long time.

'I say Thompson, I don't suppose you could get together for me some old workman's clothes- no, I'm not going to do some work in the garden, but that's the sort of thing I had in mind. One other thing; could you see if you could rustle up some ammunition suitable for this revolver.' Other than a cocked eyebrow, Thompson gave no indication that he thought the request odd. He returned shortly, carrying several articles of clothing, and a small cardboard box of ammunition. 'Belonged to you uncle, sir; the clothes as well. You'd be about his size, now.'

Dressed in the gardening clothes of his departed uncle, Charles Warner had felt painfully self- conscious as he set off from his aunt's smart Knightsbridge address. Not just the clothes, but his limping wooden-legged gait – it all served to bring him a bitter reminder of his inadequacy. He tugged down even lower the cloth cap he had borrowed from Thompson, dreading some chance meeting with an acquaintance. The excruciating conversations, explaining about his leg, making light of it – not to mention why he was dressed as he was - he couldn't bear the thought of it; it was the reason he had kept away from London since his return from the Crimea.

As soon as possible Charles boarded a horse-drawn public omnibus which soon bore him away, travelling along the Embankment. On reaching the City, Charles dismounted, as this was as far as the horse omnibus went.

'I'm afraid it's shank's pony, from now on, matey,' the driver has offered as he nudged his horses into a tight circle, ready for the return. 'Don't get no passengers from down around Whitechapel, eh.'

As he turned to go, on impulse Charles took from his pocket a sovereign; 'I know this is a probably a strange question, but I'm looking for a man, ah, a lost relative you see,' Charles extemporized, 'and my question is, where would my relative, a gentleman actually, to what part of the East End might one profitably begin one's search, do you think.'

The tram driver gave him a scornful look, 'Well,' he began, one hand on hip, nose pointed arrogantly up, 'One might go round in circles and go right up one's fundament, one might,' to the amusement of several bystanders. Furious at such unwonted impertinence, Charles checked himself from his sharp reminder; it remained unspoken, as he remembered his attire. Without making a show of it, he allowed the driver to glimpse the coin in his palm, then swiftly closed. The result was instantaneous.

Whipping off his hat, the man now had a different tone altogether, in his eye a gleam of avarice. He jerked his head, indicating that Charles should come closer.

'Sorry guvnor, but I took you for some sort of chancer, like,' as his eye travelled down the clothes of the man before him. His inquisitive eye noted the wooden leg, and he then asked; 'down there at Salamanca was you sir, by any chance?' Startled, Charles had to nod but the effect was positive.

The man's demeanour now became completely different. 'Well I was there too an' all sir,' and his eyes now regarded Charles with real warmth. Perhaps for the first time, Charles felt a surge of pride that he had served with men such as this in that terrible war. Although strangers, men from different levels of society altogether, they'd both felt that instant comradeship of men who had faced common horrors, and survived.

'I usually leaves the horses wiv nosebags on 'ere for a bit; could I suggest a pint of landlord's best sir?' and he led Charles into the nearby public house. Seated upon a corner bench, In the fug and pipe smoke of this workingman's pub, Charles felt at ease; his companion had volunteered to fetch across two pints of beer. In the clothes he now wore, Charles felt practically invisible. The driver returned, and as he sat down, he bumped pots with Charles.

'Sorry about outside – there's a lot out around, always tryin' to take a man down, know what I mean?' He took out a stumpy clay pipe, and after carefully stoking and lighting it, took his first contented puff.

'Now about your question squire; if your gentleman is in some sort of trouble, 'ed most likely might 'ead off towards Whitechapel somewhere; lots of cheap lodgins see, some right doss 'ouses as well. Don't see 'as it's a good plan though – if 'e is a gent, 'e would stand out like dogs bollocks - pardon my French,' and they both laughed. 'Now if your gent say, 'as got 'isself addicted to opium or somethin' – no offence, guvnor, but some what 'ave been wounded, they come back 'ome alive, see, but addicted something fierce. You know what I mean, bein' amputated – sorry sir, no offence, but perhaps it's goer, know what I mean?'

'I took no offence my friend, you told it to me straight, and yes, the morphine can get quite a hold on one. And yes, perhaps you're right; it may turn out that the Limehouse area could be a good place to begin. ' said Charles.

' No - , put your sov. away squire, no need for that; I'm just sorry I didn't at first recognise an old soldier like myself.' The man was pleased when Charles put out his hand for a firm handshake, ' you should call me Ernie, sir if you will,' 'very good' – grinning, as he indicated his clothes – ' and you shall call me Charlie, if you please'. The two old soldiers put their mugs together, and drank off their beer.

Charles spoke again, 'It's just a shame that it takes a nasty war for us to be able to shake hands,' as he called for another pint. 'Now, just in case your point about some possible addiction is correct, where *would* one go exactly, in search of opium?' The driver looked at him, amused, 'you really don't know your way around the East End, do you squire. Like I said earlier, the place to go is along by the docks, down around Limehouse. Can't give you no address, 'xactly, but its around there where you'll find the Chinese opium dens.' He looked concerned, '"beggin' your pardon guvnor, but I should tell you, a gent like yourself might get hisself into a bit of trouble goin' down there on his own, know what I mean?'

After finishing his beer, Charles managed to stand without too much awkwardness. Once again he took the hand of the man still seated before him. 'Thank you for the warning Ernie, well meant I'm sure, but – ' Charles leant forward, 'I have brought my service revolver with me.' And bidding farewell, Charles went quickly out through the door out into the street.

The driver looked down, a smile slowly spreading across his features.; - *the peg-leggged gent, obviously a former officer, had left a gold sovereign in his palm* -

'Landlord – one for the road, eh?'

Only the driver, and perhaps the lone drinker at the end of the bar noticed Charles leave.

CHAPTER FOURTEEN

'Well gents, if I may, I would like to summarize what we have between us discovered, to see just what we 'ave to work wiv.' 'You Izzie,'you 'ave 'ad the unpleasant task of learning of our mark's latest victim. There's another avenue of investigation cut off, certainly, but what we *can* deduce from that,' said Birtles, 'is that one, he is still in the area, and two, by taking the trouble to cover his tracks, he means to stay. This, despite that he obviously is aware that we are on his trail.' He turned to Shiloh Coombes. 'What 'ave you got?' Shiloh sat for a minute, marshalling his thoughts.

'I have picked up several things; I have learnt from my conversation with that Scotland Yard man – no, not directly, but by induction – that the intended victim of Werth was none other than the prince of Wales himself.' At this, Birtles sprang to his feet; so perturbed by this news that he picked up his hat and flung it to the floor. Feigenbaum threw Shiloh a quick amused glance - It was clear that in Ned Birtles, there stood a true royalist. As Shiloh went to continue, he hesitated a moment; he had no wish to offend the prickly Birtles, who might find the next part offensive. Nevertheless he went on.

'I believe it was his Highness, the reason he was in that get-up on the train, you see, I had heard somewhere was he has been in the habit of disguising himself to come up from Brighton from time to time, *incognito,* to visit his mistress, the actress Lillie Langtry.' Shiloh awaited Birtle's reaction.

'Well that's 'is business, innit,' scowling at the others, daring them to say something. 'What of it?'

'As you so rightly put it, Mr. Birtles,' began Shiloh, 'It is the business of the Prince himself whomsoever he chooses to er, visit' his smile was sardonic,' However, when someone sets out to assassinate that same royal personage, it becomes very much the business of others, am I not right? The police, the Foreign Office – probably the Prime Minister, and of course ourselves. For we probably the only ones who know for certain that the man who has become our enemy, is this same assassin. I would venture that all of this growing attention by the police etcetera upon the situation may hinder rather than help us. Do you agree, Mr. Birtles?' Sitting on the sidelines of this discussion, Feigenbaum was once again struck by Holme's ability to clarify any complex situation, and judging by the sententious nodding of Neddy Birtles head, to gain agreement with his point of view. Having smoothed the royalist hackles of Birtles, Shiloh continued.

'I think it give us something; we know that Werth has been paid - no I don't think so, it is not a personal vendetta, or some maniac on the loose – no, as Mr. Feigenbaum has made clear, this man is motivated solely by money. According to that Scotland Yard inspector, the police are convinced that the assassin, whom we know as Werth, will try again.' Feigenbaum broke in, '- yes, he wouldn't be acting off his own volition; obviously someone, some agency, perhaps foreign, has offered him lot of money to assassinate the Crown Prince. And as Shiloh here just said, Werth doesn't give up easily,' looking up at the other two, 'and from our perspective, it could be any number of agencies. It could be some jealous admirer of the actress, but my instinct – tapping his nose – 'tells me it might be some foreign interests. My supposition is that this is the initial reason that he is in this country. Werth has been somehow compromised; perhaps arrested, and them offered a way out. The Prussian Secret Police come to mind; they like to operate like that.' The three sat looking at each other; they all realized this whole business was getting ever more serious.

'I think it is time I fixed some more tea,' cried Feigenbaum, getting swiftly up,' we all need to have a bit of a think.' The tea was always a good tension breaker, and they were soon ready to go on.

'Of course there is the other development we have discovered, Ned. It's the reason we thought we should get together, a council of war. You see, we have just this morning been given the name of Werth's henchman – the one who was seen by the boy – yes, I know we've already got that. Yes, it's that very same boy what came earlier to warn Coombes here about this fellow Cholly Kemp. He has been overheard threatening to kill him', pointing to Shiloh as he spoke. Birtles pounced on this new piece of information like a terrier upon a rat, worrying at it, testing it's value. His dark beady eyes eyes darting from one to the other. 'And this information – are you sure it's kosher? Who else knows abaht it? Could be a trap, couldn't it?'

Feigenbaum broke in, waving down his arguments; 'Yes of course we must tread carefully Ned, you're right. But I'm pretty sure it's straight. We happen to know for a fact that the boy hates the brute, for several good reasons. I had a young fellow keep an eye out round their place; this Kemp article is always lurking somewhere around their place, Sparrow sez.' Apart from a fierce snort at mention of the Sparrow, Birtles listened in silence. 'Kemp and the mother have a sorry sort of arrangement, that's for them to work out, but he's always knocking the boy about. Shiloh once stopped the brute from thrashing her nipper in the street - very humiliating it was for him, and he's likely had it in for Shiloh ever since.'

Birtles thought this over, still darting sharp looks from one to the other, 'I know of this turd Kemp you speak of – nasty enough, but 'ardly up to this sort of caper. Murder; that would be a big step up for the likes of 'im. Might be all talk, like,' Birtles was still doubtful.

'No Mr. Birtles, I don't think so,' Coombes insisted, 'the boy heard him boasting that he was going to kill me, and that somebody was paying him to do so. But you say, and it is a good point, its not his usual go. But then, that's possibly because nobody has previously offered him money to take it on. My guess is, he has committed himself to attempt my destruction; he did this for two reasons - as much to ingratiate himself to Werth, as for the money.' Shiloh grinned suddenly; 'plus he doesn't like me much.'

The other two looked at one another, nodding their heads. It was a logical set of assumptions. Both Feigenbaum and Ned Birtles secretly impressed, at the cool objectivity with which this young man could describe the how and why of his planned death. Now Coombes continues;

'The thing is, this gives us the advantage. We know who he is, where he hangs about. if we get him first we could turn him over to the detectives. Perhaps he could be induced to incriminate the man who hired him.' Feigenbaum shook his head. 'No, that might at best lead us to Werth's main henchman; he'd be the one who put him up to it. Werth most likely would have kept right out of it,' he finished, with Ned Birtles vigorously nodding his agreement.

'Now I have something else as well.' Birtles spoke again after a small pause; they had again come to a stop for a moment or two, thinking over the problem, "and it might be pertinent. I 'ave been in touch with my other principal, and 'e is very concerned, 'e sez; 'e is concerned about what we seem to 'ave uncovered, it's wider ramifications, 'e called it – and 'e wants me to keep 'im posted.' Birtles paused;

- how much was he permitted to divulge...

'Look, my principal – 'e is someone over in Whitehall, see. E' also said 'e was going to 'ave a word or two about the whole situation with the chief Superintendent at Scotland Yard –here Birtles gave a vigorous snort, before continuing,' 'e seems to place great stock in them. We are to call for their assistance if and when required, 'e said.' Birtles looked directly at Shiloh, 'and 'e is very concerned for your safety.' Coombes looked intently at him for a second or two, but then burst out laughing.

'Thank you for the message, Mr. Birtles, but as you said earlier, we are in this together, and we'll stick it out together. About the offer of police assistance - it could be very useful, but I think we all agree that calling them in right now could scare off our quarry; I think we are also agreed that things have gone too far for the escape of Werth to be a satisfactory outcome for any one of us. Nevertheless, it will be very useful if we can call upon the assistance of the detectives when the time comes.' A sardonic half smile

crossed his features, as he rose and made his way towards the door; '
oh, and please inform my brother that I am perfectly all right, thank
you very much.' This last hung in the air, as the other two digested
it's meaning; Birtles dumbfounded, with Feigenbaum none the wiser.

Lady Violet and her young guest had just arrived back from
their shopping expedition. As she changed from her street shoes, she
noticed the envelope addressed to her upon the hall table.

'I say this is too much! Here's a note from Charles; he says
he's going into the East End for a reconnoitre - alone. Does he think
this is some sort of military exercise or something – or does he
imagine that women are too weak and silly to be consulted - oh I'm
sorry my dear, I am very fond of my nephew, but I think this is
irresponsible of him – here, do read it yourself, and please ring for
the someone to arrange some tea. I must go and find Thompson,
he'll have some idea what Charles thinks he's up to - he'd better not
keep anything back from me.'

Olivia had to smile, as she watched Lady Violet go marching
off, in pursuit of her hapless butler. Charles had risked the
displeasure of his aunt in going it alone, but unlike Aunt Violet,
Olivia was not all that displeased; she read it as a sign that Charles
cared for her still, that he wished to shield her from danger. Ever
since Charles had unexpectedly arrived the evening before, it was as
if a great weight had dropped from her shoulders. And not just
Charles, but his aunt as well. Beneath the guise of the imperious
Knightsbridge dowager, Olivia had begun to catch glimpses of a
formidable woman, a woman of considerable acuity, with inner
reserves of strength. The staunch support offered by both had given
Olivia renewed strength to go on in search of her friend Shiloh
Coombes. Alone for so long regarding her fears for Shiloh's well-
being, it was just such a relief to have these two to share her task, to
pool ideas with.   Nevertheless, Olivia had no intention of hiding
behind anyone's back.

When Lady Violet returned from her interrogation of

Thompson the butler, she was able to give an account of Charle's movements – but only up until he left the house.

'Apparently he didn't tell Thompson where he was actually off to. On the other hand, we do know that he has gone of disguised as a gardener would you believe – oh that's unfair I suppose, but Thompson did say he went out dressed in some old gardening clothes of my late husband. I think we can assume from that and from his hasty little note, that Charles has gone charging straight off somewhere into the East End slums. I suppose he imagined he will be taken for one of the locals – oh, I wish he had only waited...'

As she spoke Lady Violet had been pacing the floor, suddenly to her guest's surprise, she opened a drawer and without more ado, took out from a small wooden box a slender cheroot, lit it and before long was puffing out a considerable smoke cloud.

'Oh dear me darling, you look so shocked – yes as Charles might tell you, I sometimes take a cigar or two,' she grinned at Olivia, 'at times like this when I need something to calm me. Well what are we to do, do you think? Wait about like meek little lambs until my nephew decides to return?' She answered her own question, as she stubbed out her hardly begun cigar. 'I should jolly well think not, eh? – good girl, let us get ourselves togged out in our safari kit – well it is a sort of safari, isn't it. Into darkest London?'

A short time later the two ladies ventured forth to take themselves across London towards the East End. Neither would admit it, but they both felt not a little trepidation. Thompson had brought Lady Violet's brougham around to the front of the house, and they prepared to enter it. The butler in person had thrown on a voluminous coachman's cloak and hat, and was himself taking the reins.

Olivia felt she had chosen quite sensible clothing for their outing; tall black boots, a wide skirt of dark woollen material, a dark blue vaguely military jacket, and a bonnet, also suitably unobtrusive. Her companion on the other hand, looked as if she were off hiking in the Lake country. Olivia didn't wish to offend her hostess, so she kept private her opinion of the Tyrolean hat with the tall feather...

The gas lights were getting further and further apart the deeper he progressed into this sinister area. Limehouse; it was a London Charles Warner didn't recognize. He'd entered into a maze of narrow streets, haphazardly turning and twisting this way and that, seemingly without any plan or logic. As he made his way along yet another ill-lit street, Charles was beginning to regret his impulsive actions of earlier in the day.

He had thought that if he could make some inquiries amongst the mah-jongg gambling houses and opium dens of the dockside area, surely he would hear something of Olivia's friend Coombes, something to go on with in the morning. If his worst fears turned out to be correct, there was no telling what condition in which he might find the man they sought. Charles certainly didn't want to bring either Olivia or his aunt anywhere near this dreadful dockside area. As it was, he was beginning to think that he was himself hopelessly lost. Earlier Charles had attempted to speak to several people along the way, but as soon as he had spoken, as if by some unwritten rule, all had without exception rapidly distanced themselves from him. He'd called after a couple of them, even tried to catch up with them. Limping along though as he was, taking care not to fall on the slippery wet cobbles, they had soon outdistanced him, disappearing into the darkness ahead. He had soon given up these attempts to communicate with the locals. Charles had actually managed to enter one low place which he assumed to be an opium den, but the Chinese at the door, extremely courteous, had denied all knowledge of English. Charles was thankful that he had been keeping up a daily schedule of long country walks; it stood him now in good stead. It had been such a frustrating evening. As a former military officer, Charles felt he had at least gained a basic mental map of the Wapping docks and surrounding streets. Nevertheless, he'd come to the point where he had to admit that he had achieved very little more than this, and that there seemed very little more for him to achieve, this evening.

- decision made – now see if I can find my way out of here...

'Why are we stopping, Thompson?' came the exasperated voice from within.

'I think that this is as far as the horse tram comes, Lady Violet. As I mentioned earlier Ma'am, I saw him get aboard the tram, and I imagine young Mr. Charles might have come this far, then perhaps proceeded by some other means, your Ladyship.' Very spry for her age, Lady Violet sprang from the carriage.

'I say well done Thompson; splendid!' but then she fixed him with a stern eye. 'And now what?' 'Well your Ladyship, I should imagine Mr Charles would make some inquiry around the square here, as to how he might continue down to the docks around Wapping. Ma'am did say he might be going in that direction.' Although very proper in these useful observations, Lady Violet could see that he was still smarting over her earlier brow-beating of him. Impulsively she took him by the hand, 'you have been very helpful Thompson, and I'm sorry I was a little stern earlier, but I am a little worried about my nephew. Why don't I, together with miss Truscott wait here in the carriage, door locked, while you make a few inquiries - in those two inns across there for a start.' Still holding his hand, she thrust a couple of coins into the hand of her surprised butler. 'Off you go, don't try and rush it, buy yourself a pint of ale – yes, we will be perfectly alright, Thompson, you shall lock the doors yourself.'

He was not fully happy with this, but without further discussion, Lady Violet's butler Thompson, dressed as he was as a coachman, crossed the roadway and entered the public house on the opposite corner. Entering without pausing at the doorway, sure sign of a stranger, he passed into the public bar of the smoke filled pub without particular notice. He ordered a pint at the bar, and it was only then as he asked a few questions of the barman, that he became a figure of interest to a tall figure hunched over a beer. In the dim lamp-light available, partly obscured in his deliberately chosen dark corner.

'I might be able to help you there – couldn't help overhearing like. A gent with a wooden leg, you said? I thought so, and I said to myself, hey, I think saw a gent like that.' Elated at such early success, Thompson was about to ask further questions when he noticed the stranger dart a glance at his empty pint pot. 'Oh, let me get you a re-fill – yes, and a pint of Old Ordinary for myself, if you please landlord.'

The man told him of seeing this peg-legged man in this very pub – 'yes, early this very evening, it was. He had a drink or two with another cove, then he went off. Going down dockside, I believe he said,' he smiled encouragingly at Thompson, 'and is this someone you are concerned about, for his safety…'

So eager was he to quiz his informant, Thompson told the stranger the outline of the situation, which really began to interest his informant. And Thompson made the small but fateful mistake of mentioning the carriage outside, with the two ladies waiting – securely locked in. Thompson's interlocutor looked about, as one concerned,

'well that's probably a good idea – this is a rough neighbourhood, especially after dark. As a matter of fact, you'd best go out the back way; never know, like. Could be some blaggers waiting for you to come out, eyes still not used to the night..' Thompson finished his pint, and rose, 'That's sound advice, and I thank you for it -' oh thanks, much appreciated,' as the other man offered to show him out through the back of the public house.

Crouching over the inert figure lying in the alley, Werth couldn't help chuckling to himself. A quick firm pressure from behind at the carotid artery, within seconds the unsuspecting victim was down, unconscious. At moments like this he sometimes felt himself to be a master puppeteer, manipulating his puppets. That sublime feeling of power, as he decided: to kill, or not to kill. It was so easy; he'd had to make an effort of will not to kill this fool – he needed him as a messenger. What a stroke of good fortune! Werth gave couldn't hold back another gleeful chuckle. The peg-leg this fellow had gabbed on about - was actually searching for that bastard Coombes, the thorn in his side. What luck! With these two stupid women locked in their carriage...

-this time I'll do for him -

Unhurriedly, he took out a notebook and using only the dim light from the night sky, wrote a short note. This he he tucked into the man's top coat pocket. Before leaving, he felt, almost tenderly, for the man's pulse. *There it is, he still lives.* The message would be sooner delivered by the man alive.

CHAPTER FIFTEEN

'Ere, guvnor – come down wiv me down along the docks– I just got the whisper there's a geezer goin' abaht asking stupid questions all over the manor – lookin' for you 'e is, my mate sez. I sent a message around to Neddy like you said, if anyfing came up.' Sparrow gave a cheeky grin – 'I keeps out of Neddy's way, meself.'

'E's dressed rough like, this geezer, but 'e stands aht like a sore thumb, 'e does - some sort of toff, my mate reckons. Better come and 'ave a look – I fink 'e could be dodgy, know what I mean?' Shiloh had learnt to always take note of Sparrow's observations; the youth had a very sharp nose for anything out of the ordinary. He sprang to his feet, 'come on then – I'll just leave a note for the Gaffer - alright, wait for me,' as he grabbed up his cloth cap and hastened after the fleet footed Sparrow. It could well be someone connected to Werth.

Having sent the Sparrow off on another errand, Shiloh waited impatiently at the arranged meeting place for Birtles, stamping his feet to counter the sudden cooling of the night air. Eventually the man did arrive, all bustle and arms akimbo. 'Well here we are them, lets be off,' he snorted. As they hurried together through the evening streets, he spoke again, out of the side of his mouth; 'I'll kick that bleedin' Sparrah's arse one day, I swear it. They went on in silence for a bit, 'my missus indoors don't arf get herself all in a tither when I'ave to go out at night '- he cut off Shiloh's polite apology – 'Nah, it don't really matter to me,' he glanced again sideways, 'I welcomes it.' He gave a quick grin, 'might even get an opportunity for a quick pint later – all in the line of duty, of course.'

Although Sparrow had given the general location of the suspicious stranger they sought as the docks area, it was quite some time before they caught up with the man he'd described. In fact Ned Birtles was beginning to think that they were on a wild goose chase – *I really will kick 'is arse –*

Shiloh was regretting not taking the time to grab either his scarf or a coat. Since that beautiful early autumn beginning to the day, the weather was now taking a turn for the worst. He pulled up the collar of his jacket around his neck. There was a damp chill, a turgid quality to the evening air, hinting at rain, possibly sleet. Coming up along the docks, they had just passed Methodist Mission to Seamen hostel, when Birtles grabbed the arm of Shiloh Coombes, dragglng him into the alleyway adjacent. With the bleak weather outlook, the streets had been quite empty of people; it was a fair assumption that this man limping down the street towards them could well be the one they sought.

Given the situation he found himself in, wandering, all but lost in this maze of narrow streets, some of them coming to a dead end at some dockyard entrance, Charles Warner was making his way very warily indeed. His pulse rate had increased, all of his senses alert - he had not missed the flicker of movement up ahead. He was reasonably sure that two men had darted into the dark mouth of the alley up ahead, leading off from the left side of the street. Without hesitating, Charles continued his approach, at the same time veering towards the other side of the street. At the same time feeling for the reassuring cold touch of his service revolver inside his coat pocket.

- let them come –

Charles suddenly realized that he had not felt so fully alive since the war.

She awoke with a start, to find her young companion leaning across to her, trying to shake her awake. In that same instant, Lady Violet was made aware that something was amiss. A quick glance from the window showed her that her carriage was being driven at some speed down darkened streets. Her eyes met those of Olivia; her own alarm was mirrored there. Taking up her cane, she rapped loudly on the ceiling of the carriage.

'Thompson! I say Thompson, what the devil is going on! Stop immediately.' And then a voice came down from the driver's seat. It was a deep rasping voice, with a sllght foreign, or perhaps

Irish accent – and it was not the voice of her butler, Thompson.

'Be silent you harridan – if I must I will come down and slit your miserable throat. I only need one hostage.' The laughter that followed was not one of mirth. In the gloomy interior of the carriage, there was yet light enough for both women to see the horror, the terror in the eyes of the other. Both were fully aware of the situation; they had been kidnapped.

The knock upon his front door awoke the old rag man, dozing before the fire. He had been sitting up, awaiting news from Shiloh Coombes and Birtles. He would not retire to his bed this night – he had a strong feeling that tonight things might be coming to a head. Taking up his heavy poker from the fireplace, Feigenbaum went to open the door. He did so with great care however; the heavy security chain upon it prevented no more than a narrow slit to open. Just enough to judge whether his visitor was friend or foe. The person upon the doorstep appeared to be a well set-up young man, obviously someone from the more comfortable classes. He wore a heavy all-weather coat with cape, on his head a top hat, at his side he carried a black leather Gladstone bag.

Pulling the door now wide open, Feigenbaum urged the visitor inside. He took a quick look about, before again closing the door and bolting it. Finally he turned to the waiting visitor.

'Ah, a doctor, I see. How can I help you,' he asked. 'Yes – yes I am – oh I see, the bag,' the young man answered, somewhat apprehensive of the poker still gripped by the man opposite.

'Please, allow me to present myself – I am a friend of Mr. Coombes, that is I had him in my care, some time back. He gave me your address – you are Mr. Feigenbaum are you not?' Upon Feigenbaum's cautious acknowledgement , the doctor smiled. 'How do you do,' as he vigorously shook hands. 'Coombes spoke very warmly of you sir, very warmly indeed. Actually, I called this evening to check on his well-being. Is he still in contact with yourself, if I may ask?' Feigenbaum crossed to the fireplace, replacing his poker.

'Ah yes, I believe I know of you sir – our Mr Coombes has also spoken well of yourself.' He gestured towards a seat by the fire. 'Come and warm yourself sir, for while – can I offer a glass of whiskey – no, tea then? Good, I'll just fix the tea,' as he scurried off to tend his samovar – and think over his response to this unexpected arrival. He didn't know just how much he could tell this young doctor about what they had found themselves involved in. By the time he returned with the tea, he had decided that he should tell the doctor the general outline, at least, of their drama. Feigenbaum noted with approval the way the doctor listened silently to his account, only speaking to clarify some point. He did not evince either disbelief, nor alarm on hearing some of the more extraordinary events that Feigenbaum recounted. Instead his face wore a look of intense concentration.

- a steady rock this –

'Well goodness me' was his only comment on Feigenbaum coming to an end, 'No wonder you opened your door with such circumspection,' glancing towards where the fire poker hung at the side of the fireplace. 'Look, as you say Coombes seems to be involved in something extraordinary, but in my short acquaintance with him, I formed the opinion that Shiloh Coombes is quite an extraordinary chap,' to which Feigenbaum heartily agreed. 'Yes, we are up against a ruthless highly intelligent enemy, but I also tend believe – and hope - that our mutual friend is equal to the task. He is as you say, quite brilliant.' Feigenbaum regarded his visitor; 'So, doctor, what is your plan for this evening? Are you doing house calls – oh, finished eh. Well look, Coombes is chasing up some lead, and I daren't hazard a guess as to his likely time of return. Perhaps you might like to wait here until his return.' But the doctor stood, once more shaking the hand of his host. 'No, I think I might make my way down towards the docks, I might be of some assistance.' Catching Feigenbaum's look of apprehension, the doctor was quick to reassure him, 'Oh don't worry about me; I do a lot of work down around the docks, from patching knife wounds to obstetrics. I'm well-known in the area as a harmless sawbones.' He patted his Gladstone doctor's bag. 'One instrument amongst others I always carry in this neighbourhood though, is a loaded revolver.' His fresh boyish face broke into a grin, 'You never know, eh?'

The Inspector took his feet down from his desk as his sergeant came up, saluted, and delivered a folded note. He perused it thoroughly; it was a very short note, but it seemed to sergeant Drabble that his chief hoped to look deep beyond the note, to decipher more than just it's written contents.

- I won't be surprised if he even sniffs it –

'What's going on, sergeant,' he demanded, but the question was rhetorical; he was really asking himself. ''That's the second note I've received tonight – the first one from that bloody nuisance Coombes, telling me he's out roaming the dockside, looking for a man who might, or might not be, a significant lead in this whole affair.' He glared across at his constable, still standing at attention. Sergeant Drabble wisely kept silent.

- not for me to reason why –

- 'And now this,' as he flung this second note upon the table. 'Read it; what do you make of it? Hoax – or not.' The constable felt on safe ground, as he answered. 'Well no sir, I mean I don't think so. It was delivered just now by a lad, and 'e said 'e was sent by the landlord of the 'orses and groom' pub, there where the horse trams finish their run, sir. 'Is guvnor found a man unconscious in the alley behind 'is pub, the boy sez, and this note was in this cove's top pocket.' The Inspector said nothing, but his cocked eyebrow still indicated some scepticism. He picked up and read the note again. It was short and very much to the point:

WHEN YOU RECOVER YOUR SENSES TAKE THIS NOTE TO YOUR EMPLOYERS BANK. I HAVE ABDUCTED YOUR MISTRESS AND IF FIVE HUNDRED POUNDS IS NOT AVAILABLE WHEN I NEXT MAKE CONTACT PERHAPS HER

EAR IN THE POST WILL HASTEN MATTERS TO MY SATISFACTION.

The Inspector looked up. 'Where is this fellow now, the one found with the note on him?' 'Still recoverin' in a back room, down at that pub – according to the lad, sir. The landlord of the pub thought it best to get the note around to us.' The inspector grunted – 'more likely he didn't want us sniffing about his gaff. Good move, as it turned out.'

The Inspector jumped up, grabbing his bowler from the hat stand by the door as he exited the room. 'Come along Drabble, we have work to do. I sniff that something queer is definitely going on down there tonight.'

Before long the police wagon, its blue lantern on top was galloping on its way to the London docks. The Inspector turned to his man, 'look Drabble, here's a note; give it to the night desk sergeant at Leman Street station, tell him I will need four more men assigned, and they are to be issued small arms. Bring them as quick as possible down to, let me see; Garret St and Milkyard – got that? Keep them quiet, keep an eye out for trouble, mind, but use your initiative. Good man, I will catch up with you a bit later; but first I want to go across and interview the fellow at the pub.' He leant from the window of the van, 'hey constable; let me out here.' As he turned to leave, he had another thought; 'keep a look-out for that other fellow - young Mr. Coombes; I want a word with him, as well.' A quick rap on the roof of the van, and it was off again. Sergeant Drabble knocked for the driver to continue, as he watched his chief disappear into the evening mist.

- use your initiative –not bleedin' likely – get into the shit very quickly that way… -

It had all happened so very fast; Shiloh leapt from the alley in an attempt to apprehend the approaching man. As Shiloh did so, in that same split second, he registered that the man was pulling a pistol of sorts from inside his coat. Almost in that same instant, with amazing speed Ned Birtles had ducked in behind the stranger in the street. With a flashing back-hand swing, Birtles caught him a blow with his cosh, just over the temple. Now they were crouched over the inert figure, Shiloh anxiously trying to ascertain the extent of the damage.

'Dammit Birtles, did you have to hit him quite so hard,' as he pulled down the man's eyelids checking for sign of life. Ned Birtles leant back, somewhat affronted.

'Well that's luvvely innit – 'es goin' to shoot you, and I was a villain for hittin' im. Cor, that the bleedin' limit, that is,' he leant closer once more – nah, 'es all right. Bit of an 'eadache in the mornin', is all'. Suddenly he swung about; 'Ere, grab 'is shoulder' n I'll grab 'is legs – someone else comin' down the frog and toad.' Back now in the dark alleyway, Shiloh and Birtles reached a whispered agreement; if this newcomer went on by, they would not hinder him. On the other hand, if he came into the alley…

As it turned out, neither option occurred. They watched as the new comer on the scene came to a stop before the alleyway. Suddenly he stooped, picking up an object as he did so.

- of course! They had forgotten the fallen revolver -

In a practiced movement, the man dropped to one knee, levelled the revolver into the mouth of the alley, and called in a loud voice; 'Come on out, however you are. I am a doctor, I mean you no harm, but I will start shooting if you don't come out now.' The click as the doctor cocked the revolver was heard clearly by the two men in the lane. To his astonishment however, the doctor, crouched, finger white upon the trigger, was answered by a burst of laughter.

'John! How decent of you to call out before shooting – how sporting!,' and out stepped Shiloh Coombes, still laughing, dressed in even shabbier clothing than when he had last been rescued – by this same doctor.

He shifted his bulk, still trying to sleep but still something was preventing it. Dimly through the remaining strands of alcohol induced fug, he recognized two things; a loud knocking, seemingly emanating from downstairs – either front or back door. The other thing annoying him was his woman's whining voice, timidly trying to wake him. Throwing the one to one side with an oath, he grabbed up the cudgel he kept by his bed, in preparation to deal with the second annoyance. Surprisingly quiet, and swift with it despite his bulk, he descended the stairs. The knocking still continued; it was from the rear of the house, which lead out to his yard and disused stables.

'Who is it? It better be good, or by god you be a dead man,' as he opened a sliver in the small window alongside the rear heavily padlocked door. It was just light enough for him to make out the high domed head of his leader. The man at the door hesitated a moment or two. He was beginning to have doubts lately about continuing their connection; he'd begun to think that the man was insane. Certainly it had been very lucrative, working for this man. Enough so for him to believe he might eventually have enough to get out of this shit hole, maybe buy that little pub on the coast, back in Norfolk… Borden was a former champion bare-knuckle fighter, but this man frightened him. The knocking started again, insistent, 'Alright, alright, want to wake the flamin' whole street, or what,' he snarled, more to give himself courage. The tall figure waited until he had undone the several lock and swung back the door.

'I've hit upon a really good earner here; it will be a bloody gold mine,' Werth spoke then, in his level, emotionless voice. 'I don't have time to tell the whole story, but in a carriage outside in the lane, I'm holding two ladies prisoner. I have already demanded a ransom. In addition, they will be the bait that Mr. Coombes cannot resist. I practically have him.'

His henchman stood listening, balancing the story, seeking what advantage it offered himself. He couldn't really see any. Especially when his chief went on to explain his next move – to move the carriage with the two captives in it, into his stables. 'Now then, wait up, wait a minute – someone's going to be searching for these - ladies you said – and I'm to be holding the can; I can't say I like that bit. Not at all.'

Werth struggled to hide his fury, keeping his face blank, to speak calmly with a modulated voice.

- *nobody, not even you, questions my decisions* –

'Very well, you may have a point; I suggest then that we move the equipage into your stable building, and I will remain here with them myself. It will only be for a short while. This business will be brought to a close very soon. For you I have another mission. That fool you put up for the job, Kemp, hasn't even managed to keep an eye on Coombes, let alone kill either him or those others working with him against me.' He looked directly then into the eyes of his henchman.

'I insist upon obedience, as you well know: I want them gone.' The big man's eyes were the first to slide away from the relentless glare. Knowing he had won this battle of wills, Werth continued,

'Go and get Kemp, and with take him over to Feigenbaum's gaff. He will be alone tonight, but expecting the return of Coombes. Let him think you are Coombes, and he will let you in.' Again he fixed his eyes upon those of the man before him; ' I want the old Yid killed tonight; if by luck you manage to get Coombes as well, there's a hundred guineas extra in it for you. Perhaps you might try and get Kemp to do it, but if that fails, I expect you to finish the job.'

Shortly after this whispered conversation, Werth watched from the shadows as his henchman left to carry out his orders. The fellow had been reluctant to leave open his rear door, but Werth had insisted, saying that after moving the carriage into the deserted stable, he would remain in the warmth of the kitchen until his man returned. No sooner was the man away, than Werth was bounding up the stairs; shortly a frightened squeak told him that he was in the room he sought. Swiftly he crossed the floor, catching the woman in the bed by the throat. He had heard her sharp intake of breath, and wished to forestall the coming scream. He bent low, so as to whisper into her ear;

'Not a peep, mind. Not one bloody peep. I'd as soon strangle you as look at you,' he breathed.

His hereto obedient henchman's questioning of his orders, indicated that it might be time to sever their connection. Therefore, a change of plan. Werth prided himself that he could be flexible. Almost invariably in such a case, he would kill a man who did not unquestionably carry out his orders. But this fellow was very big and strong, and another plan has suggested itself. Werth had on the spot devised a scheme whereby he would be the only winner, whatever the outcome. It was at moments like this, that he was almost overcome with joy – his brilliance shone for him alone.

Carefully he released his grip upon the terrified woman's throat, nevertheless leaving his hands in position.

Once more he spoke,' I promise I won't hurt you if you tell me where he stashes his booty.' Seeing her still petrified by fear, Werth gave the unfortunate woman a violent shake. ' - And I don't have all night, do you understand?' she nodded her understanding of her situation. With a shaking hand, she pointed at the threadbare drugget in the centre of the room. 'trapdoor', she croaked. Quickly Werth rose, kicking away the small carpet. With glee he whipped open the crude trapdoor revealed below. He began pulling out from the space beneath the floor canvas bags filled with coins, one with what appeared to be jewellery, and one solid metal box. As he did so, at the same time avidly trying to assess the worth of this hoard, a movement caught his eye. The woman was making a dash for the door. Without so much as a sound, he'd grabbed her, and no more ado, stuffed her into the floor cavity and bolted the trapdoor. Her muffled screams would cause no alarm, in the sleeping neighbourhood.

The two women were alerted by the creaking of the carriage - someone had sprung up onto the drivers seat. A slap of reins and they were once more in motion, going they knew not where. They had watched as their tall abductor had made several trips back and forth into a gateway in the alley in

which their conveyance was standing. All about was silent and in darkness, the thin moonllght allowing but a partial view of what transpired. He appeared to be loading some heavy bundles into the luggage rack at the rear. In whispered conference they had agreed that to scream out for help would most likely bring swift retribution. 'Anyhow,' said Lady Violet, 'this doesn't appear to be a neighbourhood where screams and cries in the night would raise concern. No, we had best bide our time, for now.' She squeezed the hand of her young companion, 'I do hope Thompson is all right. Perhaps he has already raised the alarm.'

The three men now helped the still dazed Charles to his feet, his false leg hadn't allowed him to easily rise from where he had fallen. After a brief examination, the doctor pronounced him sound enough – apart from the pigeon's egg sized swelling behind his left ear. Charles stood awhile, leaning back against the adjacent wall, trying to put the last few minutes into some kind of sequence;

- 'I say, who hit me over the head! Who are you people?' he demanded, as he began to take in those around him. 'If you are out to rob me, you are out of luck, damn you,' he snarled, tenderly feeling his head.

'Oh sorry - we were meaning only to speak with you, not attack you - but then you pulled out a revolver; unfortunate, that.' With a jerk of his head, Shiloh indicated his diminutive companion. 'My colleague takes a dim view of that sort of thing you see. Look, I really am sorry old chap. Perhaps we should introduce ourselves. My name is Shiloh Coombes, and – ' but he got no further, when the one- legged man burst out, 'Thank goodness! I've been searching for you all over the docklands for you, Mr. Coombes! ' He seized Shiloh by the hand, 'How do you do! My name is Charles Warner, you see, and I've been searching for you on behalf of our mutual friend, Miss Olivia Truscott!'

Ned Birtles watched with interest the reaction to this news

upon the face of Shiloh Coombes. Brilliant as this young man was, there was in his nature a certain arrogance, an air of always being a step or two ahead of the game. The look of stunned amazement now upon the face of Coombes gave Ned Birtles some considerable amusement.

-        *that knocked you arse-over, didn't it –*

CHAPTER SIXTEEN

Werth prided himself upon his coolness in such situations; it was an attribute he'd always felt gave him a special advantage in a tight corner. But this came as such a sudden shock. In that instant as he'd rounded the corner into another darkened street, he'd caught sight of something wholly unexpected, inexplicable - under a far gas-lamp, a group, these odd shapes – helmets – policeman's helmets! – his sangfroid had almost deserted him then. Quickly mastering his alarm, Werth savagely hauled back the two horses, turning them sharply into the laneway now straight ahead of them. His hopes that he had not been observed were dashed as the sound of several police whistles split the night with their urgent blasts. Furiously he lashed the horses, sending them into headlong flight down a narrow and darkened way.

Any thoughts the sergeant still retained as to using his initiative were snatched from him – as was his initiative itself. The young constables he had collected from the Leman Street station had been like beagles on a leash.

- to be called out - by the Yard! at night - and carrying firearms ...

It was a first for them, they were fairly new recruits as it turned out, much to the old sergeant's disgust. But these trainee constables had been the only men available. As soon as they'd set off, marching down to the docks, he'd had to tell them that marching was not quite what he wanted. 'Indian file, lads, if you please, and try and see how *little* noise we can make, eh – that means no talking as well, constable, if you can possibly manage to shut it.'

The police party had been waiting on the corner quietly enough until a carriage had come into sight, but then it's driver had swerved off in another direction. Before the sergeant could call them back, all were off at a run, blowing whistles, haring after the direction of the errant vehicle. Seargeant Drabble could do little except wait, fuming, for his constables to return. As it turned out, the first to come up to him was his superior, himself somewhat out of breath.

'What's happening, sergeant – I heard the alarm whistles – there they go again – what's going on?' In a quick few words, Drabble explained what had transpired. The inspector looked at him, nonplussed, before asking, 'so you let them just run off, like a bunch of schoolboys?' His sergeant was indignant,' *let* them run off, sir? No I did *not* sir, it was more a case of 'orses bolting – yes, I hear it, they are still going, but I believe they will soon tire.' Straightening his helmet upon his head, he drew himself up, 'I thought it best to remain here at the pre-arranged spot, sir. I also presume the young fools will try to return here, as well.'

Holding up his battery torch Shiloh looked searchingly into the face of this man Charles Warner. To the other two watching, the intentness of his gaze bordered upon rudeness. Then he spoke;

'Yes, I thought so. I *have* seen you before, riding in a conveyance with Miss Truscott – who is as you say, a friend of mine.' He still stared into the face of Warner, who held his gaze. 'Tell me, Mr. Warner, with regards to that lady – are your intentions honourable, sir?'

Up until this abrupt question was put to him, Charles Warner was himself confused as to how he intended to proceed with the relationship, but now he answered without hesitation;

'Yes sir, indeed they are. It is my intention is to ask Miss Truscott to be my wife.' Coombes still held his gaze, a second or so, before taking Warner by the hand once more. 'Then I must congratulate you heartily sir, and wish you my most sincere best wishes in your quest,' clapping Warner upon the shoulder, 'She is my special friend, and if she does accept your proposal, you will be a very lucky man.'

It was a strange scene in that dockside alley, as the doctor and the other who had apparently assaulted him, whom Shiloh Coombes had described as his colleague, added their congratulations. Charles accepted this hearty show of goodwill, but he heard them only obliquely, his mind was filled with heady thoughts. He felt a great sense of release, of joy even, he realized that he had set his course; he would be totally open and frank with Olivia as to his condition, giving her a basis of complete truth upon which to make her decision. In this last day or so, he had come to believe that she still held deep feelings for him, but he would accept her decision, whichever it was.

It was growing late, but after the visit by the young doctor, the old rag dealer Feigenbaum had remained seated by the fire, unwilling to go to his bed before he heard the outcome of this evenings venture. Coombes and Birtles had gone down into the docklands, following up on a tip from young sparrow; it had seemed a possibility only, but somehow Feigenbaum felt that tonight things might be coming to a head. Although confident in the abilities of his colleagues, Feigenbaum worried that they carried no weapons – then again, on the up side, the odd partnership of the tall young gentleman and the stumpy cockney had worked well; they would be a formidable team to best. He felt a faint nostalgia, a tug in his heart:-

- *ah to be young again, to be out hunting with these two-*

He had just got up from his seat by the fireside to make tea once more, when there came another knock at the door. Feigenbaum slowly put down his cup, and moved across to again take up his heavy fire iron. Earlier, he had opened up to find the young doctor upon his doorstep, but now it was getting quite late, and caution was called for. Whoever had knocked, Feigenbaum knew this; it was neither Coombes nor Birtles. He moved to just inside the door, before calling out, 'who is it?' A slight pause, then;

'I've got a message from Mr. Coombes, open up.' 'No, just give me the message through the door.' Feigenbaum, ear by now glued to the door, imagined he caught a snatch of a whisper –

- so two of them -

'I can't, it's a written note he sent, and I can't read. Come on, open up; 'e said it was urgent, like.' Feigenbaum carefullty unlocked his several locks, opening the door jus a fraction, enough to pass a letter. But they were ready for him. Hearing the rattle of locks, the powerful ex-boxer Borden set himself; the moment the door opened the slightest, he kicked it wide open, bursting the security chain from the door-frame. Borden shoved his nervous companion in first through the door, with the result that the unfortunate Kemp received the full force of Feigenbaum's fire poker over his head. Kemp dropped without a sound, but Borden was quick; he ducked the next swing and caught Feigenbaum with his knife thrust. He heard a grunt of pain, but his satisfaction was short-lived. The next instant he received a jab from the poker, a bayonet-like thrust to the midriff, leaving him completely winded. Expecting the deceptively agile old rag-man to move in finish him, Borden managed to pull out his revolver. A lucky shot in the dark, a loud cry, and the old man was down.

Now from out on the street there began a rising hullabaloo, people shouting, running footsteps. Fast losing his composure, still fighting for breath, Borden decided to cut and run. His accomplice he abandoned, as useless baggage.

It was the Sparrow who had been shouting and banging a metal rubbish bin lid, who found the old man lying in a pool of his own blood. Feigenbaum was conscious, but going into shock. ''Blimey guvnor – oh cor, you bin shot - I was down the other end of the lane, keepin' look-out like Mr.Coombes said, when I 'eard the shot - 'ere, let me look at your wound. It's in the gizzards, by the look.' Sparrow looked wildly about, 'Ave you got somethin' I can use to bind it, like?' Feigenbaum seized his hand, meanwhile

206

pressing the other hand against the wound to staunch the flow.

'Go quick down along the docks, you should find Coombes, and he should have a doctor with him. Look sharp, lad, or I might cark it before you return,' he managed a grin to calm the distraught Sparrow. This had the effect of setting the youth off at full speed to fetch the doctor. Feigenbaum lay still, his side where the bullet had struck was strangely numb, but the knife wound was beginning to hurt terribly. He dared not attempt to move from his position on the floor.

- *wish I had that cup of tea now –*

CHAPTER SEVENTEEN

Hearing the sudden sound of police whistles, the group of men standing with Shiloh Coombes looked at each other in some confusion, but the effect upon Coombes was electric. His face was suddenly transformed, the fire in the deep-set eyes, his high aquiline nose giving him the look of a hunting raptor. He took off at a run, shouting over his shoulder, 'Come along Birtles, the game is afoot!' leaving the doctor and Charles Warner standing in the alleyway.

'Pardon me, old chap, began the doctor,' but I note your lack of a leg – look, I hope you won't mind - perhaps I should go after those two' – 'No, not at all, by all means. But tell me, what on earth is going on?' It was as the doctor was hurriedly explaining the very little he himself knew, that the sound of yet another person came to them, someone running very fast along the road towards them. This time it was Warner who stepped out from the alley, holding his revolver out in front.

'Halt, who goes,' he called in his sternest military voice. The person who then came slithering to a stop before the two men in the roadway, was none other than the street boy Sparrow. It took not long to get from the almost winded youth the gist of his search, and at the urging of Sparrow, the doctor decided he must go to attend the wounded man. 'Very well, but I believe it is now I who should go along after Mr. Coombes – after all he is the man I have been seeking.' Both turned and went their ways, the doctor practically dragged away by Sparrow, imploring him to make all haste. And Charles Warner, to make his way towards where he heard the distant whistling, the shouting of the police pursuit. Determined to avoid another ambush and thump upon his still aching head, Charles kept to the centre of the dark road. He had his revolver in his hand, loaded this time. Charles strode along as briskly as his wooden leg would allow, going into some sort of confrontation of which he had only the sketchiest idea. But he was filled with a sense of excitement; one legged he may be, he told himself, but he was also a battle hardened military officer.

     –   *I can do this –*

Cursing ferociously, Werth hauled back upon the reins with all of his strength, until the spooked horses were forced to a stop. He leapt down from the driver's seat, and running to the near-side horse's head, took hold of the halter, forcing the team to back the carriage from the short cul de sac back onto the road. As he turned to regain his seat, he gave a scream of sudden pain. Lady Violet, still captive in her own carriage, flashed her companion a triumphant grin, as she grabbed Olivia's hand.

'Oh good girl! My poor horses have been so dreadfully treated – I believe Mitzi has just given this villain up there a jolly good bite on the shoulder!'

A quick glance told him that the pursuing constables had still not rounded the last corner.

     - ha! still had time - the plan would still work - and the first pleasure when it is complete – cutting that damned horse's throat, while the bitch of an owner looks on...she will see what is coming to her –

in an attempt to see what damage the infernal animal had inflicted, Werth held the reins in one hand as he unbuttoned his coat. Pre-occupied, he did not observe the man standing in the middle of the road, signalling him to halt.

As the galloping horses and carriage swept towards him, in the split instant Charles recognised the carriages as being that of his aunt Violet

     –   *yes look – that mare on the left – star blaze –*

– as at that same moment the full force of the malignant glare of it's unknown driver was turned upon him. It was a face filled with rage, a demonic fury. Staggering back against the wall, Charles narrowly escaped being ridden down. As it was, the driver lashed at him savagely with his whip as he swept past. Charles had experienced such moments before, in the heat and madness of the battle-field. He felt again that strange familiar calm, as many different impressions flashed by so quickly. The next instant brought him a fleeting glimpse of his aunt, her look of terror. Crouching awkwardly, Charles took the time to take a deep breath. Holding his revolver in both hands, as he breathed out, he took three shots at the man still standing tall as he lashed now at the horses. As the carriage thundered on, Charles was reasonably sure that his third shot had been effective. The man at the reins dropped suddenly to his seat, but the by now maddened horses plunged on into the night.

Trying to retain some dignity in face of this operation fast becoming a shambles, the inspector from Scotland Yard kept his pace to a brisk walk, having sent his sergeant on ahead to rein in his inexperienced young constables. Striding down Old Gravel Road towards the Thames, the inspector was
momentarily brought to a halt;
- *what's that – yes it was...*
he was sure that he had heard three shots fired, but it was difficult to judge from which direction the sounds had come. Troubled by this, he hastened on. Shortly after, to be met by another figure, looming out from the darkened street, off to the left.
'State your name and business sir,' in his sternest voice, 'I am a police officer from Scotland Yard.'
'Thank god for that, officer,' came back, 'my name is Warner, and I was just now almost run down by some swine – the beast has kidnapped my aunt – possibly – another lady as well. This torrent of words would normally make the experienced policeman check the speaker for sobriety, but the distraught look upon the man's face was too eloquent, to urgent to ignore. 'Did you fire some shots just now?' 'Yes, I did sir, and I believe I winged him.' The inspector looked keenly at the man before him. 'Well I have to say, sir, that I have come down this road and nobody has passed me by.'
The man before him stood blank-faced, thinking. 'Well I was over in Tarling street when the incident occurred, and I followed as

best I could,' patting his wooden leg, 'and I assumed he would turn left into that street from whence I came – hang on - there was a lane, off to the left back there – runs off towards King Edwards Stairs, and I thought that the maze of small streets down there, many leading to the river itself, would have –oh dammit! the bastard went down that way!' The inspector placed a calming hand upon the shoulder of the agitated man before him.

'Just a moment, if you will,' and producing a whistle from his pocket, gave three sharp blasts. An answering one long blast came back. The inspector then gave another set of whistle blasts. Two short , one long, and two shorts. The inspector returned the whistle to the fob pocket of his waistcoat.

'There. We shall have reinforcements. I have a sergeant and four constables somewhere around the Wapping embankment. My signal tells them that our quarry is heading their way, and also informs my sergeant that he should keep two men with him, and send the other two in this direction. I will remain here until they arrive, as sergeant Drabble will assume that I will still be in Old Gravel Lane'. Not wishing to waste a minute, Warner began to take himself off after the fleeing carriage, but the Inspector put out a restraining arm; 'I would prefer you to wait here with me sir, if you don't mind. I have a couple of questions I would like to put to you.' With ill-concealed impatience, Charles knew he had no option but to remain standing on the corner, while that fiend got further away.

'Well inspector, ask away, but please be brief. Not only my aunt but my fiancée

     -     *there, he had said it –*

- have been abducted by some madman, and you want me to stand about – ' The inspector made placating gestures, then spoke; 'yes sir I do take note of your concern, and I can tell you that I believe that the culprit is the man the police are searching the area for. We have had a note from a Mr. Coombes – oh, you know this gentleman – that something was going down this evening. May I ask your reason for being down here at night sir? And I must say, sir, you seem to have a good knowledge of the area.' This last, though cast as a statement, hung heavy in the air as a question. Despite the dramatic situation, Charles had to smile,

- 'Nothing suspicious there Inspector, in fact I had never been in this area before this evening. I am a former military officer you see, and from my time in the service, I have learnt to put together a mental map of any area in which I find myself operating.' His grin was tight. 'Saved my life, more than once'. They remained there, agonizing for Charles Warner, waiting for the arrival of the reinforcements. The night had now turned really cold, and the two men were stamping their feet, blowing into their hands to keep them warm. A powder like whiteness had also begun to sift slowly down from the heavens. 'Just great,' muttered the inspector, 'that's what they call a bloody freezing fog; see the little frozen particles.'

Several streets away, Coombes and Ned Birtles had also heard the shots, and a little later the resumption of police whistles, but only for a short burst. 'Bugger it,' cried Birtles, 'the bobbies are all over the place, it seems, but never where you want 'em.' But his companion demurred.

'On the contrary. Oh yes, earlier on they seem to have been running wild, like hounds off the leash, blowing constantly. Now however, I believe the inspector from Scotland Yard has arrived, and has just signalled his troops. Come along Birtles, I believe he will be back along the Old Gravel Road, and perhaps at this juncture, we should rendezvous with the police, and find out what the bloody hell is going on.'

No sooner had Shiloh spoken than Ned Birtles held up his hand, 'Shush! Hear that?' As he spoke, a carriage drawn by two horses came bursting out of the laneway up ahead, dashing across Cinnamon Street into another narrow way opposite.

'I don't know what is goin' on, but I think we should get after that equipage, don't you?' and without more ado, the two broke into a run, following as best they could the recklessly galloping horses down the very dark and narrow way.

The horses were fairly blown, both foaming at the mouth and rolling their eyes in distress, but still he lashed them mercilessly. Despite the pain in his shoulder and hand, Werth felt the triumph well up in him; he had shaken off all pursuers, and soon he would be home safe.

- I wish I could see their stupid faces, when I disappear into thin air –

He'd planned this for some time, tonight's fortuitous events only brought forward his brilliant plan. It once more reinforced his belief that the gods had decided to let him win. Somehow, he was invincible, *ein Uebermensch.* In this triumphalist, invincible moment, Werth glanced down at the third finger on his right hand. It hung by a thread, all but severed, by whoever that fellow back there was, who'd shot at him.

- With a fierce grimace, Werth placed the mangled digit into his mouth, chewed savagely, and spat the

- finger onto the roadway. With unchanged expression, he managed to clutch his handkerchief around the freshly bleeding stump.

- first things first -

The noise was such that conversation was impossible, the two terrified women could do little but cling to one another as the carriage lurched and bounced over rough ill-cobbled roads. The few gas lamps that had earlier brought some light into these dismal streets had now been extinguished. Nevertheless the women had some light source; the moonlight refraction from the freezing fog gave the darkened streetscapes through which they hurtled a ghostly hue. They whispered close to each other;

'Cheer up, my dear. I must say I was absolutely astounded to see dear Charles back there '–

'yes, and I'm sure he fired at our abductor back there – didn't you hear shots? He must somehow be following us – perhaps he has met up with Thompson, do you think?' All that they could do was to conjecture, but that brief sight of Charles had given them heart. At least he was aware that they had been abducted.

'Now sir' said the inspector, ' you said you have met with our mysterious Mr. Coombes this evening.' Again his beady policeman's eye fixed that of Charles Warner. 'What if I may ask, is your connection with this man Coombes?' Charles hastened to assure the inspector that he had only that evening met with Coombes, that he himself had been searching for Shiloh Coombes on behalf of their mutual friend – yes the same young lady who is in the carriage with his aunt - , and that as far as he knew, Coombes and his colleague Birtles were anxious to get into contact with the police.

'Birtles you said – Ned Birtles, stumpy little runt? – well, I s'pose 'e can't get into too much trouble if Birtles is with him.' He looked the man before him up and down, in that look only policemen and undertakers seem to have perfected. 'Then the inspector stuck out his hand; 'Well sir I'm sorry if I have been a little abrupt, but Mr. Coombes is something of a nuisance, and I am keen to have a word in his ear before the night is done.' He turned his head, listening, 'Here come my men on the double, if I'm not mistaken; as soon as they arrive, we'll set up a plan to blockade this area. I take it you are willing to be deputised, as it were? Good man. Whoever that fellow is, the one you allege stole your aunt's equipage, he can't get away, I shouldn't think. Most of these short streets lead only a short way to the river.'

As his two constables came puffing up, the inspector's mind was racing; he was plotting a drag-net operation. He had been fretting that he had only asked for the four constables, but although one-legged, this gent Warner here would come in very handy. Warner had freely admitted having a revolver with him, but had explained that as a former military officer, he was entitled to do so. Birtles was of course very useful as well; this fellow Coombes was an unknown quantity, but he could provide some help. Counting the four constables, together with his sergeant, these three civilians and himself... The inspector knew the area well, and he mentally placed four groups of two men, beginning from where they began, closing in on the only area possible for the driver of the stolen carriage to go.

- I've got him –

'Alright you two - Harkness, is it – and you – right, Merritt –, look, stand by and listen.' He paused for a couple of seconds, as the two constables, hands on knees, blowing hard.

'This here is Mr. Warner, who is assisting the police this evening. We are looking to block the escape of a stolen carriage – yes, I know you saw it, good men – but now I want one of you to run back to sergeant Drabble's position, and tell him this. Listen carefully.' The inspector then outlined his plan to the others. 'Now then; any questions – no, all clear?' He looked from one to the other of the two young constables. He was pleased when he asked for a volunteer to carry his message, when both shot up their hands, like eager schoolboys. 'You, Harkness, you've the longest legs, I see. Oh, and tell the sergeant to send me a different man – you will really be puffing by then, I should hope. Off you go!'

As they ran, Shiloh kept his head down, seeking traces left by the passage of the carriage, now far ahead. Just the light film of frosty particles sifting down, was enough to register the faint imprint of iron tires. He and Birtles had rounded the corner from Cinnamon Street, past the White Swan, all now in darkness. Signalling to Birtles, Shiloh now darted off into the short street leading down towards the Wapping stairs.

The fog was rising thick off the river, now not far distant; Ned Birtles took Shiloh by the arm, indicating they should go now with caution. Coombes shook him off, impatient; this roiling river fog, together with the still falling ice crystals, were making it difficult to pick up the sign. Suddenly a cry of triumph, as a fresh still-steaming pile of manure caught his eye. From where it had fallen, the carriage would appear to have turned into a large courtyard whose entrance now loomed before them to the left.

'Come, Birtles, this way I'm sure. And if I'm not mistaken, this is a dead end.' They paused, looking about, in the dim light available to them. The space was indeed very large, and presented several peculiarities. Surrounded by high walls of masonry, lay a great flat area; then at one end, the cleared space dipped sharply down to a lower level. They could detect no sound from the runaway carriage, but both agreed that their quarry lay somewhere within.

'Whoever this fellow with the carriage is, I wouldn't be surprised it didn't belong to him.' At Birtles querying look, Shiloh went on, 'he was lashing those horses, had no care for them. This also seems to indicate that not only was he a cruel swine, but he is in a hurry to escape the police. I'm wondering if this has something to do with Werth himself. I think we should keep on after him, don't you?'

.Spread apart, the two men cautiously entered this unusual place. Silently, using only hand signals, they co-ordinated their search. Darting from place to place, Ned Birtles and Shiloh Coombes advanced down the yard, checking all possible hiding places for a two-horse carriage. They investigated between great piles of bricks, also enormous stacks of some very heavy timber, but saw no sign of the carriage they sought. By now, all trace of it's going had been obliterated. At a nod from Birtles, they descended the steep slope to the lower level. At the far end of this lower open space, they came up to a great wooden door, of rough timber planking, padlocked, with several planks leaning on it.

'Well I'm damned,' cried Ned Birtles, 'Where 'as he flown to' – inadvertently glancing upwards, as if this had truly been the case. 'I don't suppose we took the wrong turn in 'ere?' Coombes also stood, equally nonplussed. 'He definitely turned in here, I'm sure of it.' Having no other recourse, they spent some futile minutes searching behind further stacks of lumber and bricks. 'It's a bloody wonder nobody 'as nicked some of these bricks, eh' said Birtles as they met again in the centre of the yard.

'Actually Birtles, now that you mention it – look, there were a couple of gates at the entrance, but they were just wide open. No nightwatchman; I wonder – oh, I remember now, I was walking along here with Feigenbaum once, and he explained to me about the famous tunnel under the Thames built by the great engineer Brunel and his father. The Times called it the eighth wonder of the world when it opened, it took over seven million bricks to line it's insides apparently but it fell out of use for some reason' – He turned suddenly to his companion, eyes glittering with excitement, 'this is it!'

'Somewhere here must be the entrance of the tunnel – I wonder - ' Without another word the two men raced towards the huge timber doors. Sure enough, the large padlock was indeed in place, but a nearer examination showed that it had been forced, then put back together. That and the several planks leaning in front, covered a gap large enough for a hand to reach through…

Pulling aside the pieces of lumber, Coombes very soon had tossed aside the broken padlock, and together the two men flung wide the doors. The first sight was astonishing; a vast brick vaulted arched tunnel led off into darkness, sloping gradually down in the direction of the Thames.

'Yes! This is it!' cried Coombes in triumph. Birtles rushed over to the side, and kneeling, placed his ear to the brickwork itself. He held up his hand for silence. Seconds later he was up, dusting his knees.

'E's gone down there, all right. I could hear the rumble; the 'orses 'ooves and carriage wheels vibrating through the bricks, see.' Not for the first time, Coombes was amazed at Birtles' ingenuity. Then with a nod at Birtles, he prepared to follow the quarry. He took out from his jacket pocket his portable battery torch. He had been using it sparingly, but it's light was now noticeably weaker. Silently Shiloh cursed himself; He had not thought to bring spare batteries.

'Don't you think squire we should wait for the Bobbies,' cautioned Ned Birtles. 'I would reckon whoever 'e is, e's gone and stole this carriage; 'e may be armed, and if it is Werth, well we know what a dangerous sod 'e is.' he finished. Shiloh stared at him, intently.

'Ned Birtles, from anyone else but you, I would take that as being lily-livered. But yes you are right; on the other hand, speed is of the essence, wouldn't you agree?' and he began searching amongst the various pieces of equipment lining one side of the tunnel entrance.

'Hah!' with a cry of triumph, he beckoned Birtles to him. 'I spotted these two rails here,' he indicated with his torch beam, and I assumed we might find something like this fellow,' playing the light over a curious apparatus.

'What is it then,' asked Birtles 'I've never seen nuffin' like it.' Coombes was excited, and urged Birtles to help him uncover it and bring it across to the tracks.

'Ohoh! See Ned, fortune does sometimes favour the brave. He pulled out something from the box at the side of the larger wheeled object. 'And look here, a kerosene lamp,' shaking it, 'yes, even got a bit of fuel in it. I thought they must have had somesuch, some source of lighting to work down here.' He stood back, flinging out a theatrical arm; 'and this, my dear Birtes, is a kalamazoo – at any rate, that's what the Americans call it. See, one or two chaps stand upon it, pumping the handles here up and down, and it travels along the rails. It would have been for the use of maintenance workers. Whoever this chap is up ahead, he is in for a big surprise! Come on; help me get it onto the track.'

Together they managed to settle the large trolley upon the rails, Coombes lit the storm lantern, hanging it upon the hook provided at the front of the trolley. Despite Birtles still urging caution, Coombes prepared to follow the quarry. A glance at the eager glint in his eye, told Birtles his pleas were useless.

'But of course as I said you are right,' Coombes nevertheless surprised him, 'I will keep after him, keeping a good distance Ned, keeping a good safe distance, but meanwhile it would be best if you could find our inspector, and lead the Bobbies down here.' With a quick salute, he ran for a while pushing the apparatus, and leaping aboard, was in a surprisingly short time disappearing down along the tunnel. Birtles last sight of his impetuous companion was of him energetically pumping up and down, casting strangely distorted shadows thrown by the lantern upon the tunnel walls.

CHAPTER EIGHTEEN

The horses were terrified; they'd been unwilling to enter into the dark unfamiliar place, but were nevertheless driven forward by the relentless whip-lashing they had to endure. A coachman's whip is a means of communicating with his horses; to assert authority yes, but this driver knew no mercy. In the light now cast by the whale oil carriage lamps, the blood glistening freely upon the flanks of these two gave him no qualms. Instead his smile tightened, as he renewed his efforts with the whip.

- they will know their master now -

The coach-lamps which had now been lit by Werth, also served to cast enough illumination to throw the vast curved brick vaulting into ghostly relief. The span of the arch was awesome, allowing the horses room to gallop along a broad roadway, even allowing for two parallel lines of rail track alongside. But Werth's mind did not dwell upon this engineering marvel; he was busy calculating how much of a lead he had upon his pursuers. The police were on foot, and would take time to discover the tunnel . This, coupled with his advantage of having horse transport...

But now suddenly, the odds changed; finally reaching the end of her stamina, the left side mare went down, collapsing in a tumbling heap upon the roadway. Over the screaming of the horses, the noise of the fall, Werth distinctly heard the clean snap of a leg bone break.

- Scheisse! - but he was good at this, riding his luck, keeping his cool –

Werth had almost been thrown from his driver's box, but quickly caught himself, and was down on the ground almost before the carriage came to a swerving halt. Ignoring the white faces looking out at him, he ran forward to where the mare lay thrashing about in pain, causing the other horse to also rear and scream. Lady Violet watched white faced, unflinching, as with one great slash, her mare Mitzi had her throat cut .

Then he turned; in the carriage lights, the two women saw this man in his true light, perhaps as nobody on this earth had – and lived. His features still vivid with blood lust, they saw creature from hell; evil incarnate. Then he smiled, and it was worse. For now his attention fell upon the two women in the locked carriage. His prisoners. They were useless to him; for now, he would have to put off the main plan – he'd hoped to trap the troublesome Coombes. The hastily hatched plan, admittedly made on the run, was starting to unravel, but the idea of collecting some ransom had after all been a spur of the moment idea. Now, the intoxicating thought of slitting the white thoats of these society bitches, listening to them shriek, was a pleasure he would not deny himself. Maddened, Werth rushed at the carriage, pounding upon the door with his fists. As the two women crouched back, he ran about, seeking something, a stone, to smash the lock. But then as they watched, he froze; he was peering intently back down into the darkness from whence they had come.

'Oh god help us – there is help coming!' Olivia had snatched a look through the oval window at the rear of the carriage; she had also seen a pin-point of light, growing ever growing larger.

Werth hesitate a moment or two, torn between the strong, almost overriding desire, and the urging of caution. He cast one last hideous scowl towards his intended victims, then with an oath, he ran forward, pausing only to take down the near side coach-lamp. He then began cutting the remaining horse loose from her harness.

The mare was terrified, and attempted to break free of him, but Werth held fast, with the desperate strength of a madman. Before long he had freed his mount; leaping onto her back, within moments he disappeared into the darkness up ahead.

Clinging closely to each other, the two trapped women were at the window of the carriage, to catch sight of whoever their savior might turn out to be. A squeal of rusty breaks, and they watched as a man ran across towards them, having leapt from this strange contraption upon which he had arrived. They could not make out his features, as he directed his pocket torch into the carriage. Then suddenly the voice;

'Good god, Olivia! – what on earth are you doing here – quick, where is he – has he fled -,' and following the indication of Olivia to the affirmative, he turned and ran back to his machine. Running, pushing, he was soon back pumping furiously, gone from them as he swiftly as he had arrived.

'Oh the swine! What an impossible beast!' raged Olivia, pounding fruitlessly upon the carriage side.

'Oh dear,' said Lady Violet, soothingly,' am I correct in assuming that I have just met the elusive Mr. Coombes?' At Olivia's startled surprise, she managed a smile, 'Well it was obviously somebody with whom you seemed to be well acquainted with,' her eyebrow raised, inquisitively. This broke the tension to which they had been subjected, the fear, the terror, suddenly all but dissolved by laughter; as they fell into each other's arms, the laughter quickly turned to tears of relief.

Catching her breath, Olivia began;' Oh what you saw was just so typical – the man is so mercurial, so brilliant, but so completely single minded sometimes it drives me mad.' She stamped her foot. 'One might think a gentleman's first concern was to see to our wellbeing, but no, of he goes, without even attempting to free us!' Lady Violet smiled, 'yes, but perhaps he thought we might be safer still securely locked up. When I asked Thompson – oh I hope poor Thompson is all right – when I asked him to lock us in, you know Olivia, I believe it saved our lives.' Her sombre look was mirrored upon the face of her young companion.

'But enough of that - we shall just have to wait it out,' as she began rummaging in the space beneath her seat. 'Incidentally, you know where that madman has driven us, don't you?,' she threw over her shoulder, 'I believe it's that tunnel which Mr. Brunel built under the Thames some years ago.'

'Hah! I hoped it was there,' as she pulled out a large travelling rug. 'Come and sit close dear – have you noticed how devilish cold it has become?' At the question, Olivia realized that this was indeed so; during the drama which they had endured, it had so completely overridden all other emotions and sensations; neither had been aware just how cold it was in this mad place.

To take the younger woman's mind from their situation, Lady Violet took the opportunity to broach a subject dear to her heart. As soon as they had begun to feel somewhat warmer, she turned to Olivia. 'After this little adventure my dear, I think you and I can speak plainly. I believe that my dear nephew is very much infatuated with you, and I also believe these tender feelings are mutual.' At first the older woman believed she had been too blunt, as she felt Olivia stiffen beside her. But then she relaxed, putting her head upon the shoulder of Lady Violet. 'You are right, after this evenings adventure, it seem as if we two have become so close. I don't know that I could have endured without your courage.' She lifted her head;

'And yes, it seems you have not been fooled,' she sighed, then began to tell her story.

To Olivia's account of her unfortunate relationship, how her childhood friend Shiloh had helped her with money, her subsequent going to France for a secret abortion, Lady Violet listened in silence. When Olivia told how she had decided to keep the baby, she was heartened then to continue by the tight squeeze of the arm she then received. She went on, how she had brought the infant back to England and installed her French wet nurse and the baby boy in a cottage close to her parent's property.

'You see,' Olivia finished, tears now brimming, 'I did what my conscience told me and I am glad – he's such a little darling and I miss him terribly right now' and she fell into the open arms of the older woman. After a moment or two she recovered herself sufficiently to complete that which she wished to say.

'So you see, I could not get involved with Charles, it would not be fair to him. In fact I had resolved to tell him all of this when you came upon us in the Palm Court.' And once again her tears fell.

Gently patting the back of this young woman, Lady Violet

spoke then. 'First my dear, I want to tell you how much I admire your courage in keeping your child. For I will tell you of something; something which I have never told a living soul. Many years ago now, I once had an abortion. The circumstances were different, but I have often regretted it.'

Having each bared such innermost secrets with one another, the two fell into something of a reflective silence, wrapped close beneath the travelling rug. Suddenly Lady Violet was wide awake, gently shaking her companion, who had slipped into an exhausted sleep. ' - What is it! That madman hasn't returned, has he - ?'

"No dear, I'm so sorry to have startled you so, but I have had an absolutely marvellous thought, and I must share it with you.'

Birtles had hardly reached the gates opening onto the street, when the blue light upon it's roof identified the police van as it came towards him at around the corner up ahead. On board were the Inspector from Scotland Yard, accompanied by Charles Warner. The driver came to a sudden halt as the frantic signals from Birtles almost caused the horses to bolt.

'Ah! It's you Ned Birtles. I would appreciate if you could tell me what the devil's going on down here!' And concise as ever, in a few moments Birtles had given the inspector the gist of the situation. Climbing down from the vehicle, Charles Warner was off, surprisingly nimble for a one legged man, making for the gateway leading to the tunnel entrance. As he went, Charles had already switched on his pocket torch, and was now taking from his inside coat pocket his revolver.

'Mr. Warner – Mr. Warner sir!' called the inspector, 'I don't want you going down that tunnel sir – yes I know, I did indeed deputize you – oh dammit, go on ahead then, but I urge caution sir, I do not want you going in there like some …' He sighed, turned to Birtles; 'Judging by his peg leg, I don't believe he will come to much harm. I assume the rogue is heading for the other side, over to Rotherhithe.' Ned Birtles nodded his agreement. ' Mr. Coombes 'as gone after 'im on a workman's rail trolley. By now whoever 'e is will also know we are at this end, 'e can't come back 'ere.'

Suddenly the inspector became galvanized; he'd made his decision.

'Look here Birtles, I'm going to grab the first two of my men I can, and make a dash for London Bridge. If I reach the Rotherhithe end in time, I might nab him. I want you to stay here, and inform my sergeant when he arrives' – he gave three blasts of his whistle –' of my plan. He is to follow after Mr. Warner. Got that? I'm off – driver, shortest way towards the bridge!'

As the police wagon raced away, Birtles had a great feeling of relief. For the truth was, as he had entered that awful tunnel, he'd been swept by a wave of pure terror – claustrophobia. He had not suffered it for years. A as a small boy his gin-soaked mother had once locked him in a dark cupboard for some interminable hours, and it had made Ned Birtles very wary of enclosed spaces. Yet here he was, a grown man - he would have thought that by now he would be over it, but... He had appreciated that Coombes had somehow intuited his state–and yet forbore to tease or jeer at him.

-the man is uncanny – he could read you mind -

Birtles stamped his feet, hands beneath his armpits, as he waited. Cold though it was, he was just happy not to have to enter that awful dark place.

CHAPTER NINETEEN

Olivia sat now wide awake, waiting for her companion to speak. Lady Violet was obviously very excited by some sudden inspiration, yet she took a moment or two to order her mind, to marshal her thoughts before beginning. She could not afford for it to come out wrong.

'Listen my dear; during this awful time, we two have forged such a close understanding – oh yes and friendship, which I believe will endure – that I believe I can speak the bare truth, woman to woman; what I have to say you might not agree with, but you will know that I say it with the best of motives.' Olivia said nothing, but gave a nod to go on. 'When we first met, my very first thought was; this girl could be the one to save my poor dear nephew.' Olivia's face showed her total attention, giving Lady Violet the confidence to continue.

'Charles is the son of my sister, you see, but as I have no children, he is the nearest thing, for me.' Clearing her suddenly tight throat, she continued, 'I understand you first met Charles as he underwent some level of rehabilitation – yes, under your ministrations, Charles did tell me. Losing one's leg is an awful thing of course, but the thing is, his leg is not his main worry. He's always been very brave – oh I know, I'm his doting aunt, but did you know they gave him the Military Medal – no? Typical I suppose. Always did hide his light under a bushel. But Charles is a man of courage, and certainly not a man to be defeated on account of the loss of his leg.' Olivia sat still, silent, taking in this account. She could not understand where it might lead, but Charle's aunt had now taken both of her hands in her own, as she went on.

'What I am about to tell you, is something deeply personal to my nephew. My perhaps seeming betrayal of his private secret is based on the rapport you and I have found, in such a short time.' She waited until Olivia met her eyes. 'You see, I know you and Charles are made for each other, and I will do anything to help you come together.' Finally Oliver spoke. 'You are right - I do love Charles, and any secret of his, I would guard with all my heart.' She nodded for Lady Violet to continue. Taking a deep breath; -'I *do* wish I had a cigar!' And with that, Lady Violet dropped her bombshell.

'Charles not only lost his leg upon that battle field, you see, but he also suffered a terrible wound in his groin. In short, he cannot father children.' She watched as Olivia blanched, her face showing her pain and dismay. 'On the other hand, the doctors assured me that he will still be capable of – of carrying out his manly function, if you see what I mean. All this I have ascertained by devious means; even his mother knows nothing of this. As I said, I still have acquaintances at the War Office, and managed to obtain a copy of Charles' confidential medical records. Charles had been rather depressed, you see, and my sister had been frightfully worried. She believed it was just about the loss of his leg, but I felt it must have been something else – nervous exhaustion or some such.' Olivia still sat stunned, full of sorrow for Charles.

- oh the poor dear lamb -

'That's why I had his service revolver in my house; my poor sister was afraid he might do himself harm.' Her smile was wry; 'I never for a moment thought he might.' Lady Violet leant back, she had finished her revelation, but went on, 'I haven't had the heart to tell her; and anyway, I had until this night felt that it was for Charles himself alone to do so, if ever he wished.' Lady Violet sighed; 'Now I *really* wish I had a bloody cigar.' She glanced sideways at her young companion, who has received her news calmly.

- a beauty, yes, but also a young woman of real character -

'But don't you see, darling? Providence works in strange ways. You and Charles, your two particular situations – you are perfect for each other!'

Bending to his exertions, Shiloh saw almost too late what lay before him. Jumping upon the foot brake, he brought his conveyance to another screeching halt. He had reached the lowest part of the

227

gently sloping tunnel, and herein lay the problem. Without maintenance, with the steam pumps out of commission, the tunnel has slowly accumulated water. Holding high his kerosene lantern, Shiloh found that he could see no end to it, and he also knew there was no way of gauging its depth. Suddenly from out of the shadows to the far side of the tunnel – movement. Shiloh tensed, ready for attack, but almost immediately saw that it was only a horse – a riderless horse. The poor creature stood trembling, foam about it's mouth, eyes wildly rolling. So pleased however to find itself out of the terrifying pitch darkness, it came willingly at Shiloh's soft urging. He spent several minutes calming the animal, as he at the same time tried to assess the situation.

Obviously whoever it was had ridden her, had been unable to force the mare into the dark water. Not knowing how many were in pursuit, there had been only one course open to him. Wade or swim to freedom. Still patting and rubbing the mare, Shiloh Coombes weighed up the options. For one, he was decidedly reluctant to enter the icy water, and two, he probably had no hope now of catching up with the miscreant. And three - did he really need to?

Suddenly Shiloh remembered his friend Olivia Truscott, obviously locked for some reason together in the carriage with another lady – no, he's best get back there. The mare, much calmed and grateful for his attention, allowed him to mount, despite her wounded and bleeding haunches. Allowing the stressed mare to make her own pace, he proceeded thus back up the great tunnel. Without his thundering approach on the kalamazoo, Shiloh made out a great many rats scurrying about, mostly avoiding his light, but some of the bolder rats stood on their hind legs at the horses approach. Eyes in the lamplight glittering, almost challenging.

- they smell the blood of the horse –

Shiloh gave an involuntary shudder, and he felt the horse's nervousness as she snorted, high stepping. 'Steady girl; they are only rats - we'll soon be out of this, good girl,' and soon the mare became more accustomed to the scurrying creatures. Coombes however fought to contain his own dread, the images of how a disabled man might fare...

Riding now slowly back towards where he had left Olivia Truscott, Shiloh fell to thinking about their friendship. Shiloh's strained relationship with his guardian uncle after the death of his mother, and the fact of Olivia's parent's frequent absence from the country, had initially thrown them together. It was inevitable that being both neighbours and rather lonely children, they had formed a strong bond of friendship. So when Olivia had come to him in tears at the time of her terrible dilemma, Shiloh had immediately offered his assistance in any way possible. Indeed his first instinct had been to offer to marry her. To his secret relief, she had thanked him profusely, but made it clear that she could not accept. He then had offered to find the money she needed to travel abroad to France, to obtain a discreet abortion.

It was this promise which Shiloh had made, that had eventually led him to steal the money from his guardian, thus precipitating his being sent away in disgrace. Shiloh had therefore been very much put out when one evening walking with Feigenbaum he had caught sight of her in an open carriage together with this man Warner, the same whom he had met this very evening. At the time it had disturbed Shiloh dreadfully, to see her so laughing and carefree, whilst he had been reduced to a homeless pauper.

But now, as he approached the stranded carriage, all that was in the past. He'd come to understand that circumstances had worked out for the best. For himself, he felt himself free to follow the path fate had chosen for him, and also free of any obligation to his former guardian - their antipathy had been mutual. And for Olivia, his dearest childhood friend, he wished nothing but happiness for the future.

Approaching where he had last glimpsed his friend's white face at the carriage window, Shiloh made out the figure of a woman whom he first thought to be her. The figure stood back-lit by the carriage lamp, some distance from the carriage. Coming closer, the tired mare pricked up her ears, whickering as she quickened her pace, her safe return soon to be enthusiastically welcomed by her owner.

'Ah, Mr. Coombes I presume?' the lady called up to him, 'I am Violet Bulmer, and I am so indebted to you sir, first for rescuing two ladies in distress, and for returning my horse – oh look the poor darling, oh that cruel man, blood all over her back,' as she gave her attention to comforting her mare. Coombes had meanwhile dismounted, handing her the bridle strap.

He bowed, 'My pleasure, madam. Unfortunately however, your kidnapper has escaped.' He looked about, 'And my friend, Olivia Truscott, madam? Is she not with you?' The lady put a finger to her lips, asking for silence. 'Let us walk a little Mr. Coombes; I wish to speak with you.' To Shiloh's repeated question, she indicated the carriage, but insisted they walk on down the tunnel.

'What a strange place to meet, Mr Coombes, and under such strange circumstances,' as they both looked around them, the curving vaulted tunnel eerily lit by the lamp still held by Shiloh Coombes. 'Yes, and nothing stranger for me than to catch sight of Olivia, who was obviously together with you.' He still looked back, wanting to see Olivia.

'Ah yes, in fact she it was Olivia who was searching for *you* sir. But I will let Olivia explain all that'. But then Lady Violet put an abrupt question; 'Pardon me Mr.Coombes on such short acquaintance, but could you tell me of your intentions towards Olivia?' Shiloh looked sharply at this lady, whom he had met but minutes before, and was now asking very personal questions of him.

'You seem to be very well acquainted with Olivia, madam. She has obviously told you that I did once ask her to marry me.' His glittering eyes, his imperious hawk-like nose was intimidating, but Lady Violet was of stern stuff, and pressed on, 'yes indeed sir, and if I may say so, given the circumstances, your offer does you great credit,' and she squeezed his hand.

'I see you have the whole story; In fact madam, I must tell you in confidence that I was relieved when Olivia rightly pointed out that I was not really the marrying kind. The very thought of becoming a *pater familias* quite frankly terrified me.' They both enjoyed a quiet laugh over this. As they were now well out of earshot of the carriage, Lady Violet came to a halt. She returned her attention again to patting and stroking her still traumatised mare.

'So I deduce Olivia has confided in you much of her recent – ah, history if you will.' Shiloh asked, eyebrow raised. She smiled at him; 'Olivia has told me everything.' Lady Violet now looked back in the direction of her abandoned carriage. 'I had to ask that impertinent question, and I thank you for your answer. You see, my nephew Charles Warner is a suitor. Charles arrived upon the scene some time after you took off, and it was he who broke open the carriage door and rescued Olivia and myself.' She smiled then, 'I'm not really so keen on strolling about , you know, but thought I might leave them together to sort out their situation.'

Shiloh began to offer an apology for not himself stopping long enough to force the carriage door when Lady Violet again put her hand upon his arm; '- as I said to Olivia just a short time ago, providence works in strange ways.' Her smile now was almost mischievous .

'I believe this situation had enabled Olivia and Charles to find their way together – with just the tiniest nudge from yours truly,' and now her smile was definitely cheeky, 'I do have a reputation as a bit of an old meddler to uphold, you see.'

Exhausted now, In the aftermath of all the drama and excitement of this long evening, Shiloh Coombes and Ned Birtles walked in silence. They were returning, Coombes to the house of old Feigenbaum, and Birtles to his own home. It was freezing cold, the mean streets dark, deserted; not only was it late, well after midnight, but the inclement weather kept all indoors. Almost everyone.

At *a hisst* from Birtles, Coombes looked up from his half-sleeping gait ,trudging head down, hands in pockets. Somebody was approaching, but had paused, hesitating in the middle of the road at sight of them. Shining his torch towards this figure, Birtles called, 'we are law abiding citizens – who are you?'

But in the light of the torch, Shiloh had already recognized the youth who still stood aways up the street. 'Its alright – Shiloh Coombes here. Are you looking for me?' The news which this messenger from the Sparrow then imparted, made the two forget their fatigue. Immediately they broke into a jog, as they ran, still questioning the youth. But other than the message from the Sparrow, telling them that Mr. Feigenbaum had been grievously wounded, and was asking for Shiloh, the lad knew no more. At the end of the street he took himself off.

Entering the parlor of Feigenbaum's house, Shiloh took in the scene. After the cold night air outside, the two men found the atmosphere uncomfortably stifling, and they had hastened to throw off their coats. It was then that they had seen it – a body of a man lay behind the door, his head frightfully bashed in, and obviously dead.

Feigenbaum also lay upon the floor, covered in blankets, in the centre of the room. His face so pale that at first Shiloh feared he had come too late. Seated beside him on the floor Shiloh recognized his friend the doctor.

'John! Don't tell me I am too late – ' but as his friend looked up, Shiloh saw from his expression that this was not so. 'Oh he is asleep now, but has strictly enjoined me to wake him as soon as you came.' Getting awkwardly from the floor due to his old knee wound, the doctor stood and beckoned them away from his patient.

'You'll understand nevertheless that I am reluctant to do so,; his face earnest as he went on, 'he has suffered a bullet wound to his chest, and I have to tell you, he may not see out the night.'

The heartfelt 'Oh fuckit!' which ripped from the anguished lips of Ned Birtles, caused the patient to wake, although it was easy to see that he was very weak. There was a faint smile though on Feigenbaum's face as he whispered, ' Is that you Ned my boy? Have you got Shiloh with you, is he all right?'

Coombes knelt beside his old friend, taking his hand, 'Best be quiet, old man, husband your strength, eh?' But Feigenbaum shook his head irritably. ' No no, it's too late for that - I'm done for my boy; but I have things to tell you.' Shiloh put his head low, to better hear the old man's voice.

'Remember me teling you about the Jewish story, the two strands of the Wandering Jew?' And I said I was going to look into some things regarding your antecedents? Well I have done some research over at the Bevis Marks and it seems I was right on, from the start.' Shiloh glanced across at his friend the doctor, who was sipping a cup of tea just handed him by Birtles. Shiloh wanted to ask him if the old man was wandering, but it was Feigenbaum himself who tugged suddenly at his hand. 'Pay attention, Shiloh. I haven't long, and it is important.'

'Sorry', and Shiloh nodded for him to continue. The old man's eyes, though rheumy, still held a spark of intelligence. 'Right from the start I knew it see; you Shiloh my boy, I have to tell you are yourself are a Marrano, your ancestors thrown out from Portugal most likely, centuries ago. Your original name would probably have been Gomez, you see, anglicised of course to Coombes.' Feigenbaum stopped speaking suddenly, and he was wracked with coughing. Immediately the doctor sprang up, hastily thrusting his cup into the hands of Ned Birtles.

'Here Coombes – help me to sit him up', and to Shiloh's horror, as they did so a bright gout of blood gushed from the dying man's lips onto a cloth held before him by the doctor. Eventually, sobbing and gasping, Feigenbaum eventually regained his breath, albeit with a rasp. At a nod from the doctor, the two lowered him back down. Feigenbaum lay still, trying to regulate his breath that came now in harsh gasps.

The old man's features were like wax, the flesh drawn back from the bony structure of his face, bringing his high arch of a nose into even greater prominence. Shiloh was silent, believing his friend had finished speaking. But still he held fast to the hand of Shiloh. Shiloh glanced across at the doctor, who could only shrug in resignation. There was nothing he could do. So Shiloh sat, waiting for the end. He saw the nobility of this old man revealed *in extremis* , the true character of his mentor and teacher.

Suddenly Feigenbaum resumed, his voice seemingly stronger. 'If Ned would be so good as to go into my bedroom and look beneath the bed, he could pull out a parcel. I've been having a bit of a look around, sniffing about, and I found something you might like to have.' As Birtles hurried to carry out his wish, Feigenbaum motioned Shiloh even closer. 'Your friend the doctor was good enough to get Mr. Morris - you know, Hymie Morris, my accountant – to come around, and everything is wrapped up nice and tidy – ' Again he began to cough, but managed to stifle it. 'He beckoned Shiloh even closer, so that his ear was almost at his lips.

'You see, I never brought into this vale of tears any children of my flesh – I always thought that would be a cruel thing to do. But in you I found my spiritual son, someone whom I had always sought, someone with the capacity to learn from all I had to tell.' Again he stopped, but only to catch a laboured breath or two. 'Ah Ned – good man you are, and always were,' as Birtles that fierce bull terrier of a man, silently handed Shiloh the parcel, he turned away to hide the sudden tears.

At a nod from Feigenbaum urging him to do so, Shiloh opened the package. As the wrappings fell away, they revealed a small, unframed oil painting. Shiloh looked at the painting, but he was too distracted to make much of his present, noting only that it appeared to be a well executed seascape; moody, atmospheric.

- *A decent work, but why* –

He shot a puzzled glance at Feigenbaum, who nodded, even managing a weak smile. 'Come close again; its not the content – it's the signature.'

Beckoning for Ned Birtles to hand him his battery torch, Shiloh made out the name of the painter. When he did, it was like a physical shock through him. The signature of the artist was modest and discreet, but plain enough to read: -

EDWARD COOMBES

The tides of emotion which swept his being then, the joy, mixed with deep sadness, held him entranced as he scrutinized the very brush strokes of the painting; every one the considered mark of his own father. Although it seemed an eternity, it was only a scant minute or so before Shiloh turned back, searching for words to thank his benefactor. But he saw that tired out by his last efforts, Feigenbaum had fallen asleep. Exhausted himself, Shiloh dozed there, sitting beside his old friend, still holding his hand.

He fought against it, trying to keep his precious hold on sleep, but the hand shaking his shoulder was insistent. Suddenly Shiloh was wide awake, taking in the scene. One look told him the truth; even before the doctor could employ his stethoscope, he knew without asking that Feigenbaum was dead. Having fulfilled all of his last remaining pieces of business, the old rag trader had slipped quietly from the mortal coil.

CHAPTER TWENTY

A lovely peaceful country day, the small wedding in this quiet country village had gone smoothly, the radiant bride and her groom, pink faced with joy, had just left from the church.

A group of men stood beneath a large elm in a quiet corner of the churchyard, away somewhat from the church as they enjoyed a quiet smoke. Shiloh Coombes was there, pulling upon his accustomed pipe, as was Ned Birtles, with a cigar far too big for him. Doctor John Watson was also there, although making a show of disgust at the clouds of tobacco smoke.

Watson had been intrigued earlier to be introduced to Mr. Clarence Mycroft, the bulky quiet figure who stood with them, as to the brother of his friend. No two men could look more unlike, yet there was something indefinable about them seen together, which suggested the truth. The smokers watched as a long-legged figure detached himself from the group at the door of the church and headed in their direction. 'Allo 'allo, 'ere comes the Inspector' grunted Ned Birtles as he recognised the man .

'Good morning to you gentlemen, all, he nodded around the group – 'well I never, Mr. Mycroft. I didn't believe you ever came out from your lair.' Mycroft seemed not to be discomforted by the sarcasm from the Inspector. 'Well Lestrade, as Olivia absolutely refused my suggestion that they might marry in my office, I really had no choice, old boy,' as he shook his colleagues hand. 'He looked about; 'Still bloody miserable out here, anyhow, I see ,' and they all laughed.

'Well inspector,' began Shiloh Coombes, 'how are things coming along with all the official stuff, the coroner's enquiry etc?' Instead of answering, the Inspector jerked his head, indicating that Shiloh should step aside with him. They walked away a pace or two. 'You were right about checking Liverpool. I struck a bit of luck. One sharp eyed booking clerk was able to recognise from our detailed description, a passenger who left for America '. The inspector noted the look of intense frustration upon the face of Shiloh Coombes. It mirrored his own feelings exactly. 'Why wasn't this fellow questioned, detained? 'asked Coombes, trying to mask his chagrin.

'Good question, Coombes, but this fellow as we know is diabolically cunning. He didn't apply for his boarding ticket as coming from England, see, but as an Irish navvy, come over the water from Dunleary to get ship for America. His ticket put him down in steerage with the other Irish.' In answer to Coombes' cocked eyebrow; 'of course I've sent a telegraph message to the New York authorities, but I don't entertain very high hopes. They have thousands landing every week; to tell the truth, I don't think they neither the man- power, nor the will-power, to make any but cursory checks.'

Despondently, Shiloh nodded his head – he pretty much agreed with this assessment. He looked up; 'Yes, in fact there seems to be a broad unspoken attitude that when one lands in America, one gets another chance, the slate is wiped clean.' Coombes then seem to fall into a deep introspection, before stirring himself. 'Inspector, did you by any chance ascertain the name under which Werth travelled to America?' 'Yes, as a matter of fact we did. He called himself Maloney –hang on - no not Maloney, Moriarty.'

The sun now quite warm, as the two men strolled back to rejoin the others beneath the shade of the great elm. 'You know,' the inpector began, there was something almost hesitant in his tone, making Shiloh turn, curious. 'I have to admit I had suspicions as to yourself, Mr Coombes. In fact I had you down as a very suspicious character, and I was looking forward to having a good heart to heart – nothing nasty, no, no smacking about, sir; no, I was just thinking I should be giving you a good grilling. Never hurts I say, to give a suspect a good grilling.' His eye was once more the cold fish eye of the professional policeman.

'Of course, since Mr Mycroft – fancy him being you brother, eh, well since he told me you were working undercover for him on a parallel course to the police; - well I've had to revise my conclusions, haven't ?' Coombes realised that the Inspector was making some sort of attempt at an apology.

'My dear Inspector Lestrade, I assure you I was never offended by a conscientious officer in the line of his duty. As a matter of fact I shall make mention of my attitude in my report to Mr. Mycroft -' he smiled at the inspector; - 'who is as you say my brother, but I might tell you is also a hard taskmaster.'

- Mycroft , you dear old scamp! – working for you indeed ...'

'Thank you,' from a gratified LeStrade, 'I only wish Mr. Mycroft had informed us at the Yard. I understand of course why his office became involved, after the attempt upon the Prince – oh yes, I know I didn't believe you at the time, but it was a genuine attempt.'

'So what in fact was the focus of the police interest in Mr. Werth?' The inspector gave him a sharp glance, then relaxed. It was all over now, anyhow. 'Well I suppose I can tell you now – especially as you have been working for the secret service, and all.' The inspectors face was bland,

- ha! He wasn't completely taken in by Mycroft's tale –

as he went on. 'We have had Werth under observation since he arrived in the country, more or less. We had some information from the Prussian authorities. We are aware of his doings, we could see what he was trying to do here in the east End.' 'Oh, and what exactly do you think that was?' asked Shiloh, curious to see whether his own intuition had jibbed with the police assessment. Unlike Birtles, he had a healthy respect for the professional attitude and the modern police methods of Scotland Yard.

'Well, we had reached the opinion that this Werth was going to be a major problem unless we thwarted him.

From what we have heard from our Continental colleagues. Coupled with his malevolent influence in that short time he has spent here in London, we at the Yard began to regard him as an evil genius, an emperor of crime, and we had to stop him.' He looked shrewdly at Coombes, 'Rightly or wrongly of course, we are held back by the restraints placed upon us by the law. The swine was very cunning, and we could not touch him without real proof.' The inspector again glanced at Shiloh ' – unlike yourselves.' Shiloh continued on without speaking further with the inspector, who upon doffing his hat to the others of the group, took his leave.

Shiloh met the level, expressionless eyes of his brother. 'Everything all right with Mr. Lestrade, I trust?' A smile then broke over Mycoft's broad face then however, as he greeted a newcomer to the smoker's circle.

'Ahha! I thought I smelt tobacco smoke,' cried Lady Violet, who then proceeded to scandalize Ned Birtles as she demanded of him a light for her cigar. Within minutes however she had thoroughly captivated Birtles, who proceeded to give her a blow for blow account of the whole affair.

'Could I also have a quiet word with you Shiloh?' asked his brother.

'Yes of course, but I can tell you that my good friend here Doctor Watson enjoys my full confidence.' Both brothers were secretly relieved not have a face to face, just the two of them. It would come, but neither was quite ready for it. This lovely day, a joyous wedding day, was neither the time nor place. 'Very well, Shiloh, I will be brief. It seems our bird has flown, but if I'm not mistaken, he will be back. Regarding that earlier business, I have information that he was acting in the pay of some element of the Prussian Security Service, and it has caused a veritable hullabaloo over there, I can tell you. I also know that with a sizeable German community in New York and indeed all over the United States, they will have their agents everywhere. Werth will soon find it too hot for him. Neither can he return to Europe; he has burnt few bridges you see. So trust me; he will return.' He tipped his hat to the doctor, and with just a nod to his brother, turned to go. 'I say Mycroft,' called Coombes, 'what is this about me working for you?' Mycroft stopped, half turned; 'But of course you were. My man Birtles over there, he has been most effusive regarding the help you have given him throughout this whole beastly business.' He gave a tight smile, 'as a matter of fact, so valuable have you been according to Ned Birtles, that he has put in a chit for an *ex-gratia* account to cover your minimum expenses.' 'The cheeky devil,' burst from an astonished Coombes, trying in vain to catch the eye of Birtles.

''Oh yes, and it was for twenty guineas – don't forget to claim it,' and once more tipping his hat, made his ponderous way towards the train station.

Shiloh and Doctor Watson rejoined Lady Violet, who was laughing out loud at something from Birtles. At their approach, Ned Birtles also made his brief farewell – he had caught a gleam in the eye of Shiloh Coombes, and didn't think he would tarry to learn it's import. 'Ta ta, then; I'll be in touch squire, doctor – If I get on shank's pony, I should catch up with Mr. Mycroft.' With a flourishing bow to Lady Violet, Bitles took off at a jog, his top hat under his arm. Lady Violet was still laughing as she watched him go.

'What an amusing little man, he really is!' and she was off again, laughing. Doctor Watson and Shiloh exchanged looks. Not quite how they would have described the fierce little bull terrier, at all.

Lady Violet handed her parasol to Shiloh to raise for her, and the three set off for the short walk to where a celebratory wedding breakfast awaited them. It was to take place in the nearby house of Olivia's parents. They strolled in companionable silence, enjoying the country air, alive with bird song, the shrilling and rustling of small creatures – such as nature offers to the unaccustomed senses of the London dweller.

'Well that was a lovely wedding, don't you think? All hastily arranged, admittedly, but entirely without whiff of scandal.' Shiloh laughed, 'I believe you are fishing for compliments, madam. And yes, I am aware your machinations were largely responsible .' She was amused, 'machinations, Mr. Coombes? I would have thought 'helping hand', might have been more appropriate. Certainly, I did pull strings for my nephew; the military attaché's job in Washington, the speed necessitated by the appointment …what can I say; providence works in strange ways.' She looked across at Shiloh.

'And you know, Olivia bless her, nearly undid my plan. She told Charles that if he didn't feel comfortable with the adoption of the child, she would accept his calling the whole thing off. I was a bit miffed at her, I can tell you, but as it happened Charles apparently doted on the little chap from the moment he saw him. By the time they arrive back from America four years from now, all will be well.' Handing her parasol to the doctor, she linked arms with her two escorts, and continued on, talking as they went.

'Am I correct in saying that you know my brother, Lady Violet?' began Shiloh. He had been intrigued by that look of welcome on his brother's face. Not only did Clarence seem to know her, but they seemed to be more than acquaintances. He knew his brother was very shy with women, discomforted to meet, make conversation, with women he did not know.

'Oh yes, my husband you see, was formerly with the intelligence service, and we did bump into each other from time to time; you know how it is.' Her grin was mischievous as she saw the shadow of disbelief on the face of this keen young brother of Clarence Mycroft. 'I see now that you are indeed brothers,' she teased, 'you are quite as sharp as he, I believe. ' Shiloh watched her face, wondering.

'I believe you are more than just polite friends,' he pursued, and she tapped his cheek with her gloves. 'What are you insinuating, you naughty fellow,' and she laughed at Shiloh's protesting, thoroughly enjoying herself.

'I know that silly – but yes I will admit to what you really mean; yes, I have sometimes been able to pass on to Mr. Mycroft some interesting pieces of gossip, shall we say,' and her eyes again merry at Shiloh's surprise. 'Well you did insinuate as much, did you not?' Shiloh looked to his friend.

'You know Watson, I believe at least half of London is

nothing but a sounding board for my brother.' Again Lady Violet laughed; 'oh I believe it's more than half,' and they all laughed together, making there way towards the wedding festivities.

Escaping later that evening from the general fun and gaiety of the celebrations, Shiloh made his way out onto the terrace of the Truscott residence for a quiet pipe. It was not long before he was joined by his friend the doctor. Seeing Shiloh smoking, the doctor himself took out from his dinner jacket pocket a slim silver case. Selecting a cigarette, he then coolly asked Shiloh if he could have a light.

'Ahah! You hypocrite sir – you made much of your abhorrence of the smoking habit earlier, and now here you are!' Doctor Watson laughed as he seated himself upon the stone balustrade.

'My dear chap, this is smoking,' as he waves his cigarette in the air, 'what you and your henchman Birtles were doing together was creating a toxic cloud.' And he puffed contentedly, blowing perfect smoke rings in Shiloh's direction.

He looked then across at his friend and erstwhile patient, and his manner became more serious.

'What are your plans for the future, Coombes? I imagine you are all up in the air at present; what with this whole extraordinary business coming to closure – not to mention the unfortunate death of your friend.' Shiloh was silent for a while, his face sombre as he reviewed his future. Turning to the doctor, he began, 'well before I go further, I would like to thank you John, for all you did for the old man,' he went on, 'I was unfortunately too caught up in things at the time, but please accept that I am extremely grateful.' He put out his hand, which was firmly grasped by John Watson.

'Actually it is not quite all over, this business. There will be several coronial inquires, of course, all that long grinding process of the law.'

He chuckled, albeit sardonically, ' Inspector Lestrade told me that it was ironic that if Feigenbaum had lived, he would have had to charge him with the murder of that low-life swine Kemp he managed to bring down, whilst he himself was attacked in his own home.' The eyes of Holmes glittered dangerously in the moonlight, 'they have arrested the other one, Borden. Apparently the fool had kept the murder weapon; he's been charged over the murder of Feigenbaum.' He looked intently at Watson; 'I don't know whether to be pleased over that news or not – I intended to hunt that bastard down myself.' The doctor was shocked at the intensity of the other's gaze.

'Well perhaps it is better so,' he offered, 'or we should perhaps be seeing yourself in the dock. Do you think your friend Feigenbaum would be pleased at that result?' he ended gently.

Having finished his cigarette, Doctor Watson decided to change the painful subject.

'Actually Coombes, I wanted to talk to you about your immediate future; you do know I hope that if you find yourself momentarily out of funds, -' Coombes had also been happy to change the subject, and responded to his friend's offer with a wide smile.

'Very handsome of you John Watson; if any good can be said to have come out of this whole dreadful business, it is your friendship,' and once more they clasped hands.

'But as a matter of fact, I have been contacted by Mr. Morris, Feigenbaum's accountant, and he has revealed that my old friend has left me a considerable sum of money- yes, quite a sum, apparently, enough for me to maintain myself as a gentleman of leisure, as Mr. Morris put it.' Shiloh's smile was rueful, as he went on, 'the old man had put it all aside, but himself lived frugally. Funny, what – that I should profit by his death.' The doctor put a consoling hand upon his shoulder. 'From what I heard of his last conversations, he was only glad he had found someone to whom he wished to leave it all to.' Shiloh looked up, 'Yes, I suppose that is true. We had forged something very unusual, a special bond, the old chap and I.'

Then getting to his feet, Shiloh Coombes took his friend's arm as they strolled back towards the festivities. 'He was very thorough, it turns out, very particular in his instructions to Mr. Morris. One of the women at the laundry, a person I know well, is a very competent Irishwoman called Molly Malloy. He has left it to her to manage that end of his old business, to be advised by Mr. Morris, and to my surprise, he has appointed that young fellow – you met him, Sparrow - to handle much of the rest.' Suddenly he laughed out loud, 'when I think about it though, I believe that Sparrow was one of his long term projects – much like myself. I believe that the scamp will make a go of it, under Mr. Morris's tutelage. I know he has been courting a lass – that should focus his mind.' He turned to Watson, 'Nevertheless, I thank you for you offer; I might have to take you up on it. I should imagine that it will take some time, probate and all that.'

' Yes of course you shall, and let me congratulate you on your good fortune. The other thing I wanted to suggest, I am taking over rooms – actually a whole set of apartments – to use as both as my visiting surgery, and my accommodation. As the living quarters are more than enough for my requirements, it occurred to me you might wish to share the accommodation' he chuckled, 'and the rental, of course.'

Having secured his friend's enthusiastic acceptance of his proposal, Doctor Watson then went on to suggest that he proceed with having a brass name plate made up. At that, Shiloh paused, taking his friend by the arm. 'An excellent idea as well, but before we go in, I think I should explain a decision I have made.' His face was grave, as he began;

'As you know, that revelation of Feigenbaum's – oh you remember, as to my true heritage - well it gave me real pause. To honour him, I decided to change my name. So it must now be revealed for our brass name-plate. My first thought was to be defiant, to call myself Shylock, and be done with it, but I seemed to hear the voice of the old fellow, 'don't set yourself up for punishment,' and I then came up with Sherlock, close enough. I didn't wish to revert to the original family name Gomez, you see, for the same reason nor did I wish to retain Coombes. So for a surname I have chosen Holmes. Sherlock Holmes. For any old acquaintance who might in future encounter me, it would sound at least very similar.' Laughing, the two friends went to rejoin the wedding party.

'Baker Street you say; where's that - Marylebone?'...

END

EPILOGUE

Is it kosher, as Feigenbaum might say, to appropriate characters invented by other writers? Is it intellectual theft? I think not. As a young art student I early on became aware that there is in fact no such a thing as a completely original piece of art. All art is self referential, it arises out of its cultural milieu; an art form grows almost organically from its predecessors. We see and comprehend the art forms of our particular cultures only through a pre-determined cultural viewpoint. Art is a continuum.

With regard to the art of writing, all western prose literature can be traced back to Homer's Iliad and odyssey. And original characters? There are no such things. Like their real human exemplars, they are made up of a marvellously complex spaghetti bowl of influences, inheritances, cultural and temporal. We are a composite of an infinite number of influences.

Only by applying Chaos Theory, a lot of genome work and a fair bit of luck might we one day be able to understand all of it. But then again, do we really need to? For me as a writer, it is an endless, boundless field of exploration, a marvellous mystery; every single human is totally individual, in all those myriad ways.

Isaac 'Ikey' Solomon was an English criminal who became notorious as an extremely successful receiver of stolen property. He was known all over London for his crimes, his daring escape from arrest, and his high-profile recapture and trial. He is widely regarded as the model for the character Fagin in the Charles Dickens novel Oliver Twist.

Solomon's trial at the Old Bailey in June 1830 caused a sensation and was extensively reported in the newspapers and the pamphlets of the day. As there are strong similarities between his trial and Fagin's trial as portrayed by Dickens, it is considered highly likely that Dickens used this as the basis for that of Fagin. Solomon was tried at the Old Bailey on eight charges of receiving stolen goods, found guilty on two, and sentenced to transportation for fourteen years. The Judge castigated Solomon from the bench as being evil-disposed, an indication of the man's widespread notoriety. Solomon was transported to Van Dieman's Land – or Tasmania as it is now - back to Hobart where he has already spent time, and indeed had a family. Ikey Solomon died in Hobart in 1850.

The name Fagin is deemed for the purpose of this novel to be a corruption of the Yiddish name Feigenbaum, denoting fig tree.

Adam Worth, as he was known to the detectives of Scotland Yard, was described by detective Robert Anderson as the Napoleon of the criminal world, also commonly referred to by others as the Napoleon of Crime.

It has been widely speculated that Arthur Conan Doyle used Worth as the model prototype for his character Professor Moriarty, Sherlock's nemesis. Worth was born into a poor family in the then Kingdom of Prussia, his original surname is thought to have been Werth. The family immigrated to America; while still of tender years, young Adam turned to the life of crime. But when the Pinkerton detectives began to make things too hot for him, he fled New York City and moved to England.

There Worth, or Werth, established himself under the name of Henry Raymond. After a lurid life of crime moving between England and the continent, Worth finally settled quietly in England, where he died on January 8, 1902. He was buried in Highgate Cemetery in a pauper's grave, under the name of Henry J. Raymond. All this - and more of this man's remarkable criminal life, demanded that I should also use him for my arch villain – That plus I was serendipitously delighted to find we share the same surname.

The great Victorian engineer, the man who epitomized the Spirit of the Age, that splendidly named Isambard Kingdom Brunel, worked for several years as assistant engineer with his father the chief engineer on the project to create a tunnel under the river Thames at London.

To drive a horizontal shaft from one side of the river to the other under the most difficult and dangerous conditions, was a bold concept. It proved almost impossible to achieve. The composition of the riverbed was often little more than waterlogged sediment and loose gravel. Two incidents of severe flooding halted work for long periods. The latter incident, in 1828, killed the two most senior miners, and young Brunel himself was seriously injured, and spent six months recuperating. This disaster brought work n the tunnel to a standstill fort several years.

In time a tunneling shield was designed by Marc Brunel to give protection to the workers from further collapse. In December 1834 Marc Brunel succeeded in raising enough money - including a loan of £247,000 from the Treasury - to continue construction.

Starting in August 1835 the original rusted shield was dismantled and removed. By March 1836 the new shield, improved and heavier, was assembled in place and boring resumed. Threatened by further floods, on 23rd Augustv1837, another on the 3rd November 1837, again on 20th March 1838, also on the 3rd April 1840, the work still forged on. The project also had to overcome problems such as fires due to leaking methane and hydrogen sulphide gas. Nevertheless the remainder of the tunneling was completed in November 1841. Upon its grand opening, it was enthusiastically acclaimed by the Times as the Eighth Wonder of the World. Although one of the greatest feats of engineering – not to mention of sheer determination – the tunnel was actually something of a white elephant. Horses were not happy to enter it, from a fashionable drawing card, the tunnel slowly lost favour, it deteriorated into a haunt of prostitutes, mountebanks and thieves, and was finally closed. As the tunnel was in disuse at the time, I decided to borrow it for my novel.

Built between the years 1825 and 1843, the tunnel measures thirty five feet, or eleven meters wide, twenty feet or six meters high and is 1,300 feet, or 396 meters long. At its deepest, it is at a depth of seventy five feet , or twenty three meters below the river's surface at high tide. To line and support the tunnel arch, an estimated more than seven million bricks were used. It was the first tunnel ever to be successfully constructed underneath a navigable river. Eventually the tunnel came back into use, to become part of the London Underground system.

In all humbleness I pay tribute to these three great Victorians, Brunel, Conan Doyle, and Dickens. They are immortal. I also take direction from their equally great American contemporary, Mark Twain;

'Never let the truth get in the way of a good story,' Sam said.

John Worth

The Secret Journal of Dr Watson

www.mxpublishing.com

Two of the world's leading Holmes writers, Andriacco and
McMullen come together for the first in a series of traditional
Holmes mysteries – The Amateur Executioner.

www.mxpublishing.com

Also from MX Publishing

In paperback and hardback, 300 wonderful Holmes cartoons.